CW00495625

FALL FROM GRACE

© Charlie De Luca,2021

My Cup of Tea Press

Also by Charlie De Luca;

Rank Outsiders

The Gift Horse

Twelve in the Sixth

Making Allowances

Hoodwinked

Dark Minster

www.charliedeluca.co.uk

Ad astra per aspera

Chapter One

The surgeon's grey eyes were very serious. Nat pushed himself up in the hospital bed, breathed in the medicinal scent of the place, overlain with the smell of polish and took in the starched sheets, the bright lights and the blue checked curtains that surrounded his bed. His head felt full of stones, his left thigh ached, a gnawing, searing pain that worsened as he tried to bend his leg. His whole body ached and his brain felt like it was filled with cotton wool. His left hand was bruised and he realised that was because he had a cannula inserted into his vein which was attached to a drip.

'You've been very lucky, Mr Wilson. Very lucky indeed. Do you remember what happened?'

Nat nodded trying to decipher the man's Scottish burr. He vaguely remembered a trip to Shetland of all places with his best mate Finn McCarthy. A titian haired beauty was with them. What the hell was her name? That was it! Hattie. Except it wasn't a holiday, he remembered their intent determination, hardly the right mood for a vacation, they had been on a mission of some sort. Memories filtered into his consciousness. Christ, something to do with unmasking a criminal, wasn't it, a kindly looking chap who had not turned out to be kindly at all. And then he remembered Finn being tied up and trying to cause a distraction, a blond heavily built man aiming a gun at his friend Finn, he leapt in front of him and then there was a flash of light, a cracking sound like a whip lash and then a terrible, searing pain in his thigh. Christ, what had happened?

The white coated, kindly man with delicate hands and rimless glasses sat down by his bedside and surveyed him.

'I'm Dr Munroe. You're in hospital in Aberdeen having been airlifted from Shetland. You've been shot in your left thigh.' He shook his head. 'You've been very lucky, yer almost bled to death, if it weren't for the wee lassie having the foresight to make a tourniquet and going for help like she did...'

Christ, that was it. The wee lassie must have been Hattie, he supposed. He must remember to thank her, he really must. God, all sorts of questions ran through his mind.

'And the others? Are they OK?'

Dr Munroe nodded. 'They are all fine. Talking to the police as we speak. Now, I've removed the bullet from your thigh, it damaged the bone, shattered some of it. The surgery was very tricky. But you've had a transfusion, been packed full of antibiotics and you'll be grand. You'll need a long recovery period, rest, relaxation, that sort of thing. Yer see, the bone was shattered in part, which is worse than a complete break, so we've added a rod in there to shore things up.'

Nat listened as Doctor Munroe went on to explain about fractures and trajectories, rods, pins, femoral arteries and exactly how the good doctor had completed his surgery which had been very difficult. He was clearly an expert and Nat was grateful, he really was.

'So, you'll need total rest, I recommend no weight bearing for several weeks, so a wheelchair to begin with then crutches and you'll be as right as rain. You might struggle to walk as long as others, yer might have some pain, but I'm pleased to say that you will make a full recovery.'

Dr Munroe smiled beatifically, so Nat grinned back, questions running through his brain.

'But will I be able to ride?' he asked.

Dr Munroe looked confused. 'Ride? Ride what exactly?'

The good doctor was clearly not a racing fan.

'A horse, of course.'

The doctor frowned and shook his head as he pondered this question. 'I should imagine, you can. Yes, if it's so important to you.' Nat beamed. Christ what a relief. 'As long as you don't go mad, that is.'

Nat sighed heavily. Go mad? Of course, he needed to go mad. He thought of all the horses he'd ever ridden, all the winners, how he was famous for finding a gap, how he was nicknamed 'The Magician' because of it. Mad was certainly one way of describing his riding. Would his leg hold up to this now, he wondered?

The doctor was still looking at him quizzically. 'What is it that you do for a living exactly, Mr Wilson?'

'I'm a jockey. A jump jockey.'

'Ah.' Dr Munroe nodded, surprised. 'Are you any good, then?'

Nat smiled. 'You could say that.' The doctor studied him, willing him to say more. 'I've been champion jockey six times on the trot and ridden two Grand National winners and three Cheltenham Gold Cup winners, and I intend to continue riding…'

The doctor frowned and rubbed his chin. He looked mystified and bemused.

'Are you absolutely sure about that? I did tell you that you nearly died, didn't I?'

Several months later the racing world was fizzing with excitement for the first big National Hunt race of the season, The Charlie Hall, a Grade Two, three mile Steeplechase held at Wetherby. It was October and although the six times Champion jockey had been back since the start of the season, and had already racked up several winners, this was The Charlie Hall after all. This race always had a competitive field of first class steeplechasers, many of whom went on to win prestigious races like The King George, The Gold Cup and even The Grand National. The racing public and pundits alike, were waiting in their droves to see if their hero, Nat Wilson, still had that competitive edge, sufficient to win on his fancied mount, Saint Jude. Would The Magician be able to find a gap, and ride one of his legendary finishes to win?

The racing community had been given limited information as to the cause of Nat Wilson's injury, just to say that it was a gunshot wound which occurred during a hunting trip to the Shetland Isles. Although the gist of the race fixing betting scam had been publicised anonymously, the exact details of how the culprit had been captured, had not been revealed in order to protect Finn McCarthy and Harriet Lucas, who ordinarily worked as a jockey coach for the British Horseracing Authority, the BHA, and dietician for the Professional Jockeys' Association, the PJA, respectively. It turned out that they might be called upon to do some investigative work for the powers that be, who sometimes used staff already employed in racing to carry out inquiries where wrongdoing was suspected. So, very little information had been given out to connect Finn, Hattie or Nat with the race fixing scandal.

The racing press had been gripped by Nat Wilson's 'accident' and subsequent rehabilitation, there had even been a documentary made about it, and there was a great deal of speculation as to how he had been shot. The official line was that Nat had been shot accidentally at a clay pigeon shoot. His comeback focused on the recovery and gave little detail of the real cause and nothing that could link it to the crime which would be in court in a few months' time. The press were bored by the official explanation of his injury and instead had cottoned on to the name of Nat's mount in the race, Saint Jude, who was the patron saint of lost causes, and his nickname of 'The Magician' to create the following headlines;

The Magician is hoping to conjure up a win on Saint Jude.

Saint Jude unlikely to be a lost cause for The Magician's comeback.

The Magician's return on Saint Jude much anticipated.

Nat had had four runners already at the two day meeting at Wetherby, a win and a second so far and was feeling confident for his ride in The Charlie Hall. The good doctor's somewhat gloomy prognosis at Aberdeen had been proved wrong after all. Nat had, of course, required a wheelchair whilst he waited for his thigh bone to knit, graduated onto crutches within six weeks, then he'd had to backtrack to a wheelchair because of a set back which meant he'd needed intensive physio for months, but by July he was back riding at home. His friend, jockey mentor Finn McCarthy, had cast a critical eye over his riding and on his advice, he had hired a physio, and had been given a diet plan from Finn's friend, Harriet, and after lots of gym work building his fitness back up, he was back racing competitively for the start of the season. He had effectively written off last year and had had to watch as a younger jockey, Colm McNally, had taken his champion's crown and he had looked on as second jockey, Jamie McGuire, had taken his rides for the trainer he rode for, Michael Kelly. Jamie had made a decent fist of things on the whole. This had made him doubly determined to follow his rehabilitation plan and come back with a vengeance, despite his fiancée, Livvy's mixed feelings. She, of course, had been desperately worried about his health and would have been far happier if he had accepted the TV presenting job he had been offered. But Nat would have been miserable in such a role if he still had the ability to ride. He had been utterly driven and determined to regain his crown for this season and persuaded her that the TV job would still be there when he eventually retired many years hence.

Besides, as soon as he was racing, he had been welcomed back with open arms, and he had regained his top position next to the heater in the weighing room. His mates, Charlie Durrant, Tristan Davies, Jed Cavendish, Gerry King, and a handful of good conditionals, Sam Foster, Kyle Devlin and Harry Jarvis, were there and there were also some other up and coming lads, Colm McNally, who had come from nowhere to take his crown for last season, Jamie McGuire, and several he didn't recognise. As he surveyed the jocks in various stages of undress, he reflected that things moved quickly in racing, so quickly, it actually worried him. Several of these lads he hadn't even heard about and now they were up and coming, ready to usurp him given any opportunity. It was always the way, he realised, but he felt unsettled, threatened because of it. Sometimes, he found it hard to admit, he even felt old. Get a grip, he told himself, just get on with it. He was The Magician, after all, someone who found a gap and rode a finish like no other. He would be back on top in no time. And then there were the female jockeys, Beth Lloyd and Rachel Murphy who were doing very well and had reasonable rides. Still, call it male arrogance, but Nat wasn't too worried about them. He always felt that males would have the edge when it came to physical strength and sheer guts.

'How do yer fancy yer chances on Saint Jude? Yer do know who Saint Jude was, don't yer?' asked Jamie McGuire.

'I do, the papers are full of it.' He was beginning to wish he'd chosen a different horse to ride. As the stable jockey to Michael Kelly, he'd had the choice of Centurion and Saint Jude and had chosen the big grey after riding him at home, feeling he had the edge. 'He was the patron Saint of lost causes.'

'As all good Catholics would know. Let's hope yer won't regret yer choice,' Jamie added. His tone was light, but Nat was acutely aware that Jamie had had his nose pushed out of joint by his return and was probably smarting from his relegation back to second jockey. Michael Kelly had hinted that Jamie had suggested he should stick with him as his fellow countryman rather than welcome the Englishman back into the role, but Michael was having none of it. At least, that was what Michael had told him. Nat realised though that this was only contingent on results and if he didn't produce the goods, then this would certainly change.

'I was gggonna ask yyer,' added a young, pimply conditional whose name Nat didn't remember. He had a reasonable mount, Great Expectations, Nat had noted. 'Hhow wwas it that yer got yerself sshot?'

The lad was confident with horses, but nervous and reserved around adults, even his colleagues. Amazing that he had said anything at all really. He was skinny, pale with a crop of acne on his chin, poor lad. Nat resisted the urge to take the mick out of his stammer, the lad had enough to deal with and had endured a nasty fall in the first race, Nat remembered, so he could do without the hassle. It was a reasonable question and one that Nat had hedged around before.

'Wouldn't have anything to do with an irate husband, would it?' added Charlie Durrant, his friend and a highly competent jockey, with a wink. 'Yer never did tell us.' By now all the changing room were listening in and waiting with great anticipation.

Nat shook his head, wondering how much to reveal about what had happened. 'Nah, nothing like that. Besides, Livvy would have me guts for garters.' There was a ripple of laughter at this. Nat, as they very well knew, was the least likely of them to be hen pecked.

'And the Shetland Isles? What on earth were you doing there?' asked Tristan Davies.

'Bird watching,' replied Nat. 'I've always loved birds.' It was the best excuse that Nat could come up with at the time, although rather unlikely. He hoped no one asked him any further questions. He didn't actually know his coot from his cormorant but he also suspected that none of the other lads did either.

The lads nudged each other and laughed. 'Never, I wouldn't have yer down as a twitcher!' added Charlie with genuine amusement.

'Well, it's true,' replied Nat. 'Finn and I decided to make a weekend of it.'

Gerry King, a serious journeyman, who looked much older than his 35 years frowned. 'Surely, you don't mean the feathered variety?'

'Yes, I do actually.'

There was a shocked silence as the jockeys exchanged glances and whispered to each other.

Maybe it was stretching things, but in the heat of the moment, bird watching was the best Nat could come up with to explain his trip to The Shetland Isles. It was famous for wild birds, he knew.

'Just tell us what you've done with the real Nat Wilson, will yer?' exclaimed Charlie Durrant with a puzzled expression on his face.

'Oh, believe me, I'm still the same as you are about to find out on the racecourse,' added Nat cryptically. He only hoped that this was the case. With that they heard the bell sound and beaming at everyone in his pink and green colours, Nat clipped on his helmet.

'Come on lads, let's be having yer. May the best man win, eh?'

Nat Wilson strode into the parade ring and made his way to his guvnor, Michael Kelly, who was standing with Saint Jude's connections, a well dressed, middle aged couple, gathered with two small boys dressed in miniature tweed jackets and caps.

Nat grinned broadly and shook the hands of everyone, admiring the young boys' clothes.

Michael smiled. 'So, we're here for a good run, Nat. Just try and cover Saint Jude up, he'll pull, mind, then three from home, he should still have plenty of running. I reckon Centurion, Pythagoras and Daisy Clipper are the competition.'

Nat had studied The Racing Post and agreed, all things considered.

'Just do yer best,' added the serious, bespectacled Mr Owen.

'Yes, but we'd be so delighted if he won, wouldn't we?' added his wife hastily, eye lashes fluttering coquettishly at Nat.

'Well, I'll see what I can do,' added Nat with a grin. The next second, he was legged up and was soon cantering down to the start.

After a circuit, Nat was feeling good and more importantly Saint Jude was full of running and Nat'd had to rein him in to track the leaders. They were in about sixth but well positioned and tracking the other grey, Pythagoras, ridden by Charlie Durant, Jamie McGuire on Centurion, a huge bay and Colm McNally on Daisy Clipper, the bright chestnut. The going was good to soft, but very soft in places and Nat had to wipe his goggles a couple of times. He saved the spare pair he always wore round his neck in such weather, for the last few fences when he really needed clear vision. The young stammering conditional was catching up on his mount, Great Expectations. Nat let them go then followed along, pinging over the fences well. He was glad of the schooling he'd undertaken with Saint Jude, as the horse was jumping very cleanly.

Three fences from home, Nat felt his thigh aching but ignored it whilst he kicked on and tracked the leaders, keeping his wits about him. Nat positioned the huge grey to hug the rail, spotting a gap which appeared next to the stammering conditional. Riding close to the rail on the bend made such a difference to the distance travelled and Nat was a past master at positioning his horse and using this to his advantage. He yelled at the young jockey to move and the lad looked behind him in panic, as Nat pushed Saint Jude forward in the gap before they hit the straight and leapt over the third last fence. The conditional had lost concentration and his horse, Great Expectations, left a leg behind and pecked on landing sending his rider straight over his head. Bad luck,

12

thought Nat, the lad should have been paying attention, but he could see the small figure rolling up tight and it looked like he would avoid serious injury. Nat saw the stands looming to his right and could just pick up the roar of the crowd on the wind. He felt a surge of adrenalin and he kicked on to pass Charlie Durrant's grey, Pythagoras, who was tiring rapidly. Saint Jude moved up a gear and leapt over the second last, landing just ahead of Daisy Clipper, who having led for most of the race, was a spent force. That left Jamie McGuire ahead on Centurion, the black horse in the red and yellow colours. Nat felt he had the race in the bag and an added impetus to his determination to win was that he couldn't let Jamie triumph, the loss of face would be unimaginable in the first major contest of the season. Jamie shifted to the outside almost veering into Nat's path. Nat pulled on his left rein to move his mount to avoid the black horse. Jamie shouted something to him, some obscenity or other but it was lost on the wind. As they approached the last fence, Saint Jude did an almighty leap landing just ahead of Centurion. Nat flicked his whip in his mount's eye line and began to ride out strongly. He thought he spotted Centurion in the corner of his eye and kicked on, the pair neck and neck as they fought it out. Nat continued to press Saint Jude who just edged past and went on to win by a short head. Euphoria coursed through him as the crowd cheered uproariously.

He pulled up his steaming mount as Michael and the horse's lad, Archie, ran up to him. He rode into the winner's enclosure, accepted all the plaudits and congratulations but not before noticing the scowl on Jamie McGuire's face. Serves him right, the little upstart, thought Nat, thankful that he was able to put the man in his place. Even the young, spotty conditional scowled at him too, as he walked back limping slightly, passing Nat as he was being interviewed. Nat ignored him and patted Saint Jude's neck as a fluffy microphone on a long stick was thrust into his face.

'Just a few words if we can Nat. What a cracking race! What did you make of it?'

It was the journalist and commentator, Tim Giles.

13

'Ah, I'm just thrilled, Tim. He gave me a great spin and the best horse won in the end.' Not to mention the best rider, he thought but it would be boastful to say so.

'So, any plans from the guvnor for this horse? Will he go in The King George?'

'I hope so, but it's up to the guvnor and the owners and let's just hope he stays fit.'

Tim nodded. 'And for you personally it must be a great feeling to win such a prestigious race on your comeback. How are you and how's the leg, that's what the public all want to know.'

'There's no problem with the leg. I've had a lot of support to get back and I need to thank so many people including Finn McCarthy, Harriet Lucas, my physio, and my girlfriend Livvy but especially Michael Kelly for having faith in me. And, of course, the public for their many messages of support.'

'And I take it you will be competing for the Championship this year, hoping to knock Colm McNally off his perch?'

Nat smiled widely for the camera. 'You'd better believe it.' He checked himself. 'But of course, Colm is a great lad, but he'll have a hard job catching me.'

'And any thoughts on Jamie McGuire, he's been doing a good job in your absence and ran you pretty close today.'

'He did, he did. He rode a good race. We're all good friends, and he's done a grand job whilst I've been off, but I'm back now.'

He really was. He felt a stab of satisfaction as he read the headlines after the race.

The master teaches his apprentice a hard lesson.

The Magician worked his magic in The Charlie Hall.

Wilson wins thriller and aims to regain his crown.

14

The subtitle read,' *and on that thrilling performance, he is well placed to do just that.'*

He was back and it felt wonderful!

Chapter Two

Hattie sat in the small shared office in the Professional Jockeys' Association and took a moment to take stock. After all the fallout, the exhausting drama following the case involving the chef, which she and her friend Finn had helped solve, Hattie was really pleased to have a short breather. Her new job at the PJA as a dietician had come at just the right time. But she was under no illusions as to why she'd been appointed, her office manager Julia Rylance had been fair but blunt on her first morning.

'Look Hattie, you did a good interview, but you weren't actually the first on the shortlist.' Julia was a middle aged woman with short salt and pepper hair and a lived in, healthy looking face with a minimum of makeup. Julia managed the PJA office in Walton which was a sort of one stop office where all jockey related issues were co-ordinated. Julia had pursed her thin lips and frowned as if carefully weighing up what exactly she could say. 'We usually employ staff who are pretty experienced as our dieticians. People who have worked with a range of clients, from NHS clinics, to athletes in all manner of fields. But it seems that you are particularly valuable. I don't know t' details but I was leaned on pretty heavily to take you and the BHA are funding half your post.'

Hattie had felt the burst of elation at finding her dream job vanish as if Julia had stabbed her balloon with a pin. The BHA or British Horseracing Authority, policed racing thoroughly and had made her and Finn the offer to complete inquiries into any fraudulent activities on their behalf whilst carrying out their current roles. Finn worked as a jockey coach and was already employed by them, but they had also been keen to procure Hattie's services. However, she hadn't expected them to fund half her post.

'Oh, I'm sorry... I didn't realise. I hope you're not unhappy and that someone didn't miss out on the job because of me...'

Julia had grinned. 'Don't fret lass, we've taken someone else on too, Carol, full time like you. You see, I understand you'll be working for the BHA when the need arises. But let's see how this goes, I'm not that keen if you have to keep buggering off on jobs for them... I mean how's that going to work?' Julia narrowed her eyes. 'I don't want to know what yer will be doing for 'em either. I mean, I can guess, but best not say anything. Alright?'

Hattie smiled in relief. She could see that her boss was suspicious, but her manner was warm, practical and seen from her point of view, Hattie could imagine how irregular this must seem. But Hattie was also sworn to secrecy. Working undercover for the BHA when the need arose, required absolute discretion, she simply couldn't reveal details of the cases that she and her friend, jockey coach, Finn McCarthy had worked on. For one thing the legal process was only just beginning, and the culprit involved was in custody, his trial set sometime next year, so any leak could prejudice proceedings. It was expected that more might come out as the case progressed, but until then the BHA had to keep silent. After all the case involved betting fraud which was a highly sensitive issue.

'Well look, I can't imagine anything much is going to happen. Probably, it won't take up much time.' Hattie was keen to appease her new boss. She thought back to the tense ending to the investigation, when Nat was shot and she and Finn thought they'd be next. It may

17

have seemed like months to her because of the danger and threat but in reality the time it had taken up was a matter of a month from start to finish. The emotion and tension involved had possibly made it seem much longer. 'Listen, I'm here to work really hard, to learn as much as I can, being a dietician is my dream job, you know.'

Julia patted her hand. 'Yer said in yer interview. But I think we need a cover story should the need arise. Reckon you might have to have time off for health reasons or summat every so often, that do yer?'

Hattie who was generally extremely healthy and definitely had no medical conditions, gasped, her mind whirling. She actually felt quite offended. 'Well, what do you suggest? I'm actually very fit.'

Julia laughed. 'We don't need to say. Lots of health conditions are highly confidential, so it's probably best to say nothing if anyone asks. Right, you'll do. Now let's get Carol in and I'll go through the new employee handbook with you both and then we'll sort out some work.'

Now a couple of months on, Hattie was enjoying herself. She was determined to work hard and impress Julia. The team were all friendly and she was starting to take on her own clients. She hadn't realised that the role would involve so much travel but she and Carol, as the only two dieticians in the area, covered most of the north of the country. They had links with The National Horseracing College in Doncaster, ran drop in sessions there and also had liaised with Liverpool John Moores University too. Hattie had now had to drop her work with the Racing to School initiative but she felt she was on her way, doing a valuable and useful job. To begin with she shadowed Carol, who was an efficient and well presented 40 year old who always reminded Hattie of Fiona Bruce, the news reader. She had sat in on training and drop-in sessions with her and could tell that her new colleague had a great depth of experience. Carol had worked with the Team GB Cycling team and had a lot of interesting titbits of gossip about them and funny anecdotes. She was always extolling the virtues of that 'nice Chris Hoy' and telling her about Bradley Wiggins and his wicked sense of humour, and had what Hattie recognised as a real need to keep dropping their names into the conversation. Still, Hattie liked her and was learning a lot and crucially Carol did not seem the type to ask a lot of personal questions so wrapped up was she in her own life, which would be a blessing if she was called upon to investigate any matters for the BHA.

Hattie ran through her notes for her assessment of one of the young conditionals she was going to see later. Joel Fox was concerned about how much protein to eat and was worried that his weight training and extra whey based protein shakes might make him bulk up too much. She had a proforma to guide her and would be asking questions about his dietary and nutritional history, his exercise, medical issues and was then going to help devise an individualised meal plan for him. Then Carol had passed on notes about another client, a woman jockey who was worried about her diet and frequent chocolate yearnings. Hattie could sympathise with that all right. She was just printing off some information about the Eatwell plate, a guide for balancing nutrition when she heard her phone beep. She glanced down and smiling opened a text from Finn.

'You free for lunch? Blacksmith's at 12?'

Hattie smiled and replied. She would have time to meet him before seeing Joel at two. She felt a rush of excitement, after the two recent dramas of their last cases, she'd had a quiet couple of months and hadn't seen much of Finn. She wondered how he was. It was hard to describe their friendship, for it was a friendship rather than anything romantic, she thought of him as a big brother, in a way and she liked his company though he could be grouchy at times. Her mood lifted. It would be good to catch up.

Finn was waiting at a table by the window in the traditional, reasonably busy pub. He wore a dark denim shirt with chinos, topped off with an old Barbour and his usual scuffed suede boots and was poring over The Racing Post.

'Hi Hattie, how's it going?' He looked well, she noticed, relaxed and calm. Hattie saw the young barmaid handing out the menus give him an appreciative glance.

They ordered food and Hattie sipped the half pint of shandy Finn had ready for her.

'How's the job?' he asked, folding up his paper. 'Going OK, so far?'

'Fine.' Hattie went on to explain about her role and Finn listened, nodding every so often with interest. It had been him who had spotted the job advert and she suspected he'd been influential in helping her land the role along with his boss, Tony Murphy.

'What about you?'

Finn put down his beer. 'Yeah, I've got a whole crop of interesting new conditionals to work with. Quite a few girls, this time.' He smiled. 'Should be easier to manage than the lads anyway.'

Harriet grinned back. Some of the lads Finn had mentored had certainly caused him a great deal of stress and worry. The brother of one of his conditionals had been murdered which had set off a whole chain of events which they were all still reeling from, as fraud was uncovered. The young conditional, Gavin, had struggled emotionally as a result of his brother's passing but also his involvement in crime.

'How's Gavin?'

'Oh, doing OK, coping much better considering, riding well.' They chatted for a while about their mutual acquaintances as Hattie knew many of the lads that Finn, formerly a jockey, now trained in his role as jockey coach. 'You heard about Nat?'

Finn opened the paper and showed her an article which dominated the front page with the headline 'The Magician Works his Magic in The Charlie Hall.'

'He only went and won, the lucky sod.'

Hattie laughed. 'You know as well as I do that luck has very little to do with it. Fair play to him. He was the first jockey I helped in my new role, you know.' Hattie had advised the ex-Champion jockey on his nutrition for his recovery from a serious injury.

'Here's to many more winners,' Finn raised his glass and then leaned closer. 'There was something I wanted to talk to you about…'

Hattie felt her body stiffen, she was suddenly intently alert, bursts of energy dancing around her body. 'Yes. Anything for the BHA?'

'Not as such.'

A young girl arrived with their food and Hattie waited until she'd put down their bacon and brie baguettes and helped herself to mayonnaise before saying, 'Go on then Finn, what is it?'

Finn picked up his knife and fork. 'There's been a few rumours. Nothing concrete, comments from a jockey, repeated, passed around but when she was asked outright, she then changed her tune and denied that she'd said it.'

'She?' There were, Hattie knew, a growing number of very competent and highly skilled women jockeys who were making names for themselves in the sport and competing very much alongside men, in the same way as female three day event riders and show jumpers had always competed. And not before time in Hattie's view.

Finn lowered his voice. 'A female jockey, whose name is not known, has told several colleagues that she thought there should be a 'Me Too' movement in racing and made allegations against another jockey. Tony Murphy just wants us to keep our ears to the ground, ask about a bit. I thought you'd be well placed in your role. I was going to sound out my new conditionals. I've just got a new one actually, Sinead O'Brien, who might be troublesome. But I thought the young women might talk more to you, especially about more sensitive stuff…'

Hattie swallowed a bite of melted brie. 'I know just where to start. I have a new female client. Anyway, what's the deal with this Sinead O'Brien?'

'Well, she's had a difficult background, been in care, can ride well, but has an attitude problem. She's prickly and doesn't like being told to follow the rules. She's at Robert Johnson's, I haven't even met her yet and he's rung me twice to complain about her already.'

Harriet frowned, wondering where Finn was going with this. He seemed uneasy about dealing with potentially awkward females and Sinead certainly sounded tricky. Maybe he feared allegations being made against him and needed a sort of chaperone.

'Why do you think I could talk to her?'

'You're female, sympathetic, and you know what young women are bothered about.'

'Hmm. Fine. Though you and Robert need to talk to her about expectations and the demands of the role, of course.' Harriet knew that a conditional's life was very hard and competitive and many would drop out. 'Still, I can easily see her on the guise of talking to her about her diet.'

Finn grinned and seemed relieved. 'So, why don't you come to my BHA session on professionalism and introduce yourself?'

'OK, when is it?'

Finn told her. He studied her carefully for a minute.

'So, you're not put off by your run in with that other idiot?'

22

Hattie sighed and tried hard not to show that she suddenly felt as if ice cubes where sliding down her spine and her stomach lurched and then dropped alarmingly. Her hands shook and her food felt like plastic in her throat. Her appetite suddenly vanished like water down a plughole. She picked at her meal listlessly. She took a deep breath and tried to act normally.

'Nah, it'd take more than a jumped up moron to frighten me, Finn.'

If Finn noticed the fact that she had left her chips, or her changed demeanour, he did not comment. Hattie was trying desperately to appear nonchalant and detached but there was no getting away from it. The casual mention of their last case had upset her. Christ, she couldn't lose her nerve, not when everything was going so well, not when she'd got her dream job. She wasn't about to tell him about the nightmares either or her restricted social life and her anxiety about meeting new people, specifically males. Her friend Daisy had noticed, tried to talk to her and her mother was constantly asking her if she was all right. But surely it was just a blip, something to be expected. She needed to work through it, everything would be OK if she just refused to think about that room where she'd been held captive. To stop thinking about that bastard. But what was worse was that she had been taken in by him! She had even thought he might like her. More fool her! Finn was staring at her quizzically.

'Right, keep in touch and I'll text you to confirm the date and time.' Finn got up to leave.

'Yeah, good to see you.' Her voice even to her own ears felt too bright, too loud, fake. She wondered if she was going to be ready to help Finn and the BHA, to investigate any integrity concerns when they arose in racing. That was, after all, why the BHA were paying half her salary at the PJA, so that she could be released to do just that. In the wake of what had happened previously and the nightmares and panic

23

attacks this had caused, she was beginning to think that she couldn't do it and that she might have got the job on false pretences.

Chapter Three

Finn rose early and made himself some toast and a cup of coffee. As he sipped his drink he thought back to his meeting with his friend, Harriet Lucas. Worry gnawed away at him as he realised that there was something very wrong. Although she had valiantly tried to hide it, she had stiffened and had become overly upbeat, but he hadn't missed the devastating effect his mention of the man who had held her hostage, had had on her. The tell tale sign was the tension in her body and the fact that she had left the remainder of her meal, which was so unlike her. One of the things he liked about her was the fact that she was unaffected, and all her emotions showed on her face and it was very clear that she was in distress. They had been involved in two previous cases but in this one, the chap had realised that they were onto him. He had wanted to pull off a huge betting coup. The man had killed several people and attempted to murder at least two more, himself included, and he knew that Hattie might struggle when the court case was on and the horror of her ordeal was relived. Still, he was aware that she had been offered some counselling and he knew several psychologists himself, so he would make sure she was offered a discreet service to help her move on. As far as he knew, she hadn't taken anyone up on their offer of counselling, she probably was hoping that over time she'd improve on her own, but he was sceptical about this. She might have PTSD, but her pride had been dented too. She had been taken in by the man's charm and interest in her and this misjudgement of him was a real smack in the face. His role as a jockey coach and hers as a dietician for the PJA were perfect to undertake undercover work for the BHA Integrity unit, but not if Hattie was still traumatised. Still, it was unlikely that anything would happen like that again. OK, there were the rumours of sexually inappropriate behaviour toward female jockeys but that was something he could deal with on his own, so perhaps he wouldn't need to bother Hattie? Except, of course, it would be so much easier for the women to talk to Harriet. He frowned as he remembered the tension in her face. He needed to talk to his friend, Charlie Durrant whose girlfriend, Tara Regan, was a psychologist. Tara was such a lovely person and he felt sure that she and Harriet would get on really well. He believed she would help. He texted Charlie whilst it was in his thoughts and felt his mood lift. Hattie would be fine, all she needed was time and an expert to point her in the right direction. Satisfied he rang several jockeys he was due to see and finished off his coffee.

First on his list was Sam Foster, a young conditional jockey who was well on his way to becoming a professional. He'd had a difficult start in his professional career and his old guvnor had tried to blackmail him to pull races but had moved yards and gone from strength to strength in his new place. He rode for Robert Johnson now and having ridden almost 35 winners was on his way to riding out his claim. Conditional jockeys needed to have 75 winners in order to do that and as this was the end of October and just at the start of the National Hunt season, so Finn reckoned he had a good chance of making it as a professional this season, barring accidents or some other misfortune. Conditionals had until they were 26 years of age to make this target ordinarily.

He could also introduce himself to Sinead O'Brien if she was there, just make out he was in the area. He pulled into the layby at the communal gallops at Walton. He glanced at his watch, it was just before seven and he knew the gallops would be teeming with horses and work riders and suspected that Sam and Robert Johnson would be amongst them. He spotted Robert watching his string and made his way over to him.

The shared gallops were situated in the heart of the town. Most of the twenty or so yards used them except for some of the stables which were too far out to transport their horses into the town centre on a daily basis. Land was plentiful and some trainers had their own gallops or shared with other outlying yards. It was a fine October day, but Finn was glad of his Barbour at this time of the morning and enjoyed the breeze as he walked up onto the gallops. There were three tracks, one to the left, one that rose in front of him and a track that led to the right which had an all weather surface. The place was a hive of activity as horses galloped in groups, their coats gleaming as their hooves pounded the earth. The tracks were on an incline and were perfect for training. As the National Hunt season was well underway, the horses there tended to be rangier than their counterparts on the flat. There were a series of hurdles arranged on a small circuit and several horses and riders were practicing over jumps. The sight was so familiar and exciting that Finn was filled with anticipation.

Finn spotted Robert Johnson and strolled over to meet him.

'Hi. How's it going?'

The trainer nodded. 'Fine. We're hoping for a good season and yer lad, Sam, is doing really well.' He glanced at a bay horse negotiating the row of hurdles and recognised Sam's curly hair sticking out from under his helmet, covered with its customary blue silk. He rode extremely well, and Finn watched him fly over the fences in style.

'How's Niall?'

Niall Finnegan was Johnson's stable jockey who had had a crashing fall at Doncaster almost at the start of the season and was likely to be out for at least a couple of months with a broken leg.

Robert grimaced. 'Pissed off being out so early on, but at least it gives Sam a chance to shine.'

Finn nodded knowing that Sam would make the most of it. Racing was like that; a game of snakes and ladders and you just had to take your chances when they came. Still, it was bad luck for Niall.

'So, how long will Niall be out for?'

Robert shrugged. 'A good couple of months and that's if everything goes well.' Robert sighed. 'Listen, Sinead is here too, if you want a word. She's only been with me two weeks and as I said she's upset the other stable staff, been late twice and argued with the Head Lad. She's had a verbal warning already. And she's got a bloody social worker visiting and supporting her, asking me to make allowances for her background. I ask you…' Robert scowled, clearly demonstrating what he thought about this. 'I mean, I'm a fair man, but she's already rubbed me up the wrong way.'

'Which horse is she riding?'

Robert nodded and pointed to a slight figure galloping on a fine grey horse.

'She came well recommended, I read the report from the Horseracing College.' Finn had studied the document carefully and there seemed to be no doubt about her ability, to be fair to the girl.

'Hmm. It's her attitude, though. She's very lippy and I'm not sure how long she'll last actually, and she has a chip the size of Yorkshire on her shoulder.' He frowned. 'I reckon you'll have yer work cut out with her!'

Finn nodded. The National Horseracing College formerly the Northern Racing College trained jockeys and they were firm but fair. Finn knew the staff well and felt they would not have recommended her for the position if she didn't have some redeeming features. Finn wondered if Sinead felt she had to be like that to compete on equal terms with the men. He thought about what Tony Murphy had said about sexual harassment and a 'Me Too' type of movement being uncovered in racing. He counted at least three females amongst his cohort of conditionals this year and wondered if he should hold a joint session for them. He could talk about any difficulties they might encounter and invite Hattie along to discuss their dietary requirements, but also thought the girls might be able to confide more easily in her. He was brought up to respect all women and was really worried about the prospect of women being subjected to sexual harassment in order to gain the same privileges that males enjoyed. Besides, such a plan would really help Hattie and he could do with her input as he was beginning to feel out of his depth. He was a passionate supporter of women in racing but knew that prejudice and outmoded beliefs still existed in the sport in some quarters and there was no point denying it. He was determined that his female conditionals would be given exactly the same opportunities as the males. Yet he could also see Robert's point of view about Sinead. Conditionals of either sex had to be respectful and work hard, with no exceptions, otherwise they'd soon find themselves out on their ear. It wasn't an easy life and there was only a small percentage of conditionals who made it as professional jockeys. Owners and trainers expected good race riding and politeness. It did no harm to have some social skills as owners, who after all held a great deal of sway with the trainers, were paying the bills and often had fixed ideas about who they wanted to ride their horses. Owners liked jockeys they could talk to and who worked hard and didn't create a fuss. Sinead obviously had a lot to learn. He sighed. He had thought that maybe his female mentees would be easier to handle than the lads, but now he was not so sure.

He spoke to Sam Foster, Connor Moore and Liam Flynn, watching as the lads negotiated the row of fences, some more successfully than others. It was completely different race riding rather than show jumping and the key was to get over the fences quickly with minimum deceleration. It was a hard skill to acquire and once he had gained consent from the jockeys' respective guvnors, he schooled the lads over the fences. They queued up as he talked them through riding the circuit of fences. Sam Foster, was easily identified in his blue hat silk, handled everything with poise and confidence, Connor Moore had improved but still needed help with positioning, whilst Liam Flynn needed to go back to basics and did not have a stable enough seat for

29

fast jumping, so could benefit from more Equiciser training. He talked through their performances, encouraging them to evaluate it themselves, trying to give positives before telling them what to work on. He made a note to see who required individual attention and decided to book them in for some basic lessons, Connor Moore and Liam amongst them. He noticed the pale faced, slight figure of Sinead O'Brien watching them as she circled on a handsome grey horse. He decided to introduce himself.

'Hi there, I'm Finn McCarthy. Are you Sinead? I think you are assigned to me under the conditional mentoring scheme.' He smiled and held out his hand. She sniffed and shook it somewhat reluctantly.

'Alright? What is the conditional jockey mentoring scheme when it's at home?'

Finn told her, thinking that he was sure that Robert, Sam and The National Horseracing College would surely have explained this to her already.

'So, the idea is that I support conditionals and help them with all aspects of riding, racing, insurance, using an agent, dealing with the press, maintaining your weight, anything really about your wellbeing. How are you finding things at Johnson's?'

The girl had blue eyes, bleached blonde hair and a very wary expression. In fact, she radiated insolence and hostility. She was chewing gum incessantly and looked like she would rather be anywhere else than where she was.

She shrugged. 'S'alright, only been there a couple of weeks.'

'And yer guvnor said that you'd come from The National Horseracing College. How was that?'

'OK, I s'pose.' The girl managed a spectacular sneer and it was then that Finn noticed that she had a nose ring and an eyebrow piercing still in situ. Finn wondered how to tackle the subject. The girl's manner made him angry. How many other kids would have given their eye teeth to be in her position? She was in danger of squandering her opportunities, he realised.

'You shouldn't be riding with piercings, Sinead. I'm sure Robert has told you that. I don't want to see you with them in future. If you fall you could end up with a piercing embedded in your skull and you wouldn't want that, would you?'

Sinead flushed. 'I didn't have time to tek them out, I were up at the crack of dawn,' she grumbled, her whole face contorting with contempt. She glared at Finn. 'It's not my fault, I couldn't get to sleep.' She yawned widely.

Finn decided that a direct, firm approach was required. He pulled out a handkerchief from his jacket pocket. 'Right, well unless you want to walk home, I'd suggest you take them out now or I will talk to your guvnor. And whilst you're at it, change your attitude. You will get a fair chance at Johnson's but he's already had to give you a warning about being late. You have a great chance here and it's up to you to make the most of it. Your guvnor and I can only do so much, the rest is down to you.'

Sinead flushed, mouthed something then reluctantly fiddled with her nose ring and eyebrow piercing. She dropped them into Finn's hand, her face contorted into a scowl. Finn ignored her expression and studied her mount, Islander, a reasonable hurdler and decided to push her harder.

'Right, now circle your horse on the right rein going from a walk to trot to canter and then pop over that row of hurdles, will you?'

He was expecting a flat out refusal but Sinead pursed her lips and eyed up the fences. Then she picked up her reins and kicked on.

Finn watched as she did exactly as was asked, trotted for a couple of circuits, then urged Islander on into a canter.

After the horse was nicely warmed up on both reins, Finn shouted at her to try the fences and she sat still, leaning forward as she

31

sailed over the hurdles. Apart from slightly missing the horse's stride at the first fence, she did rather well, she wasn't stylish and her positioning wasn't perfect. She needed a lot of work but he was pleasantly surprised. Finn knew instinctively not to be overly complimentary,

'Go again,' he shouted, 'and don't get left behind this time.'

She went again and this time she rode much better. She was prepared for the horse's take off and rode with more confidence. She pulled up and stared at him.

He handed her the piercings he had kept in his handkerchief. 'Don't let me catch you wearing these again. Right, I'll speak to your guvnor and pop down in the week for a catch up and you're invited to the session about the BHA rules at Hunt's place. Make sure you come.'

Sinead patted Islander and gave him a questioning look. She was obviously expecting some feedback. He finally relented.

'You need a lot of work, and I mean a lot,' he resisted the urge to say more. 'But you have some potential, don't throw it all away.'

He was rewarded as the girl's face was wreathed in smiles. She looked like a completely different person. He found himself smiling back. Perhaps, he'd make a jockey out of her yet?

Chapter Four

Nat Wilson gazed at Livvy after vigorous lovemaking. He took in her fine features, pale alabaster skin, shiny dark hair and slim body, with curves in all the right places. She had a slight flush to her cheeks from their activities and sighed with contentment.

'Why do you always do that?'

'What? 'asked Nat.

Livvy shook her head. 'Stare at me. It's unnerving, you know.'

'Well, sorry. I like looking at you. I do love you, you know.'

It was true. He, Nat Wilson, had had loads of affairs, had always been the one to flee from any type of commitment, he patiently ended so many relationships with distraught women and had never been in love, not properly, until he had met Livvy. The only problem had been that of course she was engaged to his best friend and colleague, Finn McCarthy, at the time. He had stolen her without compunction, taken a bullet for Finn by way of compensation many years later, but his biggest fear was that he would lose Livvy, that she would find out how unworthy he was of her. Unaccustomed to being dependent emotionally on someone else for his happiness, he reflected that it was an uncomfortable, disturbing feeling.

Livvy sighed again and kissed the top of his nose. 'I know, but not enough to give up racing though.' She threw back the duvet and stepped out of bed treating Nat to a view of her perfect, slim body. She looked back at him with a serious expression. 'I know, I know, you don't want to talk about it, and I get why you do it. Bloody Finn was the same but honestly, I just worry. It's bad enough taking a bullet for Finn and now you're back chasing the Championship, I just feel scared.'

Nat grinned. 'Don't you worry about me, sweetheart. I'm like a cat with nine lives, and besides I'm lucky, I was born lucky!'

Livvy wrapped herself in her dressing gown, her eye shining with tears.

'But what happens when your luck runs out?'

'Come on now, Livvy. Nothing is going to happen, I'm The Magician, that's what they call me. Nothing will go wrong. I need to ride whilst I can, I might not have that many years left at the top. But I'm a survivor and like I said, I was born lucky and I'll always bounce back.'

Livvy turned on the shower in the en suite and came back to hug him. It was a long time before she let him go.

'Just make sure you do.'

Nat was in a rush. Being based in Cheltenham as a stable jockey for Michael Kelly, he was on his way to Worcester for an afternoon's racing. He was riding three of Michael's horses and could also pick up other rides from injured jockeys. Injuries were very common in this game. Statistically, jockeys were likely to fall every 14 rides, so it was something they had to live with. Most jockeys kept a range of icepacks, strappings, antiseptic creams and other medical paraphernalia at home. Nat had drawers full of the stuff. Like most, Nat was a great believer in ice packs and a shot of whiskey to numb any pain. Nat also had a doctor who was a close friend and could be called upon, if the need arose, out of hours, that way he could avoid the hospital and be back riding sooner.

Worcester racecourse was one of the oldest in the country and a favourite of Nat's. It had staged racing since 1718 and was pleasantly situated on the banks of the River Severn. It featured a lefthanded oval track of about 13 furlongs. It was a short distance from the three storey Georgian home he shared with Livvy, some 40 minutes or so from Cheltenham and Nat decided to take the back roads so he could try out his new Mercedes for size. Being a top jockey meant that he had to drive a lot, sometimes as much as 150,000 miles in a year. He loved speed and relished the opportunity to put his toe down on the M5 and then the 'A' road that led to Worcester. Often jockeys travelled together if they lived within a reasonable radius and were riding at the same meeting, but Nat had made his excuses to Jamie McGuire, Michael Kelly's second jockey, as he had a presentation to attend that evening, handing out awards at a ceremony at Cheltenham racecourse. In truth he had time to go home and then head out, but something about Jamie rankled and he wanted to try his car out for size just on his own. His in-car Sat Nav alerted him to speed cameras and if he was very careful, he could avoid being caught, as he didn't want to lose his driving licence. He picked up the pace and soared through the roads at speeds of 110 mph before deciding to take it more slowly. He already had nine points on his license and didn't want to risk more, so pulled himself back from pushing the car harder, taking a much more leisurely pace into Worcester.

The weighing room was full of the usual lads, with the exception of those who usually rode further north like Tristan Davies and Charlie Durrant but some other familiar faces such as Gerry King, Jamie McGuire and Colm McNally were already there, along with some conditionals, the pimply lad who had fallen in The Charlie Hall amongst them. The lads were in a huddle as he entered the changing room, but quickly dispersed and began the usual routine of running down each other's chances, talking about owners, women and horses, the usual banter and chatter much in evidence. Nat had the strange impression that he had missed out on a lot of action when he'd been injured. Things changed so quickly in racing that he felt slightly on the backfoot but then dismissed his concerns. He appeared to have interrupted a conversation about who would be in the running for the Championship.

'So, are you up for the Championship this year, or are you taking it easy, first season back?' asked Gerry King.

'Course I'm bloody up for it,' he replied. 'The guvnor has some great horses so why not, and I'm back fighting fit.' He noticed Colm McNally listening intently to his reply, as did Jamie McGuire. They shared a complicit look, Nat couldn't help but notice.

'Thigh sorted now, is it?' asked Jamie.

Nat pulled the purple and green colours of his next ride on and patted his thigh. 'Never better lads, never better.'

'Good,'replied Gerry under his breath, 'because there are those that really wanna take your crown.'

Nat nodded. Presumably, he meant Colm and Jamie, but he noticed the pimply conditional giving him dirty looks and wondered if he was still sore about him stealing his ground in The Charlie Hall. He had no regrets about that, the lad just needed to bloody well grow up, that was all.

'Alright?' he asked him, catching his eye, daring the lad to speak out. The lad flushed and muttered some response. The blush accentuated his spots, so his face looked like it had craters all over it. Nat resisted the urge to comment upon them and shook his head. It was no good taking his anger out on the kid. He did feel irritated. Damn, what was the matter with these guys? OK, he had been off but for a very good reason. Now he was back, and he sensed resentment and intense rivalry from every quarter. He realised that the very thing he

36

needed to do was for him to show his superiority rather than simply talk about it. They all needed a lesson from The Magician, he decided, and he would give it to them. He squared his shoulders as the buzzer went and he led the walk out into the clear November afternoon.

Nat rode Harlequin for a syndicate in the first. The syndicate wore matching scarves and were fizzing with excitement. Nat shook what seemed to be about 20 outstretched hands and smiled broadly.

'Can't believe we've got you riding,' exclaimed one of the women, an attractive brunette. 'It's like a dream come true! Now we just need a win!'

Nat grinned back and said he hoped he would do well for them. Sadly, the horse was something of a novice, but managed a creditable fourth after a lot of pushing. He was confident that the horse would win in the future, however, and said as much to the assembled group of owners who looked less downcast after that. He managed a second place on High Fidelity in the third, just missing out on a win by a short head. It did not improve his mood that the winner was ridden by none other than Colm McNally. At least he was on the favourite for the last race, Mercurial, a beautiful dark bay that Michael thought highly of. Nat had ridden the gelding at home and knew he really had potential but was little raced. He saw that he was 3-1 favourite and was pretty certain that he could end the afternoon with a win and reassert himself as the top jockey.

The owners were a lovely middle aged couple, the Harrisons, who owned several horses with Michael Kelly, but Mercurial was their best. They were buzzing with excitement and anticipation and Nat didn't want to let them down. Michael gave him his instructions which were pretty brief.

'Well, we're hoping for a win, so let's get on with it.'

'That's why we wanted you to ride him, we wanted the best rider,' explained Mrs Harrison with a coy smile. 'We're so glad you're back. Jamie did his best but…'

37

Nat nodded, pleased at their view of Jamie. He looked out for his rival and saw that he was riding a reasonable horse, The Editor, for another stable. The horse had won a few times but preferred softer ground than today's going. He studied the big bay as he circled in the parade ring. He was on his toes and looked very well. He noted the green colours with the blue cross of Lorraine and also spotted the pimply conditional talking animatedly to his trainer as he took his instructions. He was riding a little raced horse called Jack The Lad, which had been placed last time out. On the whole, he felt there was little to beat them today. He'd soon show them who was boss, he decided, vowing to win with the bay by hook or by crook.

The race was over three miles, so Nat knew he had to judge the pace correctly and keep the horse mid pack until it was time to strike. Mercurial had good stamina but was a little one paced. He was also a reliable jumper and was well schooled, recently by Nat himself, so he planned to pace his race so that he was pushing for the lead well before the last fence. The three miles equated to almost two circuits of the track. After the first circuit, it was so far so good. He was midway and behind the leaders; a front runner ridden by Colm McNally called Marmaduke and second, the conditional's mount, Jack The Lad and Jamie McGuire's, The Editor. The ground was good to soft and softer in some places, so Nat regularly wiped his goggles and kept his wits about him as he maintained his place. Coming up to the third last, he kicked on from his position by the rails and joined the leading pack of three horses. By now the front runner, Marmaduke, had given his best effort and he passed him and Colm easily, pushing his horse up to catch the leaders. Coming up to the second last, he showed Mercurial the whip and kicked on, jumping well to settle into second place behind The Editor and just nudging past Jack The Lad on the inside. Mercurial was running on gamely, so he kicked on as The Editor's hind quarters and Jamie's green and blue colours came closer and closer into view, as they started to gain on the bay horse. In the corner of his eye, he saw Jack The Lad rallying, as he started to come back. The three horses were battling it out before the last fence. Nat pressed Mercurial into the brush fence and then disaster struck. Just as Nat saw the stride and kicked on to tell the bay horse to take off, the animal seemed to burst forward as though spooked, ruining his take off so that the horse lost his footing and in a tangle of legs and brush, Mercurial crashed to the floor. Nat curled up into a ball and narrowly missed the horse's flailing legs before the animal jumped up and cantered off. Nat gingerly opened his eyes to see Jack the Lad with the pimply conditional aboard sailing ahead.

What the hell had happened? Nat lay dazed for a minute and carefully moved each limb until he was sure he was OK and hadn't broken any bones. When he was sure he hadn't, he waved away the Ambulance staff and began the long walk back home, his throat contracting with bitter disappointment. It was so unlike Mercurial to fall, what the hell had happened? Maybe Jack The Lad coming up behind him had spooked him, in which case he'd talk to the guvnor about using blinkers, which would limit his vision and stop him seeing anything coming up behind him. He wondered which horse had won and decided that it didn't much matter. Either way McGuire or worse the pimply conditional would be full of it. Never mind, he was really glad that he hadn't given McGuire a lift now. He would have been insufferable on the journey home. As he walked back to the changing rooms, he realised that Jamie's horse had won, closely followed by the conditional's mount, Jack the Lad. He muttered congratulations to the youngster who was flushed with pride, put Mercurial's performance down to him being spooked and recommended that Michael try blinkers on the horse next time. He was upbeat with the owners, who were clearly very disappointed but explained that horses were not machines and were indeed fallible.

'We live to fight another day. He'll definitely win in the future,' he had added, which seemed to mollify the owners at least. Michael Kelly was genuinely bemused by the horse's fall too, but said he would try blinkers in the future, though he wasn't convinced that it had been the problem. Nat was philosophical. At least neither he nor the horse were injured which was something.

Jamie came late into the weighing room, holding a trophy and smirking.

'Bad luck, old man,' he muttered with a sly smile. Colm McNally caught Jamie's eye and grinned.

'Well done,' replied Nat, magnanimously, determined not to bite back. He had the definite feeling that both of them were trying to psych him out and play mind games and he was far too experienced to rise to the bait. Again, he was glad he hadn't travelled with McGuire otherwise he'd feel like smashing his smug face in on the drive home.

Feeling marginally better about things, he set off for Cheltenham, arriving at the awards ceremony in plenty of time. He was often asked to attend functions by his agent but tended to be quite selective in the season. As this one was local, he decided to accept the invitation and had been asked to give a short address and hand out several prizes. It was the local business awards and the great and good of Cheltenham and Gloucester were gathered in one of the racecourse rooms, suitably bedecked with merchandising materials and advertising banners. Nat popped to the toilets. He had taken a smart suit with him and had showered prior to leaving the races. He checked his tousled, expensively coiffed hair in the mirror, added aftershave, his Omega watch, blue topaz cufflinks and felt his concerns about his rather dismal afternoon melt away. He had a few minor cuts and bruises but that was it. His pride was dented more than anything. It was just one of those freaky things that happened and would probably never happen again. He smiled at the man reflected back at him in the men's room mirror and liked what he saw. His mid brown hair was worn to his collar, his eyes were an intense blue and he had slight stubble. The whole effect was very pleasing, the pin up boy of National Hunt Racing looked very good indeed and he was still the man to beat.

The Cheltenham and Gloucester Business Awards was a swish affair. There was a buffet table piled with pulled pork, chicken goujons, smoked salmon, vast salad bowls, crusty bread, exquisite cheeses and a huge selection of sweets, profiteroles, brownies, fruit salad and cheesecake, on another table. Waiters and waitresses dressed in black and white circulated with trays of champagne, wine and soft drinks. The place steadily began to fill up with smartly dressed people. A young woman dressed in a red cocktail dress, with her hair in a high bun and high heels came tripping up to him and showed him to his table.

'I'm Chantelle Hirst, the organiser. I've put you with some racecourse staff, the general and marketing managers and Clerk of the Course, plus the local Mayor, his wife and a couple of small business owners.' She smiled brightly and for a second he was assailed by the woman's heady perfume. 'You'll be presenting the main prizes for Business of the Year, Best Newcomer and Best Community Engagement awards. You'll be introduced by our host, Keith Shenton, from the local Business Strategy Group.' She clutched his arm. 'Nat Wilson, I can't believe it's you. I'm having to pinch myself, really I am. I'm so glad you could make it, you look even better in the flesh. Now if there's anything you need, anything at all, then please give me a shout!' She gazed at him for a fraction too long and it was easy to guess her true meaning. Chantelle made her way to her table but not before giving him a long lingering glance as she walked away. Nat smiled back and watched the curvaceous figure retreating. At one time he would have certainly taken her up on her offer, but not since he had met Livvy. He had lost his taste for easy conquests forever.

The other guests at his table were entertaining. He knew the racecourse staff, especially the Clerk, although he wasn't keen on the obsequious marketing manager with the double barrelled name, thick glasses, a rather pompous manner, and a habit of name dropping. The Mayor and his wife were full of their own self importance, but he liked the two business owners. Lewis was a young man who had started a coffee business called 'Beans' and finally there was Milly, a young rather nervous woman with a self deprecating manner who was the owner of 'Milly the Milliner', a business hiring hats out for all occasions, which included women attending race meetings such as

Cheltenham and Ascot. She looked astonishing in a pale pink tight dress and a matching, feathery fascinator.

'I can't believe I'm sitting with THE Nat Wilson,' she enthused before asking for lots of selfies. 'Wait till I tell my friends!'

Lewis was also a racing fan and shook Nat's hand very vigorously. 'I have won so much money on you, I can't tell you! I'm delighted to meet you.'

The Clerk, Stuart Dobbs, quizzed Nat on his rides and plans for the future.

'Shame about that last race today at Worcester. I thought you had it in the bag!'

Nat sighed. 'Me too.' He shrugged. 'I guess it was just one of those things. Horses are unpredictable and you can never be absolutely certain what they'll do next.'

'Oh, I agree,' added Milly as she downed yet another glass of champagne. 'I used to have a horse, but I spent most of my time trying to get him to do stuff and failing miserably! How do you cope riding different horses every day?'

Nat laughed. 'Well, experience, I suppose and if they're well schooled, it's not so bad.'

'You're so modest,' added Milly, helping herself to another glass of wine. 'God, I'm up for the Best Newcomer Award and I'm so nervous!' she confided. 'It could make all the difference to my business and give me a real boost!' She held up her hand with her index and middle fingers crossed as she took another gulp of wine.

Keith Shenton, Business Strategy Manager, certainly gave Nat a flattering introduction.

'So, our guest of honour and triple Gold Cup winner, six times Champion jockey and double winner of the Grand National, and damned nice guy, needs no introduction, but can I just say we're so delighted to welcome him to our annual awards ceremony. Thank you for taking time out of your busy schedule to be here tonight, can I introduce the one and only Nat Wilson!'

Nat got to his feet amidst rapturous applause which took ages to quieten down. He cleared his throat.

'I'm delighted to be here, to support the Annual Cheltenham and Gloucester Business Awards. I have studied the many stalls and seen for myself the creativity and skill involved in many of the businesses represented tonight. As a jockey and sportsman, I can totally relate to being in business. The highs and lows and sheer determination to succeed in business, echo very much with my own experiences of riding. One minute you're winning the Cheltenham Gold Cup and the next you're a faller in a three mile handicap at Worcester, trying to avoid flailing hooves and eating dirt, like today.' He gave a self deprecating shrug.

There was a huge cheer and cat calls from the crowd.

'But like you guys, I know that the answer is to work harder and smarter than the next guy and to never give up your dreams! So, good luck to you all and congratulations to the winners!'

Even more applause rang out as Nat read out the winners. He was pleased to find that 'Milly the Milliner' won best newcomer and she was delighted, enthusiastically kissing Nat before staggering off the stage, slightly tipsy from the wine she had drunk. The overall winner was an engineering business who manufactured precision parts and the best community project was a dinner club, called 'Lunch Bunch' that provided friendship and healthy foods to the elderly and vulnerable. Nat decided to mingle for a little longer before making his excuses. His body was aching from his fall and his left thigh was also giving him gyp. He headed off to find Chantelle who hugged him over enthusiastically and thanked him profusely for coming.

'Any time', he called before heading off. As he walked towards the door, he came across Milly staggering about in the hallway as she waited for a lift.

'Hey, Champ, I wwon. Give us a kissh wwon't youuu…'

Nat smiled politely and tried to keep the girl at arm's length. She had been celebrating with several more glasses of wine, was clearly plastered and he was rather concerned about her. She looked so young and vulnerable.

'Listen, what are you doing out here?'

'Jusst waiting for a bloody taxi, me mates have ggone…' She blinked and struggled to focus on her watch. 'The bloody man said he'd be 'ere any minute…'

Nat studied her, shaking his head. She gave a loud belch and started to sway alarmingly.

'Is there anyone I can contact for you?'

Milly shook her head vigorously and waved her hand around. 'No, me mates have gorn and left, but don't yer worry…'

Nat found that he was worried. He made a quick decision. He had seen young women worse for the wear being preyed upon by unscrupulous men too often to feel comfortable with just leaving her. If she had friends who could look after her, then that would be a different matter, but she clearly didn't.

'Where do you live?'

She told him her address, stumbling through the words. She named a street quite near to the three storey town house he shared with Livvy.

'Look, it's on my way home, I'll give you a lift.'

Milly beamed and kissed him. 'Oh, that's grand! Best night of me life, winning and meeting yer an' all! You're me hero!' Her face was transformed by a huge smile.

Nat supported the girl as she swayed and fell into him. Her hair had fallen out of its bun, her fascinator was awry, and her makeup was smudged. She was still clutching the small trophy she had won.

'Yore a proper star! Wait till I tells me mates!'

He put his arms around her and tried to steer her in a straight line as they made the long walk to where his car was parked and drove her home. He helped her to her door. She would have one hell of a hangover in the morning, he thought. He was concentrating so much on keeping Milly upright, that he completely missed the sound of the camera shutter clicking in the distance.

Chapter Five

James McGrew's hands shook as he tried to light his cigarette. Bloody thing. He tried again, flicking the lever on the cheap orange Bic lighter he'd just bought. He took a deep breath, tried once more, lit the fag and then inhaled, as he leaned back against the wall of the grey nondescript building, home of The Yorkshire Echo, the newspaper he worked for. The familiar smell, the hit of the tobacco as it reached his lungs, made him cough slightly. No matter that this was his first fag for two years. Today he bloody needed it. It would be just the one, just while he thought of something, anything to get him out of this mess. You've been here before old son, you'll think of something. But what?

As he smoked, he began to calm himself, his breathing slowed and the sick feeling in his belly eased. Along with this came a litany of jumbled thoughts. They can't do that to you, not the legendary Topper McGrew! He pulled his tweed jacket closer and pulled up the collar to keep out the cool November wind, watching the browning leaves from the acer tree, tumble about in the small grey courtyard. But the editor, Christian Lamont, newly in post, young, ambitious and utterly ruthless had been clear in this morning's meeting, billed euphemistically as a 'little catch up to get to know all the stalwarts of the paper'. Catch up, my arse. What Lamont really meant was that he was giving out ultimatums, write something sensational, sell more papers, get more downloads for the online edition or else you'd be out on your ear. Topper pictured the young editor in his t shirt, joggers and trainers, sweaty from having jogged to work. Lamont was about to take a quick shower, a new bathroom having been installed in his office at the new editor's behest. While he'd been talking Topper had noticed the toiletries on the desk, Nivea Moisturiser for Men. What sort of men wore moisturiser?

Topper felt distinctly old and out of step with the modern world. He hated social media, loathed having to use Twitter and had no Facebook or LinkedIn presence. And as for some of these young new journalists with their degrees, he just couldn't relate to them. How could you do a degree in journalism for God's sake? All you needed was a nose for a story, an ability to knock out quick, clear prose, a knack he'd picked up years ago as a cub reporter, and that was it. Topper McGrew had worked here for 20 years, building up a considerable name for himself in racing journalism and as a tipster. Topper's Tips were famous. Everyone wanted to know which horses Topper fancied for the big races. He had contacts across the whole of the North especially in Walton, knew all the trainers, most of the jockeys and had a network of reliable spotters to help him. People who knew which horses were working well on the gallops at home, which ones were lightly raced, which ones might land a surprise and win with healthy odds. So, he'd had a couple of lean months, lost his touch a bit. It hadn't helped that one of his best spotters had got himself shot and killed. But Topper knew he could rise again, like a phoenix from the ashes, he could be great once more. He just needed a break. Heartened, Topper finished his fag and planned his comeback. He'd always had a good nose for a story, and he needed a big one, something sensational to improve his stock and he needed to work extra hard to sniff something out. He threw his cigarette stub on the ground, went inside to grab his stuff and set off for Wetherby races. Topper strode off in his rather worn Church brogues, check shirt and tweed jacket. He had the appearance of a rather affable country farmer with reddish curly hair, along with his rather jaunty expression which gave him the appearance of a rather friendly prize pig. Today he was on a mission and eager to get going, like a truffle pig picking up on a scent. He'd have a quick spot of lunch at the course and have a mosey about, listen to the gossip, nose round and about for another story. Something sensational, Lamont had said. Then that's what he would get.

Topper ordered a cheese toasty and a whiskey, as he eyed the swelling crowd at the bar at Wetherby. He leaned on the counter and nodded and waved at acquaintances. There was Finn McCarthy, ex-jockey turned jockey coach with one of his new charges, if he was any judge. Several trainers nodded over towards him, Robert Johnson, the permit holder Alister Broadie, several sets of owners who he recognised from various meetings but could not exactly put a name to, and the bloodstock agent, Declan Walsh. All around conversations were buzzing. It was a cold, November day and rain threatened so the crowd were hovering inside bars, ordering lunch and lots of drinks to fortify themselves for when the first race began in half an hour. Topper spotted the tall figure of Lofty, a freelance photographer, at the bar. He was the sort who made his money snapping owners beside their horses in the winner's enclosure, faces wreathed in smiles. He was something of a wheeler dealer and people relayed choice bits of gossip, which were often accurate, to him and he made sure it was sent to the right person for a price, of course. He made his way over towards Topper and wriggled his eyebrows by way of a greeting.

'Want another?'

Topper nodded, never one to turn down a free drink. 'Now then Lofty, how's it going?'

Lofty passed him a refill. 'Oh same old, same old…Feel like marking my card then, Topper?'

Topper took a sip of the fiery liquid whilst he thought. Today he had a good tip for the feature race and a red hot one for the last. He could probably rustle up several creditable each way tips too. He also planned to track down some jockeys for a brief chat and generally drift around with his ear to the ground for anything newsworthy. Besides Lofty owed him. Topper had always put a bit of freelance work his way, using him for photos for the paper, that sort of thing.

'Could oblige old chap, if you promise me that you'll let me know if you hear of a good story…'

'Things a bit slow at the paper then?' Lofty gave him an assessing look.

Topper attempted a rather hollow laugh. 'Well, you know me, always sniffing out some story or other.' He tapped his nose, 'always alert for the next big thing.'

Lofty nodded and his companion held out his rather podgy hand.

'Marvellous, it's a deal, now pass me your pen, dear fellow.'

Topper enjoyed the afternoon, pottering about in and out of hospitality boxes, always with his ear to the ground. There was some good racing too. In the feature race, the favourite Goody Two Shoes, was beaten by a short head by an outsider, King Rameses, ridden by a conditional. Topper had tipped the favourite ridden by Nat Wilson, the comeback kid. Topper didn't mind either way, he'd also selected King Rameses as a good each way bet in his column. Several other horses he tipped though had run into the money, so not a bad day but it wasn't the best racing, just an ordinary week day meeting, nothing flashy. He knew he still needed a good story because the reality was that with such low profile tips, even if they were winners, he was doing nothing to impress Christian Lamont and keep his job.

While he'd been at the races he'd also received a text from his ex wife, Jacqui, moaning about school fees. Topper wasn't going to have any kids of his going to state schools. He'd been educated at Rugby and the boys were going to go to somewhere at least as good. He'd got their names down for there but knew that he needed to earn more if this were to happen. Sadly, Jacqui had hired a good divorce lawyer who had forced a hefty settlement. The Jag had had to go, it was far too thirsty. And he now lived in a small one bed flat in York, while she kept the large detached house he'd inherited from his parents. He may have been a substandard husband, selfish, too fond of booze and horses but it seemed exceptionally harsh to his way of thinking.

After the last race, as Topper was heading to his car he bumped into Lofty.

'Anything, old chap? If you followed me, you should be well up.'

Lofty's face split into a grin. 'Yes, Topper's Tips were on good form today.' Lofty tapped his finger on his nose. 'Got a whisper for you too...'

Topper leaned in closer to hear the veteran photographer.

'See, the word from the weighing room is...Wilson's not quite there, lost his bottle...'

Topper's eyes bulged as various thoughts ran through his head.

'Yeah, but he won The Charlie Hall, and has been doing well since he came back, hasn't he? Surely, of all people...'

'He started well but lost a few recently, not pushing through the gaps like he used to, misjudging the stride, falling, it's a sure sign.' Lofty raised his eyebrows. 'Heard it from a good source...'

'Well, I'll do some research then. Thanks, old son.'

He gave Lofty a wave and made his way, slightly tipsily, to his second hand Astra. Wilson, he thought? Now Lofty mentioned it he had wondered about the loss on Goody Two Shoes today. Had Nat Wilson really ridden the horse to the best of his ability? Had The Magician lost his touch, his knack of finding a gap and riding through it like the devil, which was his trademark? And hadn't there been a big loss at Worcester the other day? Mercurial, he thought the horse was called, which had fallen. It might not be true, Wilson was a consummate professional after all but just suppose it was? What you need to do, old thing, Topper told himself, is look back at those races and any other cockups Wilson has made recently and have a good nose about. If Topper felt a pang of guilt about looking for dirt on the former Champion jockey, he pushed it down pretty quickly. OK, so Wilson had always been fair to him, given him interviews and quotes and so on, but he was, Topper knew, a ruthless rider and maybe he had finally lost it. Maybe the thigh injury had been the last straw? Such things did happen and this could be a big scoop, just the job to boost his floundering stock with Lamont. He felt his spirits lift. It was a pity that the man himself wasn't around, he'd probably left as Topper had stayed behind to conduct some research.

Back home, he leafed through his Racing Post, studied the card and started to make some notes after a meal of fish and chips washed down with whiskey. He sat concentrating with the fervency of a man who had undergone a religious conversion. If there was a story, then he, Topper McGrew, was the man to chase it down. After all, his career might well depend upon it.

Chapter Six

As Hattie sat down to an evening meal with her parents, Bob and Philippa and younger brother Dominic, she was unsurprised to hear another voice from the kitchen and found it was an impromptu visit from her brother, Will. He often dropped in around meal times and Hattie couldn't help thinking that his very stylish wife was probably a lousy cook, whereas her parents were both excellent chefs, Philippa particularly. Nothing was ever said by her parents though, who were nothing if not fair.

'Come and join us darling, there's plenty of casserole,' said her mother hastily setting another place and finding a wine glass.

'Smells great, as usual Mum.' Will pulled up a chair.

Bob poured him a measure of red wine. 'How's it going, Will?' Hattie's older brother was a Detective Sergeant in the CID and based in North Allerton. They all knew he wasn't supposed to give details about his work. This was a police family after all, her dad Bob, had spent his entire career in the force, but they also knew that bland questions were allowed.

'Oh OK, busy as ever, you know…' Will spooned the aromatic, thick beef stew onto his plate earning a frown from Dominic.

'Hey save some, you greedy sod.'

Hattie laughed. 'Honestly you two, you've never quite grown out of your competitiveness about food have you?'

Will rolled his eyes. 'And what are you doing back here, bro? How's the course?'

Dominic, Nic as he was known, was in his final year studying Forensic Science.

'Good, just thought I'd come back for the weekend and sample Mum's lovely cooking…'

'Oh, you need some dosh, I s'pose,' joked Will. 'And I bet you've brought mum tons of washing.'

'Someone's got to keep him in beer,' said Bob with a grimace.

'You were just the same, Will,' added Mum.

Hattie tuned out as the brothers indulged in their usual good natured banter and her parents assumed an air of being long suffering but were, Hattie guessed, secretly pleased to have their family all back together albeit briefly, and immensely proud of their brood.

'Anyway, I bumped into Gabriel Taverner today.' Will spoke casually.

Hattie felt her body stiffen like a pointer. Taverner was an Inspector, one who had been in charge of the last case she had worked on and a friend of Will's. God, she hoped they weren't going to start all that again. She put down her cutlery, her appetite draining away like the tide going out. The family all knew what had happened with the last case, about her being lured away from safety because of her own vanity and stupidity. This had happened a few months ago but Hattie still found herself reliving the experience, sleeping badly even though she put a brave face on things. She had caught her parents looking at each other with concern a few times and Mum had asked her if she needed help.

53

'Anyway, he asked after you, Hattie. He also gave me the number of a psychologist, someone the force uses up here. Reckons she's brilliant. There's no harm in talking to her, is there?'

Hattie took the proffered card in silence. Trust Will to blunder in, sometimes he could be so tactless. God, why wouldn't they all leave her alone? She would deal with the nightmares, the panic she felt around strange men, it just took time, that was all. The last thing she wanted was a stupid, over helpful, too sympathetic psychologist breathing down her neck, asking her if she was OK. She just didn't need it.

'Sounds like a good idea Hat, you should consider it,' said Nic, serious for once.

'It does, doesn't it? It would be good to just talk about what happened.' Mum had a way of announcing things as if they were already settled, as if Hattie had agreed. Christ, she knew they were only trying to help, but why couldn't they just let her sort it out herself? What she really feared was that by talking about it, the whole, distressing memory would engulf her, just as she was sealing it away. That was what scared her. She also knew that suppressing bad memories was not a long term solution, but it might just help for now.

'Right, who wants apple crumble?' Dad rose to fetch the dishes, by way of changing the subject.

Hattie stood up. 'No thanks, sorry, I've got a headache, I'm just going to lie down.'

Her family exchanged worried glances as they watched her leave.

Alone in her room she tried to take deep breaths and calm her racing heart. It was as if the mention of Taverner had unleashed an explosion of images, which seemed branded on the inside of her eyelids. The thought of what might have happened scared the hell out

54

of her. But I've been in danger before, she told herself, in the first case she'd worked on with Finn, and she'd had no after effects then at all. So why was the latest situation so different?

Fiddling with her phone she called her best friend, Daisy. A breezy chat would set her up. Daisy was a lively and positive person who had a zany sense of humour and always made her laugh. But it was not Daisy who answered, it was a male voice, Neil, her boyfriend.

'Hey Hattie, Daisy's teaching in the indoor school at the moment. Shall I get her to phone you back?'

'Yes, if you would…' Christ. Neil was someone else she didn't want to talk to right now. In fact, he'd been a suspect in the last case and somehow hearing his voice made her more anxious, not less. Bugger. She rummaged in the drawer of her bedside cabinet and pulled out a pack of paracetamol and took two with the water she'd brought upstairs. Maybe a nap would help? The person she could really do with speaking to, someone who would understand but not go on at her, was Finn. He knew because he'd been there, he'd seen what had happened. Could she bother him now? Quickly she grabbed her mobile and found his name on her contacts list. He answered at the second ring.

'Hi Hattie, you must be psychic, I was just going to phone you. I know we're meeting up at the joint session, but I wanted to give you some notice so you can sort out a dress or whatever. Wondered if you wanted to go along to a party. You remember my mate, Charlie Durrant, well, he's getting engaged and the party is this Saturday. I thought it might be a good opportunity for us to ask questions, find out any whispers about this 'Me Too' stuff.'

Maybe a party was just what she needed?

'Oh yep, why not? He's one of your jockey friends, isn't he? You've talked about him. Who's he getting engaged to again?'

'Tara. Tara Regan. She's a great girl. Some sort of psychologist. Her grandmother's Caroline Regan, you know her, the former Bond girl. It should be a great party and everyone'll be there, including lots of women jockeys and conditionals. It's perfect. Hattie, are you listening?'

Somehow, Finn had sensed her distraction. Hattie dragged her mind back to the conversation. 'Yeah, fab, I'll come…' But she was distracted. Tara Regan, that was the name of the psychologist on the card which Will had handed over to her. It had to be her, there wouldn't be two people of the same name working as psychologists in the area could there? Hell, it seemed as if she would get to meet Tara after all.

'Are you alright?' asked Finn, clearly concerned about her behaviour.

'Yeah. I just, you know, feel anxious sometimes, about what happened. You know…'

There was a long companionable silence. Eventually Finn said. 'I do know. But only you can do something about it and only when and if you want to…'

Hattie swallowed hard. She did want help, but she was also terrified of reliving the whole experience and she hated being a victim.

'You might like Tara and if you do that's half the battle.'

She noticed that he seemed to assume that she would consult Tara professionally too. First her family and now Finn.

'Yeah, maybe.'

They talked about their session on professionalism and how it would work for a while longer. Hattie felt brighter. Sod it, she thought, bring it on! She couldn't go on like this. Maybe it was time to face her fears head on?

Chapter Seven

It was a chilly autumn morning and as there was no racing at Kelly's yard, Nat was helping out by work riding. Competent work riders were always required in yards to exercise the horses, and Cheltenham was no exception, so it was ideal to have stable jockeys who would also ride out. Nat was partnered with a hurdler, Tootsie, whilst Jamie McGuire was riding Portland Bay, nicknamed Porto, one of their most promising but difficult horses owned by the yard's richest owner, Sebastian Kline, someone who had made a fortune from the pharmaceutical industry. Kline was just getting into racing and had money to burn. Porto was running in a good race at Haydock in a few days and Nat had to overcome his initial annoyance that Michael had insisted that Jamie ride him on the gallops. Did that mean that the guvnor was putting him up for the race next week? Portland Bay was a temperamental bugger, and Nat was sure he'd be much more suited to riding him than the less experienced McGuire. He damped down his annoyance at the thought. He was still in the early stages of his 'comeback' and he knew that he was the superior horseman, he was sure of that. He was of the opinion that Jamie had ridden horses beyond his competence and would fall just as quickly as he had risen. Sometimes he worried that as Jamie and Michael were fellow countrymen, then the guvnor might favour him, the Irish were sometimes like that, but then he had a firm conviction that he was the best jockey, and talent would out in the end. He damped down his worries about the few odd results he'd had lately, he was just getting back into his stride, that was all and everything would work out fine.

Michael Kelly was one of the biggest trainers in England and also one of the most successful. He had splendid training facilities which included a solarium, equine pool, several hurdle fences, plus a six furlong uphill gallop. Michael surveyed his string with a critical eye.

'Come on, then, McGuire. Let's see how this Porto fella jumps then, shall we?'

'Right, yer are.'

Jamie made an impatient clicking noise with his tongue and began to trot in circuits, progressing to canter on both reins.

'On yer go. We're not riding a fucking dressage horse there, yer know.' Michael was clearly not impressed.

There was a ripple of laughter amongst the other riders.

Nat knew what Jamie was trying to do, he was simply attempting to sweeten the horse up, to get him to obey his commands, not unreasonable in Nat's view. So far at least Porto seemed to be listening to the aids and was behaving accordingly. Jamie completed one last circuit in canter and pressed Porto into the row of hurdles. The horse appeared to be going well, he was a talented jumper, but today he was not in the mood to display these skills. He cantered towards the fence and then slammed on the brakes just before take off, almost flinging Jamie over his head. Jamie clung on to Porto's mane for dear life and managed to avoid falling into the birch fence.

Michael tutted with ill disguised annoyance. 'Come on there McGuire, go again and don't ride him like yer mammy would. Put some effort into it, lad.'

Jamie settled himself and cantered another circuit with Porto who responded perfectly on the flat. He steered him again to the first hurdle and Porto bounded towards it before again skidding to a halt, this time sending Jamie flying into the fence.

Michael shook his head and went to help his younger jockey up.

'Y'alright there, Jamie? He's taking the piss, so he is, this fella. Come on, Nat. You gi' 'im a go will yer?'

Nat jumped off Tootsie and handed the reins to Kieron, a young stable lad, beckoning for the lad to hand him his riding whip. He walked up to Porto, lengthened his stirrup leathers and bounded onto the horse. Nat began the same process of walk, trot and canter in circles and a reinback at the end. Not a lot of people knew that Nat had started life as a junior showjumper and it was at times like this, that it really came in handy. He had been useless at school, but his father had a small farm and Nat had persuaded him to buy him a pony. He had graduated from gymkhanas, to showjumping and Pony Club where he had cut a swathe through the monied Fionas and Carolines, charming them all, before moving onto hunting, point to pointing and then racing. He had actually ridden in lots of different disciplines and it showed. The lengthened stirrup leathers gave him additional control and the whip was purely there as a precautionary measure, but Porto knew he had it and that made all the difference as it showed the bugger who was in charge. He completed a further circuit, changed his rein, pushed forward with his legs and gathered the horse into a dressage outline whilst maintaining good contact with his hands, so that the horse really had to use his hind legs. Once Porto was obeying his every command, he completed the circuit and turned towards the fences. He widened his hands, used his legs firmly and urged the horse forward. This time Porto thought better of it and sailed over the fence, moving forwards to complete the four hurdles absolutely faultlessly.

Michael beamed. 'Well, what do yer know, seems like Porto just needed a decent rider, after all. Looks like you'll be on for the ride next week then.'

Nat decided to hide his delight, and merely nodded. He turned away but not before he felt Jamie's gaze upon him. If looks could kill, he'd certainly be a dead man. It was revenge for what had happened at Worcester when Mercurial fell. His spirits rose. After those strange results in the last few weeks, at the back of his mind he had really begun to wonder if he had misjudged those strides, causing him to fall on each occasion. Luckily, he hadn't been particularly injured in any of them, nothing that ice and a stiff whiskey couldn't cure anyway. He had wondered if he had lost it, he had messed it up on several occasions now, most recently on Goody Two Shoes at Wetherby, but now he knew that it was just all part of the ups and downs of racing. He whistled all the way back to the stables, noticing but not commenting on Jamie's demeanour. The younger man had the expression of a sullen teenager who had been deprived of his mobile phone.

He arrived back at his house in Cheltenham to find Livvy rushing around hoovering and spraying air freshener around. She looked rather stressed, a flush upon her cheeks.

'What's up?'

'I forgot about 'Live' magazine. They are coming round to do that interview with us. It completely went out of my mind. Did you remember?'

'No, I didn't.'

Nat sighed. Damn. He really couldn't be bothered today. His thigh was aching, he was dusty from the gallops and stank of 'eau de cheval', but interviews, attending functions and press involvement were part of the role. Besides his agent, Artie Ferguson, had arranged it, so it would be the usual slightly sycophantic interview about the life of the top jockey and his beautiful girlfriend. He was used to the drill, and ready to play his part.

Livvy removed her rubber gloves and wrinkled up her nose at the smell of him.

'Why don't you pop in the shower and I'll go out and get some cut flowers to brighten the place up and some fresh coffee. They'll be here in half an hour.'

Nat glanced at his watch, dipping his head to steal a kiss. 'OK, but don't be late.' Livvy was a natural at the PR stuff, so was he usually, but he needed time to compose himself and run through his lines. There was bound to be the usual interest in his injury, how he had been shot, what he was doing in Shetland and he needed to get all his ducks in a row, so he didn't reveal too much. He turned his power shower to red hot and enjoyed the feel of the steaming water as it battered his skin and relieved his aching thigh bone. He had just stepped out of the shower and was drying himself when the doorbell rang. Damn. Livvy must have forgotten her door keys in her haste. He wrapped a towel around him and raced down the stairs to let her in. He pulled open the door. Christ, it was then that he realised his mistake. An attractive young woman in smart clothes, carrying a briefcase, stood on the doorstep, her expression changing from awe to shock.

The woman looked bewildered, taking in his half naked appearance. 'Oh, hello. I'm Annabel Sinclair from 'Live', I've come about the interview…'

'Oh yes, of course. Why don't you come in and make yourself comfortable.'

He suspected that the towel he had chosen to wrap around his groin didn't quite cover his backside, so to avoid further embarrassment, he squashed himself against the wall whilst the woman squeezed past him.

'Go straight through to the living room, second on the left and I'll put some clothes on.' He smiled ruefully. 'As you can see, I just got out of the shower. Livvy won't be long.'

The woman settled down in the cream sofa and looked uneasily about her. She swallowed nervously.

'How long do you think she'll be?'

Looking back, Nat could almost have laughed at the comedy aspect of what happened next. He automatically looked at his watch which he wasn't actually wearing, it was still on the side of the sink where he had left it. This single one useless gesture caused him to let go of his towel as he lifted his hand, dropping the two corners of the towel which covered his modesty. In slow motion it fell and the young woman's mouth gaped open as his nakedness was completely exposed. He quickly wrapped the fabric rectangle around him, flushed and gabbled his apologies as he leapt upstairs to put some clothes on. He was hastily pulling on a clean t shirt and jeans, when he heard the door crash and assumed it was Livvy returning. Thank the Lord! She would smooth everything over but by the time he had bounded back downstairs, there was no sign of Livvy and he realised that the journalist had gone. He shook his head bemused. It was strange the way people reacted, it was an accident after all. He'd ring, apologise and rearrange. He shrugged his shoulders. He was used to the weighing room, where jockeys stripped off in front of their peers as a necessity in the quick turnaround between races, so he thought nothing more about it. Some people were just too sensitive, he decided.

Chapter Eight

Finn had gathered all his new conditional jockeys together to talk through the BHA rules on racing. Hattie had come along to introduce herself and she had brought some leaflets about the PJA and some dates about her healthy meals classes. She was going to offer some sessions to each rider about weight and diet in the future, so it made sense for her to come along and introduce herself. The PJA also offered much more in terms of support for jockeys, such as advice on insurance and agents, so she had included leaflets about the organisation. This was an important session on the BHA guidance. There was so much to think about, and an unwary jockey could end up in hot water with the stewards for infringements if they were not aware of the rules. For example, jockeys had to turn off their phones from the beginning of the first race to after the last to avoid taking calls, betting or doing anything that could impact on the integrity of racing and they could only use their whip so many times in the final furlong, and had to comply with the rules on banned substances, amongst others. Finn's role was to support conditional jockeys and assist them to navigate the rules and regulations and develop their race riding throughout their period as conditionals, to help them ride out their claim. Conditional jockeys had weight allowances of up to 10 lbs which reduced little by little corresponding to the amount of winners they had ridden. They needed to ride 75 winners by their 26th birthday in order to turn professional which was a tall order and so there was a very high drop out rate. Finn liked to support jockeys into other careers too and many could make a good living as work riders, but there were also lots of other options and Finn had developed links with colleges and racecourses. Some had gained positions in racing related roles based at racecourses, such as groundsmen or in marketing roles.

Finn had arranged this session at Vince Hunt's yard. Daisy Hunt, Harriet's friend, ran a small livery yard and they used the portacabin there for the session. Hattie went around to chat to all the jockeys and handed out the flyers that she had prepared. There was a small kitchen where hot drinks could be made and tables and chairs. They also had a white board and some suitable pens so they could write on it. This afternoon there were 10 conditionals in attendance, the new recruits, seven boys and three girls who had gained positions at the local yards within Walton, where the 20 or so trainers were based. It was a pleasant, Yorkshire town, dominated by the communal gallops and strings of racehorses which made their way there in the early mornings. Most trainers had National Hunt and Flat horses and most used the communal gallops although some of the outlying yards had their own gallops. At six in the morning the whole town rang to the sound of horses' hooves and the chatter amongst the riders as they made their way to the tracks.

Finn surveyed the group. He recognised several of the jockeys, Sam Foster, Connor Moore, Kyle Devlin, Liam Flynn, Gavin Clary and a lad called Joel Fox and three girls, Sinead O'Brien, Lottie Henderson and Maura Brandon. He nodded briefly at Lottie who he knew as she was at his friends' yard, Rosy and Seamus Ryan, and he had seen her ride. The groups were huddled together; the girls in one corner and boys in another, the lads eyeing the girls up and the girls looking at them with absolute disdain, especially Sinead who had mastered the 'who do you think you are looking at' expression with aplomb. Finn asked them to introduce themselves and to give a brief statement about what their aims were. Most of the jockeys spoke clearly and added a sentence about becoming a pro, only Sinead surprised everyone by stating clearly that she 'wanted to win the Grand National' and Joel Fox, a slight, sickly looking young man with bad acne on his face answered that ' he wwwanted to become a Cchampion jockey.' The poor lad had struggled to state his ambition and Finn motioned for everyone to listen patiently and glared at some of those who were gossiping and grinning behind their hands. Eventually the lad managed to get his words out. Finn smiled encouragingly. He was struck by the lad's lofty ambitions that belied his hesitant and nervous presentation and hoped that on horseback he was very different. He made a mental note to visit his yard and watch him ride.

Finn went through his speech about what it takes to be a professional jockey and the grit, determination and skill, not to mention luck. They all needed a bit of that.

'There are many easier ways to earn a living, that do not involve risking your neck and freezing your butt off on a daily basis and that's before we even mention the wasting and denial involved. Yet there is no better feeling in the world when it all goes right. To move on to be a professional jockey you will need to ride 75 winners by the time you're 26. Of course, your weight allowance assists you but that reduces the more winners you ride and then when you're competing with the pro's to pick up rides, it becomes that much harder. It is not a job for the faint hearted and you will all need to work incredibly hard. Another vital aspect is 'reputation'. Racing is a small community and word gets around quickly, so it is vitally important that you conduct yourself well and behave professionally at all times.' He looked round the room and was pleased to note that everyone was paying attention. 'So, what I'd like you to do is talk to your neighbour about what 'being professional' means to you for a minute and then I'll ask you to feedback.'

The conversation began and Finn watched the interactions in the room. The girls tended to stick together, more so Maura and Lottie. Sinead looked rather sullen and hostile but seemed to relax once Maura included her. The lads were at ease in each other's company with the exception of Joel who was on the fringes of the group. They all came up with good ideas for 'professionalism'. Sam suggested being reliable and having integrity, which he guessed were now very important to Sam, having been asked to pull races in the past. Connor came up with 'playing by the rules' which led Finn into a whole discussion about the integrity of the sport and how the BHA policed this. This neatly generated a discussion about BHA rules and Finn went through them and gave them handouts.

'Familiarise yourself with all the rules and guidance, so you won't be hauled in front of the stewards more than is necessary or find yourself in hot water.'

There was more discussion about the merits of various rules and regulations and how this applied equally to males and females within the sport.

'Do you think that female riders ought to be given any concessions?' asked Harriet, ignoring Finn's warning glance. She was interested in their views and hoped to prompt some discussion, but it was like throwing a match into a tinder box.

Sam nodded. 'Why not? Maybe the girls could ride at lower weights or qualify as a professional with less winners?' he suggested, immediately facing a series of howls from the women. 'I only mean that, the fairer sex are generally less strong, less muscular and could struggle to make an impact in the sport.'

'We don't need any concessions,' agreed Lottie. 'Besides we have other skills like more empathy with the horses so we can get the best out of them, I think.'

Sinead frowned. 'Piss off, Sam. Haven't you heard of equality? Women don't get no concessions in eventing or showjumping, do they? And we're all riding horses. So why is this any different? We want to compete on equal terms, we don't need patronising. Moron!'

Maura looked on, appalled at the outburst and tried to shush Sinead.

Joel had flushed pink. He rose from his seat to say something but struggled getting the words out. Finn thought he could make out the words, 'bbbloody gggirls…nno place in rracing…' The lad was met with impatience and rolled eyes from the girls, who hopefully didn't catch exactly what he had said. Gavin muttered something to him and he sat back down again, still puce. What a terrible affliction for the lad to not be able to say what he wanted. Finn wondered if one of his contacts might help the lad, a speech therapist or psychologist perhaps?

Sinead glared at him with utter contempt. 'Fffuckk off you ffucking sssspas! Jesus, you can't even speak, for God's sake! You moron! What on earth are you doing here? You wouldn't be 'ere at all, if it weren't for your rich daddy, you overprivileged wanker with your fucking hi viz hat silk and leg wraps yer mummy bought yer. Fucking idiot!'

Joel gasped as though he had been hit and immediately looked tearful. The group looked startled and then there was a groundswell of muttering and some titters as Joel tried to control his outrage at the attack. He took a deep breath amongst the hubbub of the jockeys. Hattie looked at Finn anxiously, unsure what to do.

'Now that's enough. Sinead, I suggest you go outside for a minute or two and come back when you're ready to apologise to Joel. Everyone deserves respect and that was completely uncalled for. I will not tolerate you belittling one of your peers. Do I make myself clear?'

'He started it!' Sinead spat out the words.

She scowled, mouthed something else and flounced off, her face the picture of malevolence. Hattie nudged Finn. 'I'll go after her and try to calm her down.'

'Thanks.' Finn turned to the jockeys. 'Right, I just need to hand out some questionnaires and book in some time to see you all and then we'll call it a day.'

The atmosphere began to calm and the jockeys completed their questionnaires and took the handouts that Finn and Hattie had prepared.

67

He booked in sessions with them all and course walks for those who had rides booked. As they were starting to drift off, Hattie walked back into the room without Sinead. She shrugged at Finn.

'She walked off.' She sat next to Joel. 'I hope you're alright? Listen, just take no notice.'

Finn agreed. 'Joel, I'm sorry about that. I will talk to Sinead, you can depend on it.'

The lad nodded and smiled. 'Ittt's alright. I'm uuused to iiit.' He shrugged. 'It hhhappens a lllot.' Poor lad. His spotty complexion looked far worse too, quite red as he flushed with emotion. He sighed. 'Me mmmum bbought the hhi vvviz sstuff...'

Finn shook his head. 'She's very sensible and for the record, you shouldn't be used to being teased. You have a perfect right to be here, remember that.'

'Come on, Joel. We're all off to The Blacksmith's for a quick drink. You coming?' asked Sam.

Joel grinned. 'Sssure.'

Finn and Hattie cleared up after them and gathered up the handouts, wiped the tables down and tidied up.

'Quick drink in The Yew Tree?' Hattie asked.

'God yes. We'll give The Blacksmith's a miss if they're all headed there.'

The Yew Tree was a pub on the other side of the town, a short drive away.

'Christ, that was awful.' Finn sipped his pint, relishing the taste. 'Sinead really is going to be hard work. I take it she wouldn't come back when you caught up with her?'

'I saw her stomp off into the distance, shouted her but she kept on walking. Mind you, Joel did start it with his remarks about women jockeys, I suppose.' She touched his arm. 'I'm sorry, I shouldn't have mentioned the male/female stuff, but I was just interested in their thoughts.'

Finn ran his fingers through his hair and looked troubled. 'I know but they ought to be able to have a civil conversation about it. Sinead was out of order taking the mick out of Joel's stammer, that was unforgiveable.' He gave her a searching look. 'Do you think I was too hard on her?'

Hattie shook her head. 'No. You know as well as I do that she'll need to tow the line and calm down if she's ever going to stay the course. She needs to be able to get on with people, no yard will take her on if she causes waves all the time. What did she mean about Joel's dad?'

'I think his dad is rich and has just invested heavily in a yard. He's not short of money and will give his lad all the best rides if the owners agree. He's in Walton, but I haven't met him or the trainer yet. I presume his mother is just anxious about Joel riding, hence the hi viz gear.'

Hattie nodded. 'Well, take heart. Law of averages, this crop of conditionals cannot be as troublesome as your last lot, surely?'

'Hope you're right.' Given what he had just witnessed, he wouldn't like to bet on it.

Back home, he tried to ring Sinead to catch up with her and gauge her mood. He hoped to visit the yard the next day but there was no reply when he rang her. Instead, he texted Robert Johnson so he could pass on details of his visit. Robert replied immediately.

She's not back yet, but I'll pass on the message. Thanks.

Finn glanced at his watch. It was 11 o'clock. Maybe she'd gone to the pub with the others and everything had calmed down, or perhaps she had decided racing wasn't for her and had left? He almost hoped that she had, at least it would save him a problem, and he knew that Sinead O'Brien was definitely that.

The next day he was contacted by Lloyd Fox, Joel's father, who invited him to their yard which had once belonged to a trainer who had retired. He was down to see Sinead O'Brien at Robert Johnson's place about the incident last night and maybe catch up with Sam Foster, who was at the same yard. He was really hoping that she'd seen the error of her ways, but he agreed to call in to see Lloyd Fox beforehand. The place had had something of a makeover since Finn had last been there. He had been surprised to hear from his new conditional's father, rarely did parents contact him, but when Lloyd explained that he had bought the yard, it all made sense. He wondered if Joel had mentioned the incident with Sinead and whether that was behind the invitation, and mentally prepared himself for some tough questioning.

The yard consisted of several rows of old stables and a range of new ones, set in several acres with a large stone farmhouse situated in the back. He remembered the place being rather shabby but admired the transformation, the stables were immaculate, the gardens landscaped and the house had been renovated. He realised now what Sinead had been getting at about Joel being in a privileged position because of his rich father.

'Great place you have here,' Finn added, noticing even more additions, the latest horse walker and equine swimming pool. 'Listen if this is about the session last night, then let me explain.'

Lloyd frowned. 'What session?'

'The class I ran about the BHA rules. There was an argument between Joel and another jockey. She took the mick out of his stammer and about him wearing the hi viz stuff his mum bought him.'

Lloyd frowned and wafted his hand away dismissively. 'No, I heard about it but the lad needs to stand up for himself, that's all. People will take the mick, that's human nature for you. His late mother only agreed to him riding if he wore the hi viz stuff, sadly, and he's still riding in it as a way of keeping his promise to his mother, I suppose. He always wears the hat band.' He shrugged, clearly not a man to dwell on emotional issues.

Finn took in his comments. 'Let me get this straight, Joel's mother, your wife is dead?'

Lloyd nodded grimly. 'Yep, two years ago now, cancer, that is what decided me to get into racing. Listen, I'm not messing about here. You see, I always had a passion for racing and was never able to pursue it until I sold my internet business and decided that life was too short when Jenny died. Fortunately, Joel shares my passion, so it was a way of spending more time with my son too.'

Finn felt sorry for Joel losing his mother so young and was even more annoyed with Sinead for ribbing the lad. He took in Lloyd's smart appearance. He was rich and it seemed was wearing what he thought a successful racehorse owner would wear. Most horse people were a relaxed bunch at home and wore practical boots, warm jackets and waterproofs, whereas Lloyd was dressed in a new expensive tweed jacket, shirt and tie and wore shiny, new Dubarry boots with hardly a spec of dirt on them. His greying hair was swept back and he was extremely well groomed.

'Well, just to say I will be dealing with the girl concerned, you can be sure of that.'

Lloyd nodded.

'So, have you owned horses before?' Finn couldn't resist asking. The world of horseracing was highly competitive and far from glamorous. Many yards barely scraped a living and there were the constant worries about owners not paying up, injuries, not to mention the sheer skill and knowledge involved in teasing performances out of highly strung, thoroughbred racehorses.

Lloyd gave him a man to man stare. 'Well, not exactly, but I didn't get to the top in business without learning about delegation. I bought the place two years ago now and completed extensive renovations. Most of the horses are mine but we have a few owners and I want to expand. I always say you have to aim really high to succeed, there is no limit to my ambition. It's vital that you have the right people in the right job, and I have a very able trainer. An Australian chap, you might know him, actually. Dan Richards.'

Finn chewed his lip as he thought. 'No, I don't, but it's always a good idea to employ someone with a lot of experience.'

Just at that moment a man rode into the yard on a large chestnut horse.

'Great timing, Dan. Come and meet Joel's mentor.'

A smiling, man in his early thirties advanced. He was blond haired, twinkly eyed and casually dressed in breeches, a checked shirt and olive green gilet. Dan shook Finn's hand vigorously.

'Great to meet you, mate. I've heard of you, of course. You and your battles with the great Nat Wilson were legendary, even in Oz. I'm glad that Joel is being mentored by you.'

Lloyd nodded. 'We are very pleased.'

'Where did you train in Australia?' asked Finn, making a mental note to look the trainer up in the form books.

Dan grinned. 'Ah, here and there. I was in Perth for a while working as an assistant trainer.'

'Did you ever ride yourself?' asked Finn, thinking that the Australian was probably too tall, though he was slim and wiry in build.

'Nah, grew too big, mate. So, you hung up yer boots, did yer? It's great yer can help the lads with their riding, though.'

'It is indeed,' agreed Lloyd.

He beamed broadly. Just occasionally Finn noticed a resemblance to his son, but it was very slight. Lloyd was a larger than life, confident version of his son, and Finn could see that the boy was clearly in his father's shadow. He wondered if that was the cause of his stammer.

'So let me show you round the place.'

The yard had been thoroughly renovated and the horses were all kept well. Lloyd clearly knew his breeding as he rattled off the parentage of a range of horses. Finn was impressed. The place was pretty much deserted as the horses had been up on the gallops, had been mucked out and fed early on and the yard would soon be a hive of activity for evening stables in a few hours' time.

Dan showed Finn his promising National Hunt horse, The Emperor, an impressive, black gelding.

Dan ran through the animal's latest form. He had won impressively at Haydock.

'So, we're thinking about a step up in class for him, which is where you come in,' added Lloyd.

Finn frowned. 'I don't quite follow.'

'Well, you see I want to put Joel on him, and the owners might baulk at that but if I tell them that THE Finn McCarthy, is his jockey coach, and vouches for him, then they will feel very differently.'

Finn gasped. 'Whoa, I barely know your son and I haven't even seen him ride, as yet. It's fair to say he has been assigned to me under the scheme but beyond that I'm afraid I can't make any recommendations.'

73

Lloyd's eyes narrowed and then he smiled. 'I thought you'd say that, but you see I think you will be impressed with him when you see him ride. He used to have lessons with the top eventer, Freddie Oppenheimer, who thought he was outstanding.'

Dan nodded along.

Finn could see that Lloyd was someone rich and charming enough to get whatever he wanted and if he wanted his son to be a top jockey, then no expense would be spared. But he wondered why he had sent him to train with a top event rider such as Freddie, as the disciplines of eventing and racing were completely different. Surely, Lloyd knew that?

'Well, Freddie is an expert in his field, of course. However, I am here to support Joel and I will do that to the best of my ability, but any decisions about riding are down to your registered trainer, Dan, in that case, and I really can't overstep my remit. Besides, Joel's weight allowance would certainly be an advantage, one that might persuade the owners to consider him.'

For a second Lloyd looked extremely irritated at being thwarted, he eyed Dan and the two men exchanged a glance, but then his expression changed. He put his arm around Finn's shoulders.

'Of course, of course. Dan will make those decisions and quite right too.'

It was clear that he anticipated no problems in gaining Dan's agreement.

'Listen, no hard feelings, right? I'm sure we will work very well together, very well indeed,' Lloyd added.

Finn began to feel rather uncomfortable. 'I will do everything in my power to help Joel, of course, of that you can be sure,' he added rather stiffly.

They chatted about racing in general and said their goodbyes. Finn drove to Johnson's place. He felt rather uneasy about the purpose of Lloyd's charm offensive, what on earth had he expected him to do? It was clear to him where Joel's diffidence and stammer had come from, his overbearing and domineering father. He contrasted Joel's experience to another of his conditional's situation, Sinead O'Brien, who by all accounts had no one batting for her having been brought up in care. They were both from opposite ends of the spectrum. He wondered how both would fare. His phone rang as he drove and he picked up the call via Bluetooth. It was Robert Johnson ringing to tell him that Sinead was missing.

'She didn't come back last night and didn't turn up this morning. I think this is the last straw actually.' Robert was clearly furious. 'Anyway, I thought I'd better let you know. Didn't want to waste your time coming out here.'

Finn sighed. 'Maybe something has happened to her?'

Robert was clearly sceptical. 'Hmm. Or more likely she's decided to jack it in and didn't have the decency to tell me to my face. Honestly, if that is the case, good riddance, I say. I sent the head lad round to her lodgings to see if she's there, but she didn't return last night.'

Finn didn't like the sound of that. 'Really? Have you contacted her family? Asked her friends? Listen, I suppose you heard about the row with Joel last night?'

'Yes. Sam mentioned it. I told you what she was like. She'd argue with her own shadow, that girl. I did leave a message for her social worker who persuaded me to let her continue last time. She's probably rung her. Honestly, I wish I hadn't agreed to it.'

Finn took this in. Robert was clearly furious but maybe he was right and she had just upped and left and he was worrying about nothing.

'Listen, if you hear anything, can you let me know.'

75

Robert agreed to do just that. Finn spun the car round. He felt irritated and uneasy at the same time. What had happened to Sinead? He had thought that this crop of conditionals would be no trouble at all compared to his last lot, but how wrong he was.

Chapter Nine

It was nearly eight o' clock in the evening when Finn heard more. He was just settling down to study the next day's racing at Market Rasen where two of his conditionals were due to ride, when he heard the buzz of the entry phone. Finn lived in a small but stylish flat, sympathetically converted from an old chocolate factory in the centre of York. He had lived there for almost two years and his sister had helped him decorate and furnish the place. It suited him being ideally located for his work as a jockey coach and he found he liked the anonymity of it. In fact, few people knew where he lived. A handful of friends, ex's, Hattie, his family, Nat and another jockey friend, Charlie. He could not imagine who was calling round now. It seemed late for someone to visit and he wasn't expecting anyone. A voice came over the intercom.

'Hello there, Finn. This is DI Gabriel Taverner. Can I come in?'

Finn frowned. In his experience, a visit from the police was usually bad news. Taverner had been involved in the last case he and Hattie had worked on. And Taverner and his Sergeant had called round before to question him. After a frosty start, the two men seemed to respect each other although Finn was aware that the Detective was sometimes annoyed by what he called their 'amateur blundering'.

'OK, come up.' Finn released the door and waited.

The policeman looked grave as he sat down. In fact on closer inspection he looked drained, dark ringed eyes and stubbled cheeks making him seem almost dishevelled. He was tall, dark and Hattie thought him rather handsome she had once said. Now he simply looked exhausted.

'Look Finn, it's about one of your conditional jockeys.'

Finn sighed. 'Right, which one. What's happened now?'

Taverner took a deep breath. He had his sympathetic face on and Finn realised that this was serious.

'Look, there's no easy way to say this. We have found the body of a young girl, believed to be Sinead O'Brien in the road out of Walton last night.'

'What? Oh Christ. I only saw her yesterday. She came to one of my sessions. What happened?' He felt suddenly shaky and a little faint. He sank down heavily onto his sofa.

'I can't say too much but it looks like she was hit by a vehicle. Can't be confirmed though until the PM.'

'A hit and run in Walton? Christ. So, she's dead?'

'I'm afraid so. Listen, I need to ask you some questions. When did you last see Sinead, did you say?'

Finn poured himself a Scotch and offered one to Taverner, which was politely declined. He explained about the jockeys' meeting and the argument between Joel and Sinead.

'She really was a spikey, difficult girl. She started taking the mick out of Joel Fox. He stutters you see and she started mimicking

78

him and taking the piss about him wearing hi viz riding gear, so I asked her to leave and only come back when she was ready to apologise.'

Taverner jotted this down. 'What time was this?'

''Bout eightish in the evening. The jockeys all went to The Blacksmith's after, I think.'

'So, did you go with them?'

'No, we went to The Yew Tree, to avoid them actually. I tried to ring her later to see if she'd calmed down but she didn't pick up. She's at Robert Johnson's yard.' He realised what he had just said. 'Was, I mean.'

Taverner continued to make notes. 'And when you said 'we', who was the other person?'

'Harriet Lucas. She works for the PJA, the Professional Jockeys' Association, now she's qualified as a dietician. She came to talk about the organisation and offer some advice on diets.'

Taverner smiled. 'Ah, Harriet Lucas, right. So, you two won't be involved in any investigations now you're both gainfully employed, I take it?'

Finn wondered how to answer that, especially as he and Harriet were expected to undertake work for the BHA Integrity Services if any issues came up in Walton, but he decided to be more circumspect. After all, they weren't currently working on any cases.

'Of course not. We're far too busy.'

'Glad to hear it. Well, I'll probably need to speak to Harriet too. Social Services are involved because Sinead was in care, so there will be some kind of serious case review, so everything will be pored over minutely.'

Finn sipped his drink, too stunned to think properly.

'How were the parents?' It was, Finn knew, a bloody daft question but he found he wanted to know more.

'Well, let's just say not as upset as her social worker, which tells you everything you need to know.'

Finn felt like he'd been punched in the stomach at the unfairness of it all,

'Christ, poor kid. She was spikey and argumentative, but she could ride a bit, had potential. It's such a shame when she was trying to make something of herself too.' He felt guilt gnawing away at him. Had he been too hard on her, should he have been more sympathetic and cut her some slack? He wished now that he had done just that.

Taverner glanced at his watch. 'Obviously we'll investigate and try and find whoever was driving. I just wanted to ask you about her.' He gave Finn an assessing look, his gaze penetrating and frank. 'You don't know anything else that could help us, do you? Who she hung around with. Anything at all?'

Finn grimaced. 'She'd barely been at the yard more than a few weeks. I met her twice and had to tell her to remove her piercings the first time and then there was the row with Joel.' He thought back to what he had observed about her. 'She didn't seem to have any particular friends. She came from The National Horseracing College in Doncaster. She was argumentative and had a massive chip on her shoulder, probably because she'd been in care.' He thought back. 'The other female conditionals are Maura Brandon and Lottie Henderson, they might know something. Robert Johnson will certainly be able to fill you in on Sinead's time at the yard.'

Taverner stood up to leave. 'But you'll let me know if you hear anything, won't you? It's probably nothing but there could be more to it. And you and Hattie, you seem to hear things, people talk to you in the racing world. Just promise me if you find out anything at all, no matter how insignificant, you'll pass it on.'

Finn agreed. 'Yes, of course.'

80

Once Taverner had gone, he helped himself to another Scotch and mused over what could have happened. A hit and run? Poor kid. He went through his own actions and words and anxiety worried away at him. He couldn't help but think that he could have handled things so much better. He wondered whether to ring Harriet but seeing it was getting on for midnight, he decided it was too late. He'd contact her tomorrow instead. He went to bed, his mind spinning with wild thoughts.

In the end, he didn't have to ring Harriet, she rang him the following morning.

'God Finn, I heard about your conditional, Sinead. I'm so sorry. What an awful thing to happen. It's so sad. Just an accident, I suppose?'

'Yeah. Taverner called round last night. I was going to phone you but I thought it was a bit late.'

'Taverner? What did he want?'

Finn could sense Hattie's concern about the police involvement.

'Oh, you know, just wanted to know what she was like, if I knew anything. I told him about the argument last night about her mimicking Joel and storming off.'

There was a long pause. 'You don't think it was to do with that, do you?'

'No. It may well have been an accident but obviously the driver knows something and the police are looking for him.'

'God, it's awful. Poor girl.'

'Listen, Taverner said he'd need to speak to you.'

'Right, OK. Is there anything we need to do? Speak to her parents or carers?'

'I can send a card, though Taverner said her social worker was more upset than the parents and there will be some sort of review because she was in care. Obviously, if we hear anything then we have a duty to pass it on to the police and there will be a funeral, of course.'

There was a pause as Harriet took this in. She was a sensitive girl, and could take things to heart, more than she let on. Her voice faltered for a minute and Finn worried for her, knowing in her present anxious state she might get too involved. If he could get her to speak to Charlie's girlfriend, the clinical psychologist, she could unscramble some of the knots in her head. He tried to lighten the tone.

'Anyway, still on for tomorrow? I'll pick you up at half past seven. The party's at Tara's grandmother's place. You'll know her, she's Caroline Regan the former Bond girl. She lives in a big country pile and it'll be best bib and tucker.' It was the last place he wanted to be, but then again they might hear something that they needed to pass on to the police and it might be good for Harriet. Besides, Charlie Durrant was one of his oldest friends.

'Yeah. I suppose life has to go on.' Harriet sounded rather doubtful. 'I was looking forward to going but I'm not sure now. Not after this.'

Finn thought she might say that. 'But, Hattie, you were right first time. Life has to go on.'

Harriet sighed. 'Yes, alright. OK. I'll see you tomorrow.'

Chapter Ten

The first thing Hattie spotted were the lights. As they turned off the road, between two huge stone gateposts, she saw vast lanterns hung along the drive to the imposing Queen Anne building, Bramble Hall. It made the drive look like a small, classy airport runway at night.

'Heck, see what you mean, Finn, it's really impressive...'

She glanced at her companion who she noticed had scrubbed up well. He was wearing a dinner jacket and bow tie. Hattie, after much deliberation, was wearing a green velvet midi dress with wide tapered sleeves. With her red hair tousled and loose she felt she was channelling a Pre-Raphelite painting and was pleased with the effect. Finn had whistled when he saw her which had made her smile. Their friendship continued to blossom after their own recent individual romantic disappointments, hers with the chef and his with an aspiring actress, so that the atmosphere between them was relaxed and easy, borne of the fact that neither was attracted to the other, she supposed. They had met at the races when Hattie had worked for The Racing to School Initiative, getting children involved in racing and they had come across Sam Foster, a conditional jockey, who had been beaten up. They had been thrown together investigating what had happened to Sam and a friendship had developed. Finn was easy on the eye, and she respected him and valued his opinion more than anything. She thought he treated her like a kid sister on the whole, which was fine with her. They had agreed to mingle and feed anything back to Taverner if any information about Sinead's death came to light.

'You've met the girls, Maura and Lottie, so you'll know them at least and there should be lots of other interesting people invited.'

But neither of them knew exactly who would be there although Finn had described his friend Charlie Durrant, 'as a sociable beast', who he reckoned would ask the whole of the Walton racing fraternity.

Inside they were greeted by Caroline Regan, who Hattie recognised immediately as being a 'kick ass' Bond girl but also later, an accomplished actor in her own right. Tonight, she was resplendent in plum silk with her hair dressed with roses. Caroline was, Hattie noticed, still reed slim, had tanned unlined skin and had a rich, posh voice rather like Joanna Lumley's. She had her trademark, blonde bob and was dripping in jewellery, probably real diamonds. She must be in her mid to late 60's at least, but could pass as being decades younger.

'Darlings. I know you of course, Finn, and this must be Harriet Lucas.' Her eyes shone as she looked from one to the other as if assessing their suitability for one another like a veteran matchmaker of some repute. 'Finn used to ride for me Harriet, in the old days. But now I hear he works as a jockey coach. Well, who better?' She drew Hattie aside and whispered. 'And you are a dietician, I hear. Well, I could use your services myself. Wonderful, you sound like a clever girl, just like Tara.'

She gave Hattie a wink and then excused herself to greet new arrivals, ever the perfect hostess. Hattie was left with the heady smell of Caroline's perfume and the impression of a lively and interesting woman.

Hattie was introduced to Charlie who she had not actually met formally although she recognised him from the races. He was tallish, had dark hair and a handsome face, she decided. He punched Finn on

84

the shoulder and shook Harriet's hand. He looked at her with appreciation.

'Glad you could make it. Let me introduce Tara.' Hattie found herself looking into a sensitive and clever face. Tara was slim, dark and had delicate, fine features. She was quite beautiful with a lovely bone structure.

Tara hugged her warmly. 'Lovely to meet you. I've heard about you from Finn. I hear you're a dietician for the PJA. You must tell me all about it, if we get a minute later. We should meet up for a coffee sometime, maybe in York.'

Hattie nodded, thinking she'd like to get to know her better. She noted Tara's understated elegance and natural sympathy which would greatly assist in her job. She could almost imagine herself blurting out her troubles to someone who radiated reassurance and kindness. She was surprised that such slim women would be interested in her role as a dietician, as they clearly had no need of her professional input. She knew that Finn was hoping she might take to Tara and consult her professionally about the emotional fall out of their last case. Hattie would of course have to give evidence in court where she would confront her attacker and the thought terrified her. Her mind turned to Sinead and the awful circumstances of her death. Don't think about it now, she chided herself, just enjoy this lovely party, you stupid girl.

Tara, too, was whisked away to meet others and it gave Hattie time to see the huge hall which led into a vast drawing room crammed with people. The French windows were open and she could see a larger marquee in the garden, complete with heaters that billowed out hot air, much needed on this cold November evening. Everywhere lights twinkled and waiters, dressed in black, circulated with trays of drinks and nibbles. Finn grabbed two glasses and indicated that she should follow him. They passed through the drawing room and looking around, Hattie spotted several familiar faces, Robert Johnson and Vince Hunt, two local trainers and a group of jockeys including Sam Foster and Connor Moore, together with lots of other well dressed people. She

85

wished Daisy was here, but sadly she was busy competing down south somewhere. The guests all looked so familiar and then she realised that half of them were actors and had been in either soaps or detective drama series. Sam Foster nodded at her. She waved back and followed Finn through the crowd, over the lawn to the marquee. Inside a band was playing subdued, easy listening jazz and a young man was crooning away effortlessly.

'Christ, that singer is the dead spit of Jamie Cullum,' said Hattie.

Finn turned to her and laughed. 'That's because it is Jamie Cullum. The place will be crammed with celebrities, if I know Caroline.' He glanced around the dance floor where a few couples were smooching around. 'I can see that actress who played Moneypenny over there, the chap who was in Police Beat and the couple who renovated that old castle in Yorkshire, you know the programme.'

Hattie did. The pair had been turned into overnight celebrities as the public had really embraced their struggles to turn the derelict building into a home. There were even three young men who according to the press, were all vying to be the next James Bond, all gossiping and laughing in one corner of the marquee.

Hattie gulped. 'And the presenter from Lovers' Leap is dancing with Sherlock Holmes and look there's those dancers from Celebrity Dance Off.' She indicated a couple who were ostentatiously fish tailing and quick stepping around the place while a gaggle of young women watched in awe. 'This is bloody amazing. Caroline is something else.'

'Yes, she really is the real deal. Now don't forget what we're here to do. Let's go and I'll introduce you to some more people.'

Finn led the way over to talk to Tristan Davis and Jed Cavendish. She knew they were well known jockeys, but they looked different without their riding helmets. Finn introduced her to Tara's uncle, a man called Lawrence Prendergast, who was apparently a bloodstock agent. He chatted to Finn about his recent purchases and was enjoying talking about bloodlines. Finn was tapped on the shoulder by another man, so went to speak to him, and she found herself trying to follow Lawrence's conversation about a stallion called Modus Operandi.

'He's sired some brilliant progeny, he's had 70% winners, a cracking percentage. He's going to be a top class sire. I've bought up lots of his first crop, so I'm naturally delighted.'

Hattie didn't know what to say to that. 'But surely the mares are important too,' she added thinking that the sire's form could not be the only predictor of a horse's success. She felt that the mares' DNA was being completely ignored.

'Oh, absolutely. Are you in the market for a racehorse, did you say? Like I said, I have some fabulous yearlings that I bought at Doncaster,' he added hopefully.

Hattie was thinking about upgrading her old Polo, but certainly couldn't afford anything like the cost of a racehorse. 'Oh, no nothing like that. I work for the PJA as a dietician. I've not been there that long.'

She looked around frantically for Finn. He was chatting to a smart looking man and a blond, rather handsome chap. She made her excuses and went over to him. Finn waited for a gap in the conversation and introduced her.

'Lloyd Fox and his trainer Dan Richards, Harriet Lucas.' Finn went on to explain her role as a dietician in the PJA.

The two men smiled at her. Lloyd, she presumed, was Joel's father but it was hard to find much of a likeness between father and son. Lloyd was well groomed and when he spoke, he was confident and socially skilled, very unlike the nervous conditional.

'Lovely to meet you, Harriet. The PJA is a splendid organisation and your role must be very fulfilling helping these jockeys stay in shape. It must be such a challenge especially for the flat jockeys and taller National Hunt ones.'

Dan Richards agreed. 'G'day. I might be needing your services meself. I'm getting a bit heavy to be work riding these days so could do with losing a couple of pounds.' His blue eyes twinkled as he patted his flat stomach.

Hattie was surprised to hear his Australian accent and warmed to him immediately because of his open and friendly manner.

'Whereabouts in Australia are you from?'

'Perth but I moved about a bit for work as an Assistant trainer.' He grinned. 'Came here and met Lloyd and he was wanting to get into racing in a big way and bob's your uncle, here I am.'

'How are you finding things in England? Is the racing different?'

'Nah, it's pretty much the same. Competitive and hard to win races, same as here. I like the country, just need a few warmer togs. Perth is really sunny, so I do miss that. I like the mentor system that Finn runs for young jocks. Lloyd's son, Joel is mentored by Finn. Have you met Joel?'

Hattie nodded. 'Yes. I work closely with Finn and met him recently, it was the evening when the other jockey was killed. In fact, I asked the jockeys about females in racing and whether or not there should be any concessions and that seemed to start the argument between Joel and Sinead which made her storm off.'

A shadow passed over Dan's face. 'Christ, I heard about that.' He put his hand on her arm. 'Don't beat yourself up about it, Harriet. Reckon they made their own decisions, you know, so don't sweat it.' Harriet smiled back.

'It's kind of you to say that.'

Lloyd turned to Dan. He had been in a conversation with Finn but clearly wanted to involve his trainer.

'Finn was just asking about whether we are going to buy some more horses and I was telling him about the ones we are interested in the Doncaster sales for horses in training.'

Harriet spotted the two young female conditionals at the edge of the dance floor, talking to a sandy headed middle-aged man who Hattie had seen around the racecourses. She realised it was the journalist, James McGrew. The man looked like he was trying to chat up the girls and not getting very far, from their disdainful expressions. They looked like they were in need of rescue, so Hattie made her excuses.

'Anyway, I must mingle, nice to speak to you.'

Dan grinned and pointed to his stomach. 'And you, Harriet. Very nice. Don't forget to call in. Finn knows where we are. I really do need to get rid of me gut.'

Harriet smiled back and realised that he was flirting with her as he certainly didn't need her advice professionally as he was in very good shape, as far as she could tell. It felt good but she could do without the hassle just now. She caught up with Maura and Lottie.

'Hi. Awful about Sinead, wasn't it? So, what happened when you went to the pub?'

Maura and Lottie looked at each other. Lottie answered.

'Nothing much. Sinead was in there and Sam bought her a drink. She'd calmed down by then and everything was fine. She even apologised to Joel. A hit and run! I can't believe it happened in Walton of all places!'

Maura shook her head. 'Honest to God she was bang out of order but she could be alright, to be honest with yer, Harriet. We didn't know her real well, but it's awful sad, just the same.'

'I suppose the police will get to the bottom of it.'

The girls nodded and Hattie realised that she had spoiled the party mood and decided to be more upbeat. 'Anyway, you all scrub up beautifully. Looking good, girls!'

'And yourself,' replied Maura smiling. 'Jaysus, I wasn't expecting everyone to be so done up. I just put on me old togs ...' She pulled at her faded cotton skirt. 'I'm just trying to text me Mam, she'll never believe I'm hobnobbing with all these stars, so she won't ...'

Hattie took to the pale skinned woman immediately, there was something so sincere and humorous about her manner. Lottie on the other hand looked sophisticated, and rather guarded. A bit distant, thought Hattie, but probably she was just more reserved.

'I did explain what Caroline Regan's like. Her parties are always fabulous. But I was expecting Nat Wilson to be here. Have you seen him?' Lottie asked. Hattie shook her head. Lottie looked disappointed and Hattie got the impression that the young conditional had a huge crush on the former champion jockey. Finn had explained once, rather bitterly that it happened a lot, and Hattie knew that, after having a terrible reputation, Nat was now happily settled with Livvy, Finn's ex fiancée. Nat, she conceded, although not her type, had gypsy good looks and easy charm which some women loved.

'He was invited I hear, but he's chasing winners, I think. He's keen to win the Championship again. He's riding at Worcester tomorrow.'

'Oh. I see, yes, he's doing really well, isn't he?' said Lottie, mollified somewhat.

Then Caroline approached the stage and whispered something to Jamie, the real Jamie Cullum she now knew, and he stopped singing, the band paused and she took up the microphone.

Her beautiful, sultry voice rang out. 'Just a few words everyone. I won't keep you. I just want to thank you all for coming to this little soirée to celebrate the engagement of two of my favourite people, my amazing granddaughter, Tara Regan and the dashing Charlie Durrant.' She gestured over to the marquee entrance where Charlie and Tara stood hand in hand, beaming but also looking embarrassed.

'As an engagement present, I have a little something …' Caroline turned to the band, 'a drum roll, please…' The drummer obliged and a tide of expectation rose. Caroline gestured over to the marquee door. 'Ah, here he is now.'

There was a gasp as a beautiful bay horse, probably about 16.2 hands, wearing a grey and red rug, with a matching red ribbon on his bridle was led in. He looked startled at the people and his stable lad spoke soothingly to him.

'Christ,' said Finn who had just joined them, 'I think it's Saint Jude, the horse Nat rode to win The Charlie Hall at Wetherby. Caroline's got form for this, she bought Tara a racehorse for her birthday a few years ago.'

Caroline smiled broadly. 'This is my present to this wonderful couple, the super Saint Jude. As many will know, Tara and Charlie met whilst racing, so this is the perfect engagement present.'

There was a hush as everyone in the racing fraternity began to realise the monumental implications of the gift.

'I thought Charlie could ride him and Tara could cheer him on! Now everyone enjoy yourselves, let the party continue and please, take Saint Jude back to the stables.'

There was a titter as Saint Jude lunged for a flower display, raised his tail and deposited a pile of droppings on the hessian matting. He was quickly led away.

The guests clapped as Caroline stepped down and the band resumed.

'What a present,' said Hattie, looking towards Finn. 'Is he a good horse?'

'Only a potential National winner,' said Finn quietly. 'And Nat usually rides him as he's at Michael Kelly's. I suppose he'll move yards. I wonder if he knows Caroline's bought him and wants Charlie to take over the ride? That will certainly set the cat amongst the pigeons.'

The red haired journalist, McGrew, who had been chatting up Maura and Lottie, elbowed his way over, eyes glittering with the gleeful knowledge of having a tremendous scoop presented to him on a plate. You could almost see him composing his piece in his head.

'What a fabulous coup for old Caroline to bag such a star as Saint Jude. I wonder what will your friend Nat think? And will they keep him at Michael Kelly's or move him to one of the local trainers here in Walton, do you think, Finn?'

Hattie realised that the man had much more to say to Finn and remembering their brief for tonight, when Lottie and Maura headed to the loos, she decided to follow them. Thoughts raced through her head. She wondered what it must be like for Tara having such a famous grandmother. It would be lovely to be given such fabulous presents, but less so when one realised that the gift might cause a rift between two such good friends as Charlie and Nat. Would Charlie even agree to take over the ride from Nat? Who would train Saint Jude? Knowing as she did, Nat's long road to recovery after the shooting and his determination to take back the jockeys' title, she guessed he would be gutted to lose the ride. All's fair in love and war she mused as she queued behind the girls in the most luxury loo suite she had ever seen. Ahead of her, Maura was looking about her pointing at the range of makeup, hair clips, hair spray and perfumes dotted about in front of the mirror, obviously for guests to take full advantage of. Caroline had not stinted, supplying a range of luxurious cosmetics.

'Jaysus, there's Chanel No 5 and No 19. And I've never even heard of this,' she said picking up a bottle, 'The Coveted Duchess Rose', I've never seen the like.'

'Penhaligon's' said Lottie airily, unimpressed.

Hattie noticed that the woman in front was the slim, elegant trainer Lucinda Williams, who leaned forward and sprayed a cloud of 'Cairo' as she left. It smelled exhilaratingly of hot musk and made Hattie think of spices and excitement.

'You can go ahead, so you can,' said Maura to Hattie, as she was still sniffing the bottles and eyeing the cosmetics with glee.

Hattie nipped into the loo, resolving to run a brush through her hair and try out some of the perfumes on offer. Marc Jacob's Daisy, was more than up to the job, but these fragrances smelled gorgeous, utterly sensual and intoxicating. On a whole new level of sophistication, like the evening so far. She decided to take off her tights, the place was sweltering and spent an age in the toilet repairing her makeup and trying to rearrange her hair in an updo. She could hear the main door to the toilets opening and closing many times as the toilets filled up and then emptied.

As she adjusted her hair, she suddenly heard whispers from outside the cubicle. The girls must have thought she had left.

'What'll you say in your interview with the police, Lottie? We have to stick to the same story.'

'Just what you told the woman from the PJA. That we all kissed and made up and that was that. Sinead left before us, that is the truth.'

There was a heavy sigh. 'But what about what happened to Clare,' she hissed. 'Supposing it's the same person?'

'What about it? We don't know it's related. Just keep your trap shut, Maura, like we said. Let's not stir up any trouble. I mean it, say *nothing*!'

'But, still poor Sinead,' Maura sounded tearful.

'Come on, let's go and have another drink and try and enjoy ourselves. Now that Charlie's taken, I might have a go at Finn. He's a bit of alright…'

Maura laughed. 'OK. I like the look of that Sam actually.' Hattie heard them squirt perfume about and stagger off on their high heels.

Hattie waited a couple of minutes before slipping out, her eyes scanning the crowd for Finn. Her head was spinning with what she had just heard. What had happened that evening to Sinead and what did it have to do with Clare? Her eyes alighted on Finn.

She made her way over towards the entrance to the marquee and spotted him in conversation with someone tall and dark haired just outside.

'All I'm saying is, be discreet. I'll go in and get Robert and you can take him off without interrupting.'

'Right, you have two minutes,' said the man. As Hattie approached, she realised it was Taverner, the detective. She looked from one man to the other.

'Stay here Hattie, I'm just going to fetch Robert.' Finn looked grim faced.

Hattie nodded and stood next to Taverner outside the marquee. The music played on, mingling with the sound of laughter and desultory conversation. Taking in his serious expression Hattie said, 'I take it this is an official visit?'

The detective nodded. 'I'm here to talk to one of the guests. Ah, here he is now.' Taverner straightened. 'Mr Johnson, I need you to accompany me down to the station. I want to speak to you about the death of your conditional jockey, Sinead O'Brien. If you would come with me, sir.'

Johnson looked aghast. 'What? Can't this wait, Inspector? I'm at a party for goodness' sake!'

The Inspector drew himself to his considerable height. 'Mr Johnson, a young woman in your employment has died. There are no more parties for her, so I think you can spare a few minutes to talk to us, as you will appreciate, time is of the essence. I'm sorry if this is inconvenient but I have an investigation to run.'

Robert considered this for a moment, swallowed hard and then nodded.

'Christ, what an evening,' said Finn as they both watched Robert being driven away. Their mood plummeted in an instant, like a stone thrown into a lake. Both knew that there would be huge ripples as a consequence.

Chapter Eleven

Nat Wilson drove to Worcester in an excellent mood. He was engaged to ride several good horses, including Portland Bay, the promising hurdler in the fifth race and he hoped for a good run. Jamie McGuire had been sent off to ride the yard's inferior horses at Huntingdon, but he noted that his other rival, Colm McNally was in attendance. He hoped for a good run on Porto. The ride on this tricky but talented horse endorsed Nat's rightful position as top jockey and he was heartened by this. Racing was so competitive that after his year out, he felt the world had moved on, other jockeys, including Jamie had done well and he needed to reassert himself big time. Another reason was that Worcester was one of his favourite courses and he also had the opportunity to put his Mercedes through its paces as he drove there. There was a particularly good stretch of road off the M5 that was great to test it out and he came alive as the needle on the speedometer nudged up to 120 mph. Adrenalin surged through him, he loved speed and the car's receptiveness did not disappoint.

He arrived in plenty of time. The course was nestled next to the River Severn and was very picturesque. The weather was turning colder but the weighing room banter always cheered him. The usual jockeys were there, Colm McNally, Gerry King and Jed Cavendish, and some conditionals that he didn't know.

'Sounds like Caroline Regan threw a great engagement party for Charlie and Tara,' Jed told him. 'Jamie Cullum was singing and there was a whole host of 'A' listers there.'

'I know. I was sorry to miss it what with riding here today, but I sent them a case of champagne. I love a good do, but I'll be there for the wedding, wouldn't miss if for the world.'

Colm pulled his ride's colours over his head. 'Heard that wasn't the only good present.' Jed cast him a warning glance, but Colm ignored it. 'Listen, did you hear what Caroline bought them for an engagement present?'

Nat had ridden for Caroline Regan a time or two and thought she was an amazingly talented actress and icon. Mind you, she had more money than sense, so it was bound to be something very extravagant.

'What was it? A posh house, a new car, she's been paid millions for her latest gangster movie, she's loaded, that one.'

'Ah, you don't know?' Colm sighed and looked uneasy. 'Michael's not said anything then?'

'No, about what?' Why on earth would Michael know anything about Caroline's present to Charlie and her granddaughter?

Jed shook his head. 'Well, you'll have to tell him now, you idiot!'

Nat looked from Colm to Jed and back again, increasingly confused.

Colm took a deep breath. 'She only went and bought them Saint Jude.' He watched as Nat's face fell. 'Sorry, I thought Michael would have said something.'

Nat processed this information. He felt like he'd been punched in the stomach. So, Saint Jude, arguably the best steeplechaser in the last few years, prospective Gold Cup and Grand National winner, *his* ride had been sold to Caroline Regan. That meant that the horse would move yards and was likely to be ridden by Charlie Durrant. She was bound to favour a jockey who was practically family rather than him, surely? After The Charlie Hall win, he had pinned his hopes on keeping the ride and potentially winning some, if not all of those great races. Still, racing was like that. Horses changed hands all the time and hence jockeys, as different owners had other allegiances and changed trainers at the drop of a hat. Something told him that Colm had relished telling him this bit of news. A usually taciturn man with a strong Cork accent, he had been surprisingly talkative about the horse changing hands. Nat took a deep breath determined to put a brave face on.

'Ah, well. I suppose Charlie will be riding him from now on. Good luck to him. Never mind lads, there's plenty of other really good 'chasers kicking around.'

'Course there is, course,' replied Jed, slapping him on the back. 'Knew you'd take it like that.'

Except of course there wasn't. Saint Jude was the best and they all knew it.

Nat partnered Joie de Vivre in the first race and came in fifth out of a field of ten. He rode Bora Bora in the second and managed a third after mastering the horse's peculiar striding and habit of putting in short strides as he jumped. In the fourth he rode Have a Nice Day. He reflected that actually he was not having a nice day as the lanky bay had to be pulled up as he hit the third from home and became completely and utterly lame. Still, he was riding Portland Bay in the fifth and hoped that this ride would come good. He was still seething after he learnt about Saint Jude's sale. It made him even more determined to win on the large bay horse.

There were a couple of good horses in the race ridden by the usual guys, Colm McNally, Gerry King, Jed Cavendish, and some conditionals chancing their arms. The owners, Mr and Mrs Horley were excited about Nat riding for them and hopeful that from what Michael Kelly had told them, he had managed to iron out some of the horse's quirks. Not that Michael was there today, he had opted to go to Huntingdon and had sent his young assistant, Andrew Kirby. The man was in his thirties, cheerful and knowledgeable.

'McNally's horse, Hinterland, is well fancied and I like the look of Gerry King's, Capitano.' Andrew frowned. 'If Porto is up for it, he should win easily but you know what a temperamental bugger he is? You know better than I do how to ride him, so just do what you think is best.'

Nat winked. 'Great. I will.' He appreciated Andrew's respect for him in not telling him how to do his job.

He was legged up and rode round the paddock with his feet out of the stirrups to give Porto the message that he was in control. He passed the spotty kid in a huddle with a blond, smiley chap, an Australian if the accent was anything to go by. They appeared to be staring at him and Porto, probably aware that the horse, on his day, was likely to be hard to beat. He just hoped his mount was going to play ball. Once he felt the horse was listening to him, he slipped his feet into his irons and cantered down to the start, making sure that Porto was going at the pace he dictated, not the other way round.

Porto seemed to be behaving himself so far, as he flicked his ears back and forwards. Then the tape was up and they set off at a decent crack. Nat was vigilant as he came to the first fence. He would know how things were going to go once they had safely negotiated the first obstacle. He rode on strongly and Porto charged over the fence to land well up the field. Thank the Lord, thought Nat. Perhaps, this day wouldn't turn out so bad after all. By the second circuit of the three mile hurdle race, everything was going well and they had moved up the field. Porto was full of running and seemed to be enjoying the run as his ears were pricked forwards. Nat surveyed the scene, as the heavens opened, and a steady downpour made visibility even worse. He wiped his goggles and saw that there were now two horses in front. In the lead, Colm McNally's mount, Hinterland, and behind them to his left a bay being ridden by someone unknown to him, one of the girls possibly. They jumped the fourth fence and he decided to squeeze past the second placed horse on the inside as they came up to the third last. Nat positioned Porto against the inside rails and pushed forward. The horse sprang gamely on and Nat was confident that they would get through the gap and press on to win. As he pushed the animal next to the other horse, Porto seemed to surge forward, put in a short stride, ploughing into the fence and missed his take off. Shit, Nat tried to right the animal but was thrust over the horse's head and received a heavy blow from Porto's flailing near hind as the animal sailed over him. The pain in his shoulder was intense. Then he blacked out.

Livvy picked Nat up from the hospital, his arm was in a sling and he clutched a packet of painkillers. He had broken his collarbone and was facing at least a month to six weeks off. As he'd blacked out, he had been carted off to hospital and had been unable to hide his injury. If he hadn't, he'd have been tempted to strap it up himself and ignore it. He was in an absolutely foul mood. His mind was in overdrive. Not only had he lost the ride on Saint Jude, it had happened again. His mind went through the events before Porto had fallen. Things were going well, the horse was focused and full of running and the same bloody thing had happened as in the other races. Had he misjudged the stride? Was he losing it? Normally upbeat and confident, he was not prone to self doubt or introspection but something was very wrong and it had to be with him. He had heard that this had happened to other riders, self doubt, a loss of nerve was possible, but it had never happened to him before. He was the champion jockey, the best in the business, for God's sake. His mood was not improved when he found out that Colm McNally had won the race, closely followed by the spotty conditional he had seen before.

Livvy cast him a sidelong look. 'Listen, I know you're pissed off being out for a few weeks, but it could have been so much worse than a bust collarbone. You'll soon be back and winning again.'

Nat looked at her and shook his head. 'Saint Jude's been sold, so he's bound to move yards, I'll be jocked off.' A surge of anger raged through him. 'But the worst thing is it happened again. That's four times now I've missed my stride, caused the horse to fall, completely messed up. All those horses should have won. I've lost it, Livvy. The magician is no more.'

Livvy gasped. 'No, never. It's just a run of bad luck, that's all. A good night's sleep and you'll feel better in the morning. Everything will seem brighter. You'll see.'

Nat very much doubted it. Livvy patted his arm.

'I believe in you.'

He managed a grimace. 'I know.' The problem was, did he?

Matters got worse when he saw the headlines in the racing columns.

'The Magician's tricks fall flat.'

Wilson out after a bad fall. His comeback is now in question.'

Even more brutal was the column in The Yorkshire Echo. Its racing section was one of the most well respected.

'The Magician falls from grace. Is it all over for ex-champion jockey, Nat Wilson?'

It comes to us all, the time when we need to retire gracefully and leave the career we have built over many years. Most of us know when that time has come but what could be sadder than the man who is in total denial? And so it is with Nat Wilson, six times Champion jockey who has enthralled and captivated racing fans with his daring and talented riding over the years, but having watched Wilson fall in four races at the crucial time due to pilot error, on horses that could have easily won, I can tell you that, Nat Wilson is not the rider he once was. He was off for a season following a hunting accident that shattered his thighbone. We all expected him to make a full recovery, but having followed Nat's career for many years, I have reached the inescapable conclusion that he has not. Sources close to Wilson, have also confirmed my analysis of the situation. Hopefully Wilson will realise that his magic touch has all but gone. There would be no shame in a graceful retirement now.

The article went on to give a blow by blow account of each recent race he had fallen in, specifying his 'poor riding'. It even mentioned that he had lost the ride on Saint Jude but implied that was also due to his incompetence in the saddle rather than reporting that the horse had been sold. Nat scanned the article for the author's name. James McGrew, Topper McGrew! He'd thought he had a reasonable relationship with the seasoned journalist. He had always made the effort to talk to him and give him some quotes for his column. The fucking, fat bastard! For a minute he imagined punching the journalist's, fat face in. As if he could even manage to climb into the saddle, let alone race ride. How dare he? He screwed the paper up and chucked it. The implication was clear, although never fully stated. They thought he had lost his nerve. In the confusion and turmoil, he wondered if he actually had.

Worse was to come. The doorbell rang out and an ashen faced Livvy came back with two besuited and serious looking men.

'Nathaniel Wilson?'

'Yes?'

The taller man stepped forward and flashed his warrant card. 'I am DS Jones and this is DI French from Gloucester Constabulary. I am arresting you on suspicion of indecent exposure. You have the right to remain silent, but it may harm your defence if you do not mention when questioned something which you later rely on in court. Anything you do say, may be given in evidence.'

As the two men grabbed him, one producing handcuffs, Livvy screamed.

Christ what was happening? Indecent exposure? Then Nat remembered the bloody journalist from 'Live' magazine and the unfortunate incident when his towel had slipped. Jesus!

'Look, Livvy, it's not what you think.'

The rebuke in her eyes was even harder to stomach somehow than reading Topper McGrew's article.

Livvy shook her head and wiped her eyes.

'I trusted you, I thought you had changed. For God's sake, Nat, what the hell have you done?'

'Look, it's all bollocks. I'll explain it when I get back.'

Livvy gave him a long, bitter stare. 'Well, don't expect me to be here.'

Nat gasped. He felt like he had been stabbed in the heart. The pain threatened to overwhelm him as he saw his life unravelling before his eyes.

Chapter Twelve

Finn and Hattie met up at The Singing Kettle café in Walton to discuss what they had found out about Sinead's death. The café was not too busy, so they took their seats at the rear and sipped cappuccinos.

'Christ, so do you think that Robert is involved in Sinead's death?' asked Hattie. 'And Taverner turning up at the party put a right dampener on things. Why couldn't he have waited for a bit?'

'I think Taverner was just making a point to the racing community that we have to take this seriously. That's why he turned up then, to make an impact.' He shrugged. 'I presume he just wanted to find out all the details of Sinead's work with Robert and didn't want to wait. Time is of the essence, I should think.'

'Hmm. Yeah. I suppose. Sinead certainly made an impression during the time she was at Robert's, but not a good one. Great party though! All those 'A' listers, Jamie Cullum and gorgeous actors! What did you make of Caroline giving Saint Jude to Charlie and Tara as an engagement present?'

'God, it's bound to be awkward. I know Nat was banking on getting the rest of the rides on him. The horse is the best prospect I've seen this year. Still, Nat will land on his feet, he always does.'

Hattie shook her head. 'I'm really sorry for asking them about the gender of jockeys. I feel sort of responsible for causing the whole argument and for all we know it might have led to Sinead's death.'

Finn gave her a penetrating look. 'You can't think that, Hattie. Besides, the whole thing was probably an accident. Maybe, Sinead was simply run over and that's that.'

'Funnily enough, that's exactly what Dan Richards said too. What did you make of Lloyd and Dan?'

Finn shrugged. 'Well, I can see why Joel stammers. His father is very rich and very pushy where Joel is concerned. Dan seems OK though, quite likeable. The Aussies always seem so laid back, it's refreshing really.'

Hattie agreed wondering if she should take Dan up on his invitation to call in and see him. Then, she suddenly thought about what had happened afterwards.

'Damn, I nearly forgot. I was in the loos last night and Maura and Lottie were talking outside. I think they thought the place was empty. They were talking about Sinead. Maura asked if it was anything to do with what happened to Clare. Lottie told her that it wasn't and that she should keep her 'trap shut'. So, they definitely know something.'

Finn stiffened. 'Who is Clare, did they say?'

Hattie shook her head. 'No, but we need to find out, because she might just hold the key to what happened to Sinead. Perhaps, she works in the stables, or she's a friend?'

'You're right. I'll ask around.' He would have to do any investigation on his own. He really couldn't burden Hattie after everything that had happened in their last case. Finn glanced at his watch. 'Christ, I'd better go, I've got an appointment. Are you staying?'

Hattie looked slightly smug. 'Oh yes, I forgot to say. I'm meeting Tara Regan here. We thought we'd catch up after the party. I liked her straightaway and she wants to pick my brains on something.'

'Brilliant! I'm sure the pair of you will get on very well.' Finn left, his spirits lifting. He had already discussed Harriet's suspected PTSD with Tara and he was sure that under her expert guidance, Hattie would soon be back firing on all cylinders. Thank God for that!

Meanwhile, DI Gabriel Taverner was accompanied by DS Anna Wildblood to the post mortem. Sinead's body had been identified by her tearful social worker as Sinead's parents had not seen her for a number of years. The social worker, Ella Morton, had been heartbroken, but at least someone was, thought Taverner, having been met by largely blank expressions by the parents. Sinead had been found in a ditch off the road out of Walton a mile or so away, in a remote area. She had been wearing a black hoodie pulled up over her dyed blonde hair and presumably had been on her way home to the lodgings just near Robert Johnson's yard. First impressions were that she had been involved in a hit and run. SOCO had been at the scene, a road block had been set up, and initial interviews were taking place.

Dr Tony Ives was in attendance, a Scottish, bear like man who Taverner had worked with on many occasions now. He was a consummate professional and often liked to speculate on the police investigations. Taverner steeled himself for a look at the body, as Ives saw them and stopped recording into his dictaphone. He raised an eyebrow in greeting.

'So, what do you have for me?' asked Taverner.

'Well, it's an interesting one, actually.' Ives moved towards the body and pointed to a series of scratches, abrasions and bruises on Sinead's front side and marks to her crotch. There looked to be a tyre mark, just three or so inches on the left hand side edge of her back and a large wound to her right temple. 'Firstly, the poor wee lassie was

106

NOT killed in a hit and run. My guess is that she was already lying on the side of the road and had been attacked just before.' Ives pointed to the abrasions, scratches and bruises to her front, back and crotch. 'See these marks here and here. I'd say she was attacked and struggled and judging from the marks to her thighs, we can't rule out a sexual assault, but I'll need to run further tests, of course.'

Wildblood started to look distinctly queasy and Taverner found himself taking a deep breath. Sexual offences were amongst the worse he had to deal with in Taverner's book because of the psychological devastation they caused the victims and the poor prosecution rate.

'So, what about the tyre marks?'

Dr Ives nodded. 'From the crime scene, I'd speculate that she had fallen over and the car,' he hoisted the body up so he could see the back and pointed to the tyre marks, 'nudged her into the ditch.'

Taverner took this in. 'What is the cause of death then?'

Ives eyes gleamed as he pointed to the large wound to Sinead's right temple. 'That is, Inspector. There was a large stone in the ditch and unfortunately, she hit it when she fell in. The density of the bone on the temple is much lower than the rest of the scalp, so blows to that area can often be fatal, as in this case, sadly.' The big man shook his head sorrowfully. 'The wound matches the surface of the stone exactly. I made a cast of the surface and it fits perfectly. All life was extinct seconds later.'

'So, she was alive when the car ran her over?' asked Wildblood.

'Very much so.'

Taverner and Wildblood looked at one another. 'So, that means we could be looking at a perpetrator who raped and ran her into the ditch or the person driving the vehicle could be someone else entirely.'

Ives raised a grey eyebrow. 'Exactly. So, do you have any suspects? Are there any sex offenders in the area? Where had she been before she set off walking?'

'In the pub, she was last seen in The Blacksmith's Arms before walking home,' replied Taverner drily. He knew that there weren't any registered sex offenders in the area, as he had already checked, but then again many of the stable staff were transient or maybe it was a stranger or someone who had never been prosecuted before.

Wildblood's brain was in overdrive. 'Could she have been drugged?'

Ives considered this. 'It's certainly a possibility. We'll know more when the blood tests come back. I'll send my report through by tomorrow, I'd say.'

The two detectives prepared to leave. Taverner turned back. 'Assuming there are two separate perpetrators, would the driver who drove into Sinead, necessarily know they had hit a person?'

Ives pursed his lips. 'Aye, it's a good question, right enough. Possibly not. They would have known they had hit something but maybe assumed it was a deer, a badger or other animal. Judging by the tyre marks, they just caught the side of her, so there may not have been any damage to the vehicle even.'

Taverner sifted through the facts and tried to ignore the smell of the various chemicals used in the post mortem, deep in thought. 'So, what about the time of death?'

'Death occurred between six pm and midnight.'

'OK. And just one more thing? Presumably, if the impact of the car pushed her into the ditch, then even if someone got out of their car to check what they had hit, then they probably wouldn't have seen anything on that remote stretch of road.'

'Correct. Certainly not the body as it would have been dark, and she would have rolled out of sight. The poor, wee lassie. Well, it's going to be a hard case to crack, Taverner, that it is.' Ives gave the officers a wide smile. 'Gud luck!'

Taverner nodded wondering where to start. The two officers sat in the car in stunned silence. Christ, there was no CCTV or lights on the remote stretch of road that Sinead had been found on. In the end it was a postman delivering post to a farmhouse that noticed the black object in the ditch. If she'd been drugged, raped and then collapsed that meant any number of people could have driven over her and might not even have registered the fact that she was there at all.

Wildblood wound down her window and started to take deep breaths.

'Do you want me to drive?' Taverner recognised that his Sergeant was trying very hard not to vomit. For all her plain speaking and common sense, she was a very sensitive soul.

'No, it's alright, guv.' She took a few more deep breaths as she navigated the York traffic. 'It's just that poor girl. To have survived being raped and then being run over, only to end up hitting her head on a bloody stone and dying! What a tragedy! And it's not even as though she's had much of a life by all accounts!' Taverner let Anna control her emotions for a minute.

'I know, I know,' he said soothingly. 'I feel exactly the same. Don't worry, we'll get the bastard that did this, you can be sure about that.'

The sight of the lifeless body of the young woman, who by all accounts had had the most deprived of backgrounds and was just trying to make something of her life, was truly heart breaking. They owed it to her in death, to catch the rapist and driver and bring them to justice. It was the very least they could do for the girl. With renewed

determination, he began to plan out his investigation in his head, as
Wildblood wiped her eyes and continued driving back to the station.

Chapter Thirteen

It was, thought Hattie, a good job she liked The Singing Kettle as she was spending a lot of time there today, as she watched Finn walk away and waited for Tara to arrive. She'd been surprised and thrilled to be contacted so quickly by her new acquaintance. Hattie was also intrigued at the hints Tara had given about wanting to talk to her. She felt sure it would not be about her speaking to Tara as a client, as she knew that Finn, tied by the secrecy of their role at the BHA could not have given away details of the last case. So, it must be, she reasoned, about something else.

From the window she spotted Tara walking towards the shop. She saw her check her watch and march quickly along the street. Dressed in black fitted trousers and a long blue tunic top and carrying a black satchel, she looked professional but warm, not too formal.

'Hi Harriet, have you ordered? I'll have a latte please and a toasted teacake,' she said to the waitress, 'and you?'

'An Americano and a fruit scone.'

Tara sat down smiling and Hattie breathed in her discreet, floral perfume.

'Oh, isn't this a fab place. I've been past but never inside. Smells gorgeous too, fresh coffee and newly baked scones...' She looked round at the mismatched chairs and crockery, the rather thrown together décor, old black and white photographed scenes from Walton mixed, with modern splashy watercolours, Singer sewing machines and old riding gear.

'Thanks for the party. I really enjoyed it...'

Tara made a small gesture of helplessness. 'When Granny does something, she does it well. Me and Charlie, we might have gone for something more modest but well, she does so love organising a do, I just couldn't not let her. Anyway, how are you? Tell me all about your new job?'

Over the next few minutes or so Hattie found herself telling Tara about her role, about the work of a dietician. Tara, she found, was a sympathetic listener who seemed genuinely interested.

They tucked into their food, Hattie realising that she was absolutely starving.

'What a great job and really useful. I wanted to ask if you have any ideas about helping bulimics...'

Hattie put her head on one side whilst she recalled the lectures. She picked up the crumbs from her scone with her finger. 'Yes, I know a bit, but I think I would have to work closely with another professional, someone like yourself in fact. Use a multi-agency approach...'

Tara grinned and put down her mug. 'Oh, that's exactly what I'd hoped you'd say. We're looking for a dietician to assist us actually. That's why I was keen to meet you. Several of our clients have bulimia or are anorexic. So many young people feel the need to be ultra thin, a fair proportion are in racing where weight is crucial, so it is a welfare issue too.'

'Of course. My boss mentioned something.'

Tara grinned and lowered her voice. 'Brilliant. I'll suggest you for the next networking group, shall I?'

'As long as my boss agrees. We do have a load of resources we can help with, lots of diets and meal plans that ensure proper nutrition. Some of these jockeys play fast and loose with their health, but it will only cause problems in later life.'

Tara laughed. 'Don't get me started on Charlie's diet! Actually, though he's luckier than some. I have to be careful what I eat though because I don't want to annoy him. I have a whole stash of chocolate hidden about the house.' She gave Hattie a considering look. 'Are you and Finn an item? Only you seem very close.'

Hattie laughed this off. 'No, not at all. We just met at the races when Sam Foster was beaten up, you know the jockey, and sort of became friends, that's all.'

Tara nodded. 'Oh. He's a great bloke. Charlie's always going on about how much Finn taught him and what a talented jockey he was. It's marvellous that he's doing well with the coaching.'

'Yes, though some of his charges can be a little troublesome.' She went on to explain about Sinead's death.

'Gosh, that's awful. So, was it a hit and run?'

'I think so. In fact, the police came to your party and picked up Robert Johnson. Finn fetched Robert and stopped the officer from going in. He didn't want the party to be ruined, you see.'

Tara shook her head. 'Oh, I didn't know, that's so kind of him. I must thank him. Is Robert involved?'

'No. I think it was just routine because Sinead was apprenticed there. Finn and I had seen her a few hours before, so we've had to give a statement to the police, too.' Hattie was still feeling like it was all her fault. Why did she have to ask that question about whether female jockeys needed allowances made for them to compete? What was she thinking? If she hadn't said it, Sinead wouldn't have argued with Joel and they'd all have had a quick drink at The Blacksmith's and gone home as a group, in complete safety. Added to her nightmares about being held hostage in their last case, she was struggling to sleep, kept having flash backs and wondered if she was going a bit mad. If any work did come up for the BHA, she might have to duck out and make some excuse. Damn.

Tara studied her carefully. 'Do you want to talk about it?'

Harriet shook her head. 'No.' She gave a fixed smile. 'Now let's talk about something more cheerful. Tell me how you met Charlie and when the wedding is and where.'

Tara explained about her grandmother's gift. She had given her a racehorse, Rose Gold, and how she had co-opted Charlie to assist her with the raceday procedures. 'So, things just grew from there really. He's a lovely chap and I just feel so lucky.' Harriet noticed the expensive but stylish diamond engagement ring.

'Lovely ring. He's obviously got good taste too. So where are you having the wedding? At Caroline's, I suppose?'

Tara laughed. 'I'm sure granny would love to host it but we haven't really thought. Some of Charlie's family are from the Whitby area and there's loads of lovely hotels near there and a great one near Robin Hood's Bay, actually. Anyway, we've got lots of time to decide...'

Suddenly Hattie remembered her own recent visit to Robin's Hood Bay. Sweat began to pour off her and her mouth ran dry. A video memory reel of the last case, her abduction, trying to escape, the house, the images of people walking down to the beach unaware of her plight, raced through her brain. It felt as if she had been drenched by a bucket of ice cubes. She gave a wretched sob and desperately trying to breathe, grabbed the tablecloth so hard that her knuckles showed white. '

'I...I...'

Then she ran for the toilets, swerving to avoid the open mouthed waitress.

Once there, Hattie threw open the door of the cubicle, sat on the closed seat with her head in her hands, trying to control her ragged breath, her racing heart, the shaking limbs.

'Christ, it can't be a ruddy heart attack,' she told herself knowing that she was young, healthy, an ex Junior Pentathlon Team GB member for Christ's sake. She concentrated on breathing in for four, holding for four and breathing out for four, like her coach had taught her to before competition. Gradually her gasps slowed.

'Hattie, are you OK? Listen, come out. I've got some Rescue Remedy here. That'll calm you,' said an anxious sounding Tara.

Hattie opened the door. 'I'm so sorry…'

Tara grinned. 'Was it something I said?' She passed over a small bottle. 'Have a shot of that. Oh sod it, shall we go to the pub?'

Ten minutes later, the two were sitting side by side in The Blacksmith's Arms sipping Chardonnay.

Hattie turned to Tara. 'Sorry about that…'

Tara inclined her head. 'Do you want to talk about it? No pressure.'

So, Hattie began to speak, unburdening herself, explaining about the mention of Robin Hood's Bay which had triggered the reaction. Something about Tara's quiet empathy encouraged this release. She found once she'd started to talk, she couldn't stop. It was such a relief to let it all out to someone who wasn't there, she'd worried about upsetting Finn by going on about it, so she hadn't spoken to him about how she felt. Not really. When she'd finished Tara shook her head.

'Wow. That's so brave of you. Listen, I could offer help. I think your panic attacks need addressing, don't you?'

'Panic attacks? Is that what they are?'

Tara smiled. 'Definitely. I think it's Post Traumatic Stress Disorder, very common after a traumatic event. It responds really well to Cognitive Behavioural Therapy.'

'Won't I have to be referred to you through my GP or something?' Hattie knew these things were complex. It wasn't easy to access the services of a clinical psychologist.

'No need. I'll do it as a friend and because, to be honest, your story is absolutely fascinating.' Tara grinned. 'I just won't mention RHB again, honestly. You really had me worried for a moment. You have to do some work too, but it will help and you'll soon start to feel differently about what happened.'

Hattie grinned. 'I thought I was actually going a bit crazy. I can't tell you what a relief it is to know that I'm not.'

They burst out laughing and Hattie felt her spirits soar. Only then did she realise what an awful grey cloud she had been living under recently, but she now knew that her reaction was entirely normal and that she could be helped.

Chapter Fourteen

Topper McGrew slunk into the team meeting at the Yorkshire Echo, rather late. He positioned himself at the back having grabbed a quick coffee. Several pairs of eyes darted over towards him but no one commented. Too keen creeping to that prat, Christian Lamont, he thought sourly. The prat who was currently presenting a Power Point about sales and targets. It was just past nine. Topper regretted making free with the whiskey last night. Now he had a pounding headache and felt dishevelled and grubby. He had woken up in the armchair and when he saw the time, had a quick wash and raced to work. His colleagues, he noticed, were to a man or woman all clean, alert and ready for action.

The colleague, a junior reporter, was seated at the next desk, a keen 20 year old slip of a girl called Lindy was taking notes in a pink furry notebook which looked better suited to a junior classroom than a newsroom. She wore a t shirt, tight leggings on skinny legs and trainers and looked as if she'd been exercising. Probably ran to work, he thought savagely. He glanced at her sipping what he guessed was some sort of healthy, bright green smoothie, with kale in it. How revolting! She was pretty enough, he thought, with mousy hair which looked blonde at the ends, if only she didn't overdo the eyebrow makeup, which made it look as if she had two great fat black slugs balanced on top of her eyes. When he'd joked about it once, the office had gone instantly quiet and he realised his faux pas. Later Christian had had a little talk to him about his attitude which he said, 'was sexist, old fashioned and would result in a warning.' Christ, everyone these days had had a sense of humour removal, that was their problem. Bloody prats. A small laugh escaped from him and Christian, pausing looked over.

'James, have you something to say?' Topper shook his head wanting to scream it's bloody Topper not James. Only his wife and his mother called him James, and hardly ever in a good way.

'Well now, I'll start on the one to one coaching sessions. I'll call you in separately. James, you first, so everyone let's get to it and make the Echo and Yorkshire proud today. James?'

Head down, grumbling to himself, Topper entered Christian's glass walled office. There was a smell of lavender from an oil burner and he could hear the faint sound of some sort of animal wailing, running in the background.

'Soothing, isn't it?' said Christian pointing to a chair. He himself sat next to Topper on a round blue gym ball. 'Just keeping my energy flowing with this thing, the chi,' he said, 'and it's great for the back. So, James, good job with the jockey piece. What's his name, Nat Wilson? Mmm…not bad for starters…'

'I think it's one of my best stories,' said Topper, somewhat aggrieved by the slightly lukewarm reception to his piece suggesting that it was time for the ex-champion jockey to hang up his boots. He had lost his bloody nerve and it was bloody dynamite, he thought, a scoop, really hard hitting but respectful.

'So, look at it like this,' said Christian with a fake smile revealing dazzlingly white teeth in a tanned face. He held up his hand and counted on his fingers, 'Lindy's got a story about the local MP getting his brother to take his speeding points, hugely important. There's a couple of guys working on the corruption allegations against

118

the town Mayor and the crime reporter's onto the case of a hit and run murder story…' He smiled again, 'so you see hinting that a jockey should retire is a bit tame, James. I need more. Find out what's happened to him, what his weaknesses are, does he take bribes, is he into boys or young girls, does he want to change gender, is he a racist? That's what sells, James…'

Topper regarded the loathsome, smiling figure in front of him and was reminded of a piranha cruising around a lake, which fatally wounded its prey and then devoured it in minutes.

'I've got a good day's racing at Market Rasen, got some fabulous tips…' Topper lied, knowing that his tips were pretty mediocre these days. They had been ever since his chief spotter had got himself killed. The bloody idiot.

'Hey, you got any girl jocks, any lesbian action? Anything saucy for me?' Christian's eyes twinkled with salacious interest. 'Or maybe you could spice up your piece with more tasty details?'

'Yes,' said Topper deciding he'd had enough and agreeing just to get out of there. 'I can do better, there's bound to be more on Wilson. I'll dig around a bit.'

'Good job, you do that, bro' said Christian trying to sound urban and edgy. Annoying, thought Topper, when he knew full well the guy was from rural East Yorkshire.

'Have Lindy come in now.' And the editor began rolling to and fro on his gym ball. As Topper reached the glass door, he'd even begun bouncing on the ruddy thing. Tosser.

Feeling about 300 years old and completely out of step with the modern world and Lamont's style of journalism, Topper went back to his desk and gestured that Lindy should go in for her session. She skipped off like a starved pony trotting towards its feed. Topper thought desolately, I need a fag and a drink, preferably as soon as possible.

Later in the Owners and Trainers bar at Market Rasen, several Macallans in, Topper's mood had lifted. He'd seen the trainers, Vince Hunt and Robert Johnson, and asked about their runners and riders. His first tip had won at a canter and Johnson had given him a quick interview about his plans for the gelding. That would make good copy, he thought, no matter what that burk Lamont thinks. I do a racing column, I need to keep writing about racehorses. All the same, he was glad Nat Wilson wasn't riding at Market Rasen today. He wouldn't want to face him just yet. But Nat was off with a broken collarbone and would not make the trip here as a spectator, so Topper could relax. He decided to hang around the jockeys, to see if he could find out a bit more about what was happening, why Wilson had fallen four times on very well fancied runners, dead certs actually. He threw back his whiskey, grimaced and ambled unsteadily over towards the parade ring.

Watching the horses being led round, he felt a tap on his shoulder.

'Hey, Topper old pal, interested in a photo of our friend, Wilson?'

It was Lofty looking as shifty and grubby as usual. Topper's heart lurched but his tone remained casual. 'Might be, depends…'

Lofty grinned and gave him a quick flash of a digital photo showing Nat Wilson walking with his arms around a glamorous girl, who was definitely not his girlfriend, Livvy. The woman looked very young and the two were closely entwined, intimate even, and dressed in evening wear.

'When was it taken?'

Lofty pointed to the date on the photo. 'The other week, Topper. I think Wilson's got a bit of a complex personal life, no wonder his mind's not on the job. Eh?'

'How much?'

Lofty named a huge sum. Topper bartered until a more feasible amount was mentioned.

'OK, I'll take it off your hands.' Topper bluffed, knowing that this had to be the sort of thing Lamont was after. 'Email it to me then invoice me.'

'Money first.'

With a sigh, Topper made the transfer via his phone with his own money. It would, he felt, definitely be worth it and Lamont would be delighted when he saw the story, he was sure of it.

'Do you know the girl?'

Lofty laughed. 'Christ, do you want jam on it! It was at some business awards dinner in Cheltenham, that's all I know. And that's your lot. You sniff out the rest, my friend.'

And that, thought Topper, nose twitching involuntarily, is just what I'm good at. Itching to get going, he decided to repair to the bar and have a quick snifter before getting to work on what he felt would be a sensational story.

Chapter Fifteen

Nat Wilson spent an uncomfortable few hours in a police cell near Gloucester, where his mind was in overdrive. The look on Livvy's face when he had been arrested, had been enough to floor him and the thought that she might leave him, sent shards of ice through his heart. It had been awful not being able to explain about the bloody journalist from 'Live' magazine. Of course, he hadn't told her about what had happened at the time. He didn't know why exactly. To him it was no big deal and he just thought it would all sort itself out, but now he was bitterly regretting his decision. Hot on the heels of his fall at Worcester, he was still dazed and upset about the awful headlines he had read about himself. One minute he was riding high, had high hopes of a miraculous comeback, now he was in a prison cell accused of indecent exposure and his collarbone was still throbbing like crazy. He was going to be off for several weeks and his hopes of winning another Championship seemed further away than ever. Surely, this was all some sort of ridiculous joke, he kept expecting someone to pop up and shout, 'surprise!' except that he knew it wasn't. He had to face the stark reality that he might well lose the woman he loved and his racing career. What the hell was going on?

After a few hours, two officers came and led him into an interview room. One was a hard faced, auburn haired woman with a buzz cut and the other, an older, taller man with a quiet air of authority. They introduced themselves as DC Horton and DI Carpenter. After some preamble, when DI Carpenter asked if he was happy to proceed without a solicitor, he was, he told them, DC Horton gave him a malicious smirk and switched on the tape recorder. DI Carpenter read him his rights.

'So, you're here under suspicion of committing the offence of indecent exposure. Can I ask you where you were on the afternoon of the 20th of November, Mr Wilson?'

'Well, I haven't got my diary on me.' Nat made to pat his pockets but saw the hostile look on DC Horton's face and decided to play it straight. He had the distinct impression that there was no point using his charm on the female officer. 'I can't remember exactly, but I presume you're talking about the time that journalist from 'Live' magazine came to interview us. Annabel something or other she was called. I don't know the exact date, but it would have been about a week or so ago.'

'So, what happened?' prompted DC Horton, sneering unpleasantly.

'Well, I'd just come back from riding when Livvy, my girlfriend, reminded me that this journalist was coming. We'd both forgotten, so Livvy popped out to get some bits, flowers, coffee and cake, I think. I was sweaty from riding and had a shower. Then the doorbell went, and it was a quarter to two, so I thought it was Livvy. She often forgets her keys, you see, so I wrapped the nearest towel around me and went to open the door.' He ran his fingers through his hair. His collarbone was throbbing in its sling, and he was exhausted. 'Look, you couldn't get me a paracetamol and a cup of tea, could you? My shoulder is really hurting.'

'All in good time, all in good time. Let's just get this over and done with and then we'll see.' DI Carpenter gave him a stiff smile. 'So can you tell us what happened next?'

'Well, I opened the door to the bloody journalist, 15 minutes early she was. As I said I had grabbed the first towel I could find, a small one unbeknown to me and so I decided to let her in and showed her into the sitting room.' He sighed trying to remember what had happened next. 'She asked me when Livvy was back and I stupidly looked at my watch, which was upstairs anyway and not on my wrist, and I accidentally let go of my towel.'

'Just to clarify, your towel dropped, and you were standing there in the nude in front of this young woman?' asked DC Horton.

'Yes, that's about it.' He looked at the woman's sneering expression. 'It was an accident, of course. It was a bit embarrassing, so I said I'd get changed and went upstairs. When I came down a couple of minutes later, she had gone. That's it.'

'Did you drop your towel deliberately with the intention of engaging Ms Sinclair in sexual activity?' asked DI Carpenter.

'Nah. Why would I do that? Have you seen my girlfriend?'

'Strapping, is she?' sneered DC Horton.

Nat shook his head. 'No, actually. She's stunning. Drop dead gorgeous, is what I meant. Why would I look at any other woman?'

DI Carpenter pushed his chair back and gave Nat a penetrating look.

'Did you push against Ms Sinclair when she came into the house?'

'What? Course not? Is that what's she's saying?'

'It is,' continued DI Carpenter. 'And that you made suggestive movements with your hips giving her to believe that you had planned the whole thing and were intent on sexually assaulting her.'

Nat shook his head. Anger coursed through his veins. What was this?

'Look, I did no such thing. Livvy will tell you. Ask her. The woman was coming to talk to us both. She just turned up early and I stupidly answered the door with a towel wrapped round me, that's it. This is utterly ridiculous. The woman is making it all up for God's sake! She can't go around making stuff up like this. It's not right!'

DC Horton gave a slight smile as though she was enjoying his discomfort. 'For your information, this incident caused Ms Sinclair great distress. A well known figure like you indecently exposing yourself in front of her when there was no one else in the house. Lots of men, especially famous, powerful men try to intimidate young women into doing what they want, they use them as sexual playthings.'

'What? Well not me, that's for sure.' He looked from one to the other. 'You have to believe me, this is utter garbage!'

'Did you know Annabel Sinclair before the incident, was the whole thing staged?' asked DC Horton, her lips pursed.

'Of course not. I had never met her before and had no idea she would turn up on her own either. Usually there's at least a couple of them, a journalist and a photographer.'

'I suppose you give a lot of interviews, a man in your position?' asked DC Horton.

Nat shrugged. 'It's all part of the job talking to the press. My agent usually arranges everything. To be honest, it's a real pain in the arse.'

DC Horton scowled. 'And I suppose as a successful jockey, you have access to lots of pretty young women. Are you faithful to your fiancée, Livvy Jordan?'

Nat was really beginning to hate the boot faced detective. She made 'successful jockey' sound like a scurrilous profession, one up from 'child murderer'. Nat glanced at DI Carpenter.

'Do I have to answer that?'

'It would help,' came the reply.

Nat sighed. 'Listen, I have had my fair share of affairs when I was younger and I didn't always treat women as well as I should, I grant you. But what I do know is that any sexual encounter was consensual before you ask, but since I met Livvy, I haven't so much as looked at another woman and I don't intend to. She is the real deal for me and that's all there is to it.'

There was a standoff where Nat glared at them both. The pair consulted each other, then suddenly DI Carpenter announced that the interview was over.

'We'll get you that cup of tea whilst we make some further inquiries. And I'll see if I can find you a paracetamol,' he added.

'Thanks.' Nat felt relieved but then he pondered on the words the detective had used. Further bloody inquiries, what the hell did that mean?

Eventually, DI Carpenter came back with a cup of tea in a plastic cup.

'Sorry, no paracetamol, we're not allowed to give out medication unless it's prescribed to you, apparently. Anyway, your version of events checks out, so you're free to go. Just to confirm there will be no further police action.' DI Carpenter gave him a wry smile. 'Just mind how you go.'

Nat stood up. He took one sip of tea and nearly spat it out. He just wanted to get the hell out of there. He was torn between relief and wanting to punch the officer's lights out. All that fuss and bother just to be let out?

'And the journalist? What will happen to her?'

'Nothing. She's young, and naïve and she was very traumatised.' The Inspector raised an eyebrow at this.

Nat shook his head, rage building at the injustice of it all. Traumatised! In the end he shuffled out and turned his mind to the conversation he needed to have with Livvy when he got home. He had lost all track of time and realised that he had been there all night and all around him the town was waking up. It was nine o'clock when he arrived home. His heart sank when he saw that Livvy's car was not parked outside but he derived some relief when he went upstairs to find out that her clothes were still in the wardrobe, so at least she had not cleared out. Thank Christ for that! He was too wired to sleep so went back downstairs and pulled out a tumbler and poured some Scotch into it. He had an awful lot of thinking to do. It was then that he noticed a copy of the 'Yorkshire Echo' on the table which had obviously been pored over. The headlines leapt out.

Top jock's poor form linked to affair?

Nat Wilson was spotted leaving the home of a stunning, mystery brunette after an awards ceremony held at Cheltenham a few weeks ago. Wilson, who is engaged to beauty, Livvy Jordan, had a reputation as a bit of a player but it was widely thought that Livvy had tamed the six times Champion National Hunt jockey. The pair were recently featured in 'Horse' magazine when Wilson credited his fiancée with changing his life for the better. 'She is the light of my life,' he explained. The jury is out on whether the marriage, which is due to take place next year, will still be on, once Livvy finds out about Wilson's mystery brunette.

He checked the author and was not surprised to find that it was none other than James McGrew, the same journalist who had suggested he had lost his nerve and should retire. The bastard! He studied the photo. There was a grainy picture of him and an attractive brunette, dressed smartly in the half light, as he helped her into her house. It was the girl from the business awards ceremony, the milliner he recalled. All he did was give her a lift home, since when was that a crime? He screwed up the paper and flung it at the wall. Then he took a large gulp of Scotch and tried to compose his jumbled thoughts. He felt numb. That McGrew was trying to bring him down was obvious, all because he had a bad run of form for Christ's sake. But why? What had he ever done to him? He railed against the unfairness of it, took another sip of Scotch and enjoyed the burning sensation as the amber liquid trickled down his throat. He planned to drink himself into oblivion, at least until Livvy came back. Then he heard the door and Livvy came in. They stared at each other for a few minutes. He broke the silence.

'Livvy. Look, I never did anything to that stupid journalist, the police have let me go and as for that story about me and that brunette, I just gave the girl a lift from that business awards meeting. If they had waited a couple of minutes, they would have seen me leaving. You remember that night? I wasn't even back late.' He ran his fingers through his hair. 'Look, sweetheart. You have to believe me. This is all nonsense. I think I'm being set up.'

Livvy looked so pale and sad, he could hardly bear to hear her response. Eventually, she nodded.

'I know, Nat. I've spoken to the magazine. The girl was new and very inexperienced, and I remember the night of the awards. You told me about the woman and how drunk she was.'

Nat sighed. 'Thank Christ for that!'

Livvy pulled a notebook and some pens out of her capacious Mulberry bag. 'I do think someone is trying to ruin you and rather than drink yourself to death, I think we should work out who is behind this.' She wrinkled up her nose at him. 'Now, how about you get in the shower and I'll put the coffee on. I've already made some notes.' She pointed at the neat handwritten notes she had already made. 'And I've contacted Finn.' She took in his look of surprise. 'Because he knows the racing world through and through and I'm sure he'll know what to do. He's discreet and besides he's your best friend.'

Nat nodded. Finn McCarthy, of course, why hadn't he thought of that? Just the sort of man you needed around you at a time like this. He pulled her to him and kissed her forehead. The relief was overwhelming.

'I bloody love you!'

Chapter Sixteen

Finn met up with Hattie for lunch at The Blacksmith's. The place had undergone a transformation with new owners, and they had really capitalised on the huge open fireplaces and had leather seats arranged around the crackling fire. The floors were stripped and had large rugs in place and there were still smithy tools displayed on the walls, together with photos of the old forges in the town. They ordered toasted sandwiches with chips and drinks and settled down by the fire.

'So, how was your meeting with Tara?'

Hattie beamed. 'Great actually. I'm going to see if I can be part of a multidisciplinary team working with jockeys with eating disorders. Tara is running it. Not surprisingly there are a lot of jockeys round here with issues.' Hattie took a mouthful of her cheese and onion toastie. 'I think we're going to be good friends, she's a really lovely girl.' She gave him a shy look. 'In fact, I've met her again since and she's been helping with, you know, all that stuff that went on in our last case…'

Finn knew very well what she was talking about. It was clear that she had been suffering from flashbacks after being held hostage and it was he who had engineered the meeting with Tara as he knew she needed help. But he thought it wise to not mention this directly.

'Great, I knew you'd get on. It was a brilliant party, wasn't it? Shame about Taverner turning up but, he was just doing his job. I wonder who ran Sinead over, someone from the town, I suppose.'

Harriet glanced around the pub, which was full of lads and lasses from the local racing yards.

'God, I hope it was no one we know!' She gave a shiver of revulsion. 'Why didn't they stop for God's sake? Maybe she'd have survived if they had got her to hospital sooner and not left her for dead.'

Finn nodded. 'Probably the driver was scared, drunk or uninsured and they didn't want to get done, but it beggars belief that they just left the poor girl.'

'It wouldn't do any harm to keep our ear to the ground and see if we can identify the mysterious Clare.'

'You mean the girl that Maura and Lottie mentioned? I guess so.'

Harriet looked longingly at Finn's chips which he didn't seem to want.

'Can I have a chip?'

'Course.' At least she had regained her appetite. Honestly, the girl ate like a bloody horse, thought Finn but was still slender. Harriet duly leant over and stabbed a couple of chips with a fork.

'Do you think Sinead's death *was* just a hit and run?' Harriet studied him carefully.

'I think so. I suppose the police will be talking to more people and piecing it all together.'

'Hmm. Still, it would be interesting to know what Maura was referring to. She was shut down pretty quickly by Lottie which is interesting, but she might be worth talking to.'

Finn grinned. He could tell that the old curious, slightly maverick Harriet was re-emerging and for that he was extremely grateful. He was pleased that he had introduced her to Tara. He loved it when a plan came together.

He glanced at his watch. 'Well, it just so happens I'm seeing Maura later on. So, I'll ask about.'

Harriet beamed at him. 'Brilliant!'

Maura was based at Jeremy Trentham's yard. He was a very successful trainer and had some excellent horses including the classy In The Pink owned by football player, Tyler Dalton and Benefactor, a talented hurdler. The stable jockey was Tristan Davies and they had two conditionals, Kyle Devlin and now Maura Brandon. Finn knew Jeremy well and his wife, Laura, too. The yard had expanded due to its success, and he hoped that both Kyle and Maura would fare well there. Kyle was further on in his journey having been a conditional for some two years already and he had 30 odd winners under his belt at aged 20. Finn knew he'd ride out his claim successfully, but he had still joined the coaching scheme and Finn was pleased to be working with him. The yard was a few miles away from Walton's shared gallops but Jeremy had built his own, so Finn was looking forward to seeing Maura ride out and chatting to Kyle about his rides.

He made his way to the house where Laura Trentham greeted him. She was dressed in jeans, a padded jacket and a furry headband. She gave him a broad smile.

'Hi there, Finn. Jeremy is schooling with a few of the lads and lasses if you want to go down to the gallops. Call in and have a drink if you've got time later.'

'Fine, will do.'

As he approached, he saw that Tristan Davies was riding In the Pink, the yard's star and was helping Maura and Kyle with some of the 'green' hurdlers, horses who had shown sufficient promise on the flat to hurdle but were just starting out in their jumping careers. Tristan rode In the Pink and jumped over a row of brush hurdles, with Jeremy watching on foot. Then it was Kyle's turn. He warmed his rangy bay mount up and then cantered towards the fences, clearing them effortlessly and in style. He had seen the lad ride quite a few times now and felt he had the makings of a really good jockey. Jeremy saw Finn approaching and raised his hand in greeting. Dressed in a quilted green jacket with a tweed cap and wellies, he looked every inch a countryman, old fashioned and thoroughly decent.

'Devlin is shaping up very nicely.' Finn nodded at the lad.

'Now then, Finn. Yes, he certainly is, so I'm guessing it's Maura you have come to see, is it?'

'That's right. How is she doing?'

They watched her cantering aboard a grey horse before tackling the fences. The horse looked tense and approached the first fence well enough before ducking out at the last minute and cantering off. Maura managed to stay on, but it was touch and go.

'Turn him round!' yelled Jeremy. 'Damned horse can be a bit of a bugger.' They watched as the girl managed to turn the horse round. 'Go again! Follow Tristan. Tris, can you do the honours?'

Tristan and In the Pink gave the pair a lead over the fences. This time Maura and her mount jumped well.

'Better. Try it on your own this time,' shouted Jeremy. Maura rode better this time, although she wouldn't have won any prizes for style.

Jeremy turned to look at Finn. 'So, in answer to your question, Maura is a bit up and down. She started off really well but this business about the girl who died in the hit and run has really got to her. And you know what horses are like, they certainly pick up on their rider's

133

emotions.' Jeremy sighed. 'I don't think they were close, but it's still a terrible thing, a young girl being killed here in Walton.'

'Hmm. Well, I'll talk to her,' added Finn.

'Another thing is that the police are coming to interview her tomorrow and she seems very worried about it.' Jeremy frowned. 'I mean, it's just routine, surely?'

Finn nodded wondering why Maura would feel so anxious. Maybe she hadn't had much experience of the police and was genuinely concerned, or perhaps there was more to Sinead's death than they thought? He decided to frame his questions carefully.

Maura didn't give much away when he spoke to her.

'Oh, I'm just gutted 'bout Sinead,' she said later. 'The poor wee girl. I don't think she'd had much of a life, you know, being in care an' all. Such a tragedy, it really t'was.' Her eyes filled with tears.

'Well, just make sure you tell the police everything you know, Maura. The smallest detail can really help.'

'Course, course,' she responded, not quite meeting his eye.

Jeremy talked about Maura having her first public ride on a steady hurdler who was experienced and would have short odds, so her weight allowance would be very helpful. Finn arranged to meet Maura at Wetherby and do a course walk before the race, so the moment was lost as they discussed the race day routines and Maura regained some of her sparkle as she spoke about her ride, but Jeremy's earlier comments did make him wonder. Why was Maura so nervous about speaking to the police? What did she know?

Finn then went on to see Lottie Henderson who was a conditional at Seamus and Rosie Ryan's. He had known Rosie since he was 17 and trying to become a conditional, in fact it was her that had saved him from his first guvnor who was very handy with his fists and treated his staff, including Finn, appallingly. Rosie had been instrumental in moving him to Reg Hollins' yard, and from there he had thrived. He still rode out for Seamus on occasions, had already met Lottie and was looking forward to catching up with them all. The yard was about half a mile outside of Walton and the trainer usually used the communal gallops but also used a steep field at home to gallop on. Finn caught up with Seamus who was feeling the off fore of a large bay horse when he arrived in the yard. Finn recognised the horse as Cardinal Sin, or Cardy for short.

'Ah, Finn. How are yer? Just feeling this lad's leg. He's running at Market Rasen in a few days. There's some heat, so I'm just gonna get one of the lads to hose him down.' He nodded at Lottie, who was in the yard grooming a large chestnut.

'Ah right. Well, best not put him through his paces then. I wouldn't want to injure him further. Is it alright if I just catch up with Lottie?'

Seamus grinned. 'Course. Call into the house before yer leave. Rosie'll be back then. She's just popped into town with one of the lasses, but she won't be long. Shopping or something.'

'Oh right. How is Rosie?'

Seamus shrugged. 'Worrying about something, not sure what. She'll want to see yer though, it may cheer her up.'

Finn was instantly concerned when he heard this. Rosie had to be the most upbeat, cheerful person he had met. Still, the life of a racehorse trainer was not always easy and there was a lot of competition in Walton with horses frequently changing yards. He hoped that all was well with his friend and resolved to find out what was bothering her.

Lottie explained about Cardinal Sin. Finn had hoped to see her ride him but didn't want to push the horse if he had a minor injury.

'No worries. I'll just talk you through your race. Do you want to do a course walk beforehand?'

'Yep, that'd be good.'

'Market Rasen is a sharp mile and a quarter track, so it wouldn't suit a galloping type, but I reckon you'll be alright with Cardinal Sin. You've ridden there before, haven't you?

Lottie nodded, seemingly pleased that he had remembered. 'Yes, I have and I think he's in with a shout, but it's a step up in class and some of the big boys are gonna be there. It might be good to talk tactics with you before the race when we know who's definitely running.'

'Great.' Finn studied her. She appeared to be a complex girl, on the one hand confident but he sensed that this was just a front. Perhaps, she was struggling with what had happened to Sinead too?

'Listen, how are you feeling about what happened to Sinead? The police might need to talk to you, they are talking to a lot of people who last saw her before she died. What did happen in the pub?'

A shadow crossed over her face. 'Sinead had calmed down, Joel was alright with her. She sort of apologised, had a drink with us and said she needed to get going back to Johnson's. She left before we did, wanted Sam to come with her but he was chatting to some other lads.' She frowned and hesitated. 'Do you really think the police will come and talk to me?'

'I imagine so, but it's nothing to worry about. But you do need to tell them everything, even small things can be important.'

Lottie's blue eyes had clouded. 'Yep, I will. Maybe she collapsed from drugs and then was run over? She was in care and I imagine she could have been into drugs.'

Finn felt rather wary and uncomfortable that she was speaking negatively about someone who has recently died.

136

'If so, it's the first I've heard of it. As far as I know, it was a simple hit and run. If you know anything different then you must pass it on to the police, got it?'

Lottie nodded. 'Right, I will. Listen, I didn't mean anything about the drugs stuff. I don't know anything. It's just kids in care, you hear about what kids in care get up to, that's all…' Lottie looked embarrassed.

Finn wasn't sure that she was telling the truth. 'OK. But make sure you tell them everything.'

Finn made arrangements to meet Lottie at Market Rasen, just as Rosie arrived with a blonde, stable lass. Rosie's face was creased with worry but she beamed as soon as she saw Finn. The girl disappeared into the stables.

'I've just been into town with Clare,' Rosie explained. 'I'm glad to catch you. Come in for a cup of tea, will yer?'

Finn immediately picked up on the reference to Clare and was intrigued. Could this be *the* Clare, though he supposed there were lots of girls with that name working in racing yards, so it might not be significant.

'Sure. It would be good to catch up.'

Over tea and lemon drizzle cake, Rosie seemed more animated. After discussion about racing and prospects for the season, Finn probed a little further.

'How long has Clare worked for you?''

'Oh, almost two years. She's a grand girl, I don't know what we'd do without her, so good with the horses, turns them out beautifully, she takes a real pride in her job.'

Finn waited for the 'but' which came as he ate his cake. Delicious, of course.

'It's just, you know what working with youngsters is like, don't you? I'm worried about her, that's all.'

Finn nodded. 'I do know. They need a lot of support sometimes and can easily be led astray. I've had a lot of trouble with my conditionals, as you know. Perhaps I can help?'

Rosie frowned. 'I'm sworn to secrecy.' She sighed and was clearly struggling with how much to reveal. 'Listen, what would you do if you knew someone had been attacked but didn't want to report it?'

Finn considered this. 'I suppose I'd try to explain to them that although it would be hard to do the right thing, it might stop others being harmed in the future. How would they feel if something happened to another person when reporting their attack could have prevented it? That's what they need to consider, could they live with that?'

Rosie smiled. 'Of course. I knew you'd be able to help. I just didn't know what to do for the best.'

Finn had an idea where this was going and decided to take a risk.

'Of course, if any of this has anything to do with what happened to Sinead, then she really has a duty to report it to the police, you know.'

Rosie flushed and nodded.

Finn was just contemplating what on earth this all meant, when his phone buzzed and a text arrived. It was from his ex-fiancée, now Nat Wilson's girlfriend, Livvy Jordan.

Something awful has happened and the press are all over it. Need somewhere to lie low and really need to speak to you. On our way to meet you. You are our last hope. Be there at around 5. Livvy

Finn re-read it and glanced at his watch. Whatever had happened must be truly dreadful for Nat and Livvy to drop everything and drive to York. It was past four, so he would just make it in time to meet them if he set off now. He said his goodbyes to Rosie, who seemed much more upbeat and firmed up his arrangements to meet Lottie. What on earth had Rosie been referring to? Had Clare been attacked but decided not to go to the police? He hoped that Rosie would persuade her to speak about what had happened to her. Then his thoughts turned to the text message he'd received from Livvy. He drove back to York, his mind in overdrive.

Chapter Seventeen

Loathe to return to his cheerless flat alone, Topper McGrew had developed the habit of staying late at work. It served several purposes, making him look like a workaholic, superkeen journo, whilst giving him time to snoop about the empty office, looking for crumbs of information and stories to pinch, anything to impress that bastard Christian Lamont. It also shortened the time he spent in his grim, cold hovel. Topper would wave goodbye to the team, mostly rushing home to partners or indoctrinated by Christian's healthy work/life balance bollocks while Topper prowled about, put his feet up on the desk and sipped from his hipflask before staggering out to the off license, the chippy and then driving the few miles home. There he would scoff the take-away, moon about the loss of the family home, watch mindless TV, drink and then nod off.

Tonight, he was thrilled to discover that Lindy had left her furry pink notebook on her desk, in the rush to meet her boyfriend in the pub. Topper put his feet up on her workstation and began to flick through for items of interest. Swigging whiskey from his battered hip flask, he muttered softly as he stared at the rounded handwriting written in a range of colours, purples, greens and pinks featured heavily in there and if Topper wasn't mistaken, the writing was largely done in sparkly gel pen. Unbloody believable…

'Bloody pathetic. Why put circles,' he groaned, 'even bloody hearts instead of dots over i's? The girl's never grown up, I bloody well ask you…'

As he scanned the pages, he put down the flask. An interesting name caught his eye. Micky Lofthouse aka Lofty. As far as he knew Lindy was working on a story about the MP, Andrew Foster Watts, who had allegedly bribed someone to take his speeding points to avoid being banned from driving. So why had the photographer contacted Lindy? He studied the writing closely and found his own name below. *Ask Topper to ring Micky,* she had written. It was certainly a message that had not been passed on to him and he'd been in the office a couple of days this week. Bloody typical of the brainless slip of a girl. He had also lost his mobile phone charger but eventually found it under his bed which is why Micky had rung the office, he supposed.

Progress was slow as he checked the rest of her notes, just in case there was anything else worth noting. All he had after 40 minutes was a brief insight into Lindy's doodles, there were several hearts with her own and presumably her boyfriend's initials scribbled inside. Also, odd lists of numbers which were hastily scrawled down and added up with accompanying sad or happy faces. Probably her finances thought Topper, savagely. The stupid bloody girl. His stomach rumbled and Topper felt the chippy calling him. Or maybe he'd go mad and have a Chinese instead? He gathered up his stuff and put the notebook back exactly where he had found it.

Topper sipped his whiskey and rang Lofty's phone. He wondered what he wanted. The call went to voicemail and he left a message feeling somewhat deflated. He leafed through the book again and finding nothing of interest, was just about to go home when his phone lit up. It was Lofty.

'Now then, me old mate. I'm glad you rang. Guess what I've got for you? Only another bloody scoop about Nat Wilson. It's not gonna come cheap though...'

141

Topper's skin prickled with anticipation. 'I need to know what it is first, though.'

Lofty laughed. 'It's good alright. I have a photo of Nat Wilson being arrested...'

'For what?'

Lofty told him.

Topper tried to appear nonchalant.

'Might be interested at the right price...' he replied as his spirits rose. All in all, it had been a great evening, he decided. Christian Lamont was going to love it.

Chapter Eighteen

Hattie's respect for Tara had risen considerably when they'd met for a couple of brief sessions to talk about her experiences of being held hostage at the end of the last case. Tara's empathetic presence, the relief of being able to unload made her feel valued, and most of all lighter, as if the black clouds which had followed her around since it happened had dispersed. When Hattie looked back, she could not quite work out what it was about this unburdening that had helped so much. Tara had analysed her thinking and made her realise that her fears about being abducted or harmed again, were understandable but the likelihood of this actually happening was really very small, miniscule in fact. Partly, she was aware that she had felt unable to tell her parents, even her mother to whom she was very close, the full extent of her fears and distress.

'That's probably because you've been trying to protect them,' Tara had said in one of her rare interjections. 'And that is perfectly understandable.'

'So, you don't think I'm going mad, having panic attacks, being a total wuss?'

Tara smiled. 'No, absolutely not,' she said. 'It's a perfectly normal reaction to what you've experienced. I think you need to work through these emotions, stop trying to suppress them and then use the techniques I'm going to show you to help manage them, and consider the actual risks. Change your thoughts to change your feelings.'

They had spent a while identifying the sort of negative thoughts that were chasing round Hattie's head and categorising them, thoughts like, 'it must have been my fault, I should have taken better care, read the signs, this is bound to happen again,' and so on. Tara introduced her to a Cognitive Behavioural Therapy model and gave her a diary to record her emotions and analyse her thoughts. Hattie was grateful but suddenly felt better as if just being listened to by someone she liked and trusted and who did not judge, was all she had needed.

'Look, I might not do the diary…'

'See how you go, it's a tool that's all. If you don't use it, that's OK too.'

Now, a week after the last session, Hattie was waiting for another person to arrive at the multidisciplinary meeting about mental health before it could begin. Her supervisor was happy for Hattie to attend the meeting and then report back on how the dieticians could be useful in dealing with the group of young people with eating disorders, a few of whom were conditional jockeys. The last person to arrive, squeezing into a chair in the Health Centre meeting room was Dr Friedlander, a psychiatrist who Hattie judged to be in his 50's. His genial expression and quiet voice gave her a sense of confidence and although she had never met someone of his profession before, she was not intimidated.

Dr Friedlander chaired the meeting after a round of brief introductions. Tara was there too and two mental health nurses and another dietician.

'So, our aim today,' began Dr Friedlander 'is to co-ordinate services for this group of four patients. We'll go through them all in

144

turn and those involved can give brief updates and we'll decide next steps, whether clinical or therapeutic.'

Hattie found herself fascinated as the patients were discussed. The first couple were teenage girls who were still at school. One had been hospitalised for anorexia and the other was bulimic. It was reassuring to witness the professionalism, and dedication of the staff involved as they gave their updates. Tara, as Hattie expected, gave information from a psychological angle and was calm, thoughtful and insightful. Decisions were made about next steps, and both were deemed to be improving.

The next two were both conditional jockeys, which made Hattie sit up and concentrate more.

'Lottie Henderson self referred via her GP with symptoms of anorexia. I carried out an initial assessment and then you've been seeing her, Tara. If you could update us?' Dr Friedlander took up his pen to make notes.

'Mmm, she's a complex character with a history of eating disorders going back to her early adolescence. There's also,' Tara paused and frowned, 'some suggestion of sexual abuse in her past. She had help aged 14 and seemed to have recovered but now at 19, the eating problem, specifically bulimia, has resurfaced.'

Dr Friedlander nodded. 'And she's a trainee jockey you say? Would this role have triggered the re-emergence, do you think?'

'Not sure. She's of small stature, eight stone wet through and can easily make the weights for conditional jockeys who ride at more than that, but she is in an environment where weight is important. This could have triggered it, but I don't know. I feel there's something else...'

'Eating disorders can be a consequence of abuse, a way of either the person shielding themselves in excess weight or of trying to control the only thing that they can when they feel powerless, under threat possibly...' Dr Friedlander was thoughtful.

'Lottie also knew the young lass who was killed in the hit and run the other week. I think that may have had a big impact on her and I feel she's rather vulnerable at the minute.'

Hattie remembered the rather superior young woman at Tara's engagement party, who she herself had not warmed to. But her prickly nature could be hiding all sorts of trauma. I shouldn't have been so judgmental, she thought and also began to worry that Finn did not know about all these complications. Certainly not the eating disorders or the suspected abuse.

Tara cleared her throat. 'I want to continue to see her weekly, and I thought that individual help from Hattie's service would also be good if everyone thinks that's a way forward.'

There were murmurs of agreement and Dr Friedlander moved onto another patient. This time he named Liam Flynn. 'I think this lad might be growing too big to be a jockey, he's six foot and still growing. He was referred for a fainting episode, but seems to be starving himself in an effort to stunt his growth, I am worried about his diet which is really poor and seems to consist of bits of chicken and potatoes and nothing else, no fruit or veg in sight. It seems to be almost obsessive. I'm carrying out an assessment but,' he looked at Hattie, 'some nutritional advice would be good.'

Hattie remembered meeting Liam in one of Finn's group sessions. 'I have met him but I'm sure me or my colleague could arrange some individual sessions with him.'

'That would be most helpful.'

The meeting drew to a close and Hattie's head was buzzing. This is exactly what she came into the job to do and whether she or Carol dealt with the two conditionals, she did not mind. At last, something concrete to get her teeth into. But she did have a few questions.

146

Before leaving, she timidly consulted Tara. 'Can I tell Finn about these two? I think he should know. He can talk to Liam about other career options for a start.'

Tara grinned. 'Oh, I should have said, they've given their permission for him to know so yes, please do. And Hattie, it's great to have you on board.'

Hattie walked out of the health centre as if on air. Once in the car she checked her phone. There was a text from Finn.

Phone me asap

Her good mood evaporated immediately. Something was up.

Chapter Nineteen

'So, you're telling me she had rohypnol in her system and that she was raped?' Taverner asked Dr Ives, the local police pathologist.

'Aye, that's about the size of it,' he replied. 'Rohypnol is often used as a date rape drug and renders the victim comatose. The body had minute traces, we were lucky to identify it, because as you know the stuff is metabolised within 24 hours usually.'

Taverner grunted down the phone. Lucky, he wouldn't describe the poor girl as lucky. Sadly, the drug was a common method of incapacitating a victim.

'I came across it a lot in London, but here in North Yorkshire, Walton of all places...'

'Aye, well you'll know more than I do about county lines and how these things are distributed. Listen, I'll finish off my report and send it through to you.'

'Was there any forensic evidence?'

Ives sighed. 'No, he clearly used a condom, so no semen. Possible skin scrapings under the wee lassie's nails, forensics mentioned footprints, they might yield results, that's about it.'

'Anything else?'

'Nothing from the body, SOCO might have more information and the only other thing was that she had old scars, likely from self harm on both arms and wrists.'

'What about timescales, is it possible she was drugged and raped, collapsed by the roadside and was knocked into the ditch by someone else?'

'Difficult to say. The rapist and motorist might be one and the same or two separate people. Pretty sick to rape a girl and then run her over, but possible. I can't help you with that. I'll leave that to your detectives, Gabriel.'

Even Ives wasn't offering any theories which was unusual for him. It made the detective feel overwhelmed. Taverner signed off and ran his fingers through his hair. He felt the weight of responsibility pressing down on him heavily. Christ, that poor kid! Leaving a life in care into a world of possibility, only to wind up raped and dead in a ditch. Life was so unfair.

He looked through the glass wall of his office and beckoned his Sergeant to him. DS Wildblood saw his serious expression and came immediately.

'Right, Anna. I've just had Ives on the phone. Sinead was drugged and raped. She had rohypnol in her system. Let's get everyone together in five.'

'Rohypnol, roofies in Walton? Christ.' She shook her conker brown curls and curled her lip in distaste. 'OK. Right y'are.'

Taverner pointed to the links board with a photo of Sinead in the centre and various other pictures surrounding her. Several were of jockeys in their riding gear. It was beginning to look like a bloody racecard, he thought crossly.

149

'Right. Ives has confirmed that Sinead O'Brien was drugged, there were still traces of rohypnol in her blood stream, the perpetrator used a condom, so no DNA evidence, but there are possible nail scrapings and footprints. Patel, can you liaise with SOCO about the evidence at the scene?' Taverner looked at the sea of faces, taking in his team; Patel, an excellent officer, Haworth the joker, Ballantyne the morose Scot, Wildblood, his trusty Sergeant and a female officer, Natalie Cullen, a relatively new addition to the team who was shaping up well under the guidance of Wildblood and Patel.

'We know that Sinead was a conditional jockey at Robert Johnson's, a racehorse trainer and had only been there for about three weeks. Her jockey coach is Finn McCarthy, who we know from previous cases. Johnson states that the girl was recommended from The National Horseracing College in Doncaster where she did her training. She had a care history and had some emotional problems. It might be worth speaking to her social worker about her family. Can you do that, Cullen? On the night in question, she and several other conditional jockeys had attended a session with McCarthy and Harriet Lucas, who is now a trained dietician. There was some sort of dispute as I understand it, an argument and Sinead was asked to leave the group because she was taking the mick out of another jockey. She went to The Blacksmith's Arms and was joined by the other jockeys later. The other conditionals were Sam Foster, Kyle Devlin, Joel Fox, Liam Flynn, Gavin Clary, Lottie Henderson and Maura Brandon. How did you get on interviewing them?' He looked at Haworth and Ballantyne.

'Och well, they're all saying the same thing.' Ballantyne consulted his notes. 'Sinead was in the bar when they went there, she apologised to Joel Fox, he's the lad with the stammer who the victim took the piss out of, had a drink with them and set off home early as she wanted to get to bed. Seems she was on a warning anyway for lateness at her guvnor's and didn't want to risk being late again. She could be argumentative and difficult, so much so, Johnson was keeping a real close eye on her.'

'Did she buy her own drink?'

Haworth pursed his lips. 'No, Sam Foster bought her a drink, a diet coke. The jockeys confirmed this as did the other witnesses from the pub. It were busy because of a quiz night, so there were lots of people in there. The pub has recently been taken over by a Steve Armitage and his girlfriend, Lizzie, been refurbed and they are keen to drum up business.'

'Hmm, anything on the jockeys that raises concerns? Wasn't Sam Foster the jockey that went missing last year?' asked Taverner.

'Yep, he had a bad boss, it seems, McCarthy and Lucas were involved as you all know, but he is settled now at Robert Johnson's too. There's nothing on the jockeys, PNC checks are squeaky clean,' replied Haworth. 'Might be into drugs, though, to keep the old weight down, not roofies, probably amphetamine or cocaine.'

'What about the lad Sinead upset? Joel Fox, wasn't it? What did he have to say for himself?'

Haworth grinned. 'Not a lot, stammered all the way through. He wouldn't say boo to a goose, in my opinion. Says he's used to being teased, weren't phased by it at all.'

Taverner taped the photo of Sam Foster on the links board. 'Hmm, right. I want Haworth and Ballantyne to check the CCTV from the pub and elsewhere on the street and bring in Sam Foster again. He is at the same yard, so should know more about Sinead. He may have been in a relationship with her and crucially he bought the girl a drink so could easily have slipped her a roofie. Patel and Cullen, find out more about Sinead and speak to her social worker, carers and so on. She may have already had a drug habit before she came here for all we know, and she might have a dealer. And find out from the Drug Squad what dealers are about locally. We still need to identify the driver of the vehicle which ran into her, but it is possible they are unaware that they hit her and if they came out to check, they wouldn't necessarily have seen anything. Are there ANPR cameras anywhere near Walton?'

Patel sighed. 'No, the nearest is on the A roads into Walton but at the particular site where the body was found, there's absolutely nothing. I think we'll be relying on SOCO, so I'll get onto them.'

Taverner bit his lip. He had got used to working in rural North Yorkshire, but it could be infuriating in areas without much in the way of CCTV or ANPR cameras, not to mention the limited budgets, of course. Still, it had its compensations too, he realised.

'Right then. We'll reconvene in 48 hours and see what's what. Now scram.'

Chapter Twenty

Finn poured whiskey into three tumblers and handed them around to Nat Wilson and his girlfriend, Livvy Jordan. Both were tired from the journey, Nat's arm was in a sling and he had the tight, pinched look of a man who had not slept very well. Livvy was eyeing up the flat with interest. She looked her usual stunning self, just a little paler than usual. Both looked thoroughly preoccupied.

'So, what on earth has happened?'

Nat took a gulp of the amber liquid. 'Someone is trying to ruin me, Finn.' He pulled a newspaper out of his bag and showed him the headlines of the latest article by Topper McGrew which revealed that he had been arrested for indecent exposure. 'They've also implied that I've lost my nerve because of those four fancied horses I had falls on.'

'You're our only hope,' added Livvy looking tearful. 'The police won't be able to help, because they don't know about racing, but we believe you can. You have all the insider knowledge.'

'These allegations can be explained.' Nat looked wildly about him. 'I mean you know me, mate. All my relationships have been consensual. I dropped a girl off after an awards dinner,' he stabbed his finger at the picture of him with Millie from the awards ceremony. 'I simply gave her a lift and dropped her off and went. And this one,' he picked up another copy of The Yorkshire Echo, 'was when some silly girl, a journalist who came to do an interview with us, came to the door. I'd just come out of the shower and wrapped myself in a towel, which slipped by accident and she goes and tells the police. I got questioned for indecent exposure!'

He looked at Livvy as his expression softened. 'Those I can prove and thankfully Livvy is a very sensible woman, but the riding and the allegations I've lost my bottle are absolutely unforgiveable.' Finn raised his eyebrows at this. 'Look, it's all rubbish. I'm thinking of suing the paper, except that will generate even more publicity!'

Finn sighed. He believed him. Livvy had once been his fiancée and Nat his best friend, well, he was still his best friend, he had made his peace with Nat after what had happened. And besides Nat had literally taken a bullet meant for him in their last case and that had to count for something. He also had to admit that Nat was different with Livvy, the carefree, womanising heartbreaker he once knew, was no more. When he was single, women were drawn to him like flowers unfurling in the sun. He was good looking, but it was also to do with the sheer force of his personality. And as for his riding, he was and always would be one of the most natural horsemen Finn had ever known.

He looked at them both. 'You can stay here away from the press for as long as you want and I will try to get to the bottom of what's going on, I assure you.' He noticed the relief on their faces. 'Right, first things first, are you hungry? Then we'll have a look at where to go from here.'

Finn set about making a carbonara and salad. Livvy laid the table and pulled out some wine glasses whilst Nat showered.

'It's a nice place you've got here.'

'Yes. I like it, anyway.'

154

Livvy smiled coyly at him. 'Do you do much entertaining?' She meant women, he supposed. He had seen her scanning the place for any evidence of a girlfriend. Finn didn't know whether to feel flattered or annoyed.

'Sometimes,' he added.

She suddenly grasped his arm. 'Listen, it's so good of you. I can't thank you enough.'

Finn shrugged. 'It's the least I can do. Do you remember when we went to Shetland in that last case? Nat literally took a bullet for me and that's why he's in this trouble, if he hadn't needed that bloody operation, he'd be riding high again.' He scratched his head. 'I mean he was doing so well to start with, The Charlie Hall win, all that press coverage, it was really positive. So, what happened?'

Livvy shook her head. 'I'm not really sure but he's been beating himself up about it for a while. Some races he should have won in but fell instead. Something to do with missing a stride. You'll have to ask him, I'm sure it'll make more sense to you. As you know I'm not much of a rider.'

After they had eaten, he did just that.

'What is it about these races that make you think someone made you fall?'

Nat sighed. 'I've been thinking and thinking about them, but I can't work it out. There were four races when I was on a fancied horse which should have won and each time the horse has got its striding wrong and fell, the last time I broke me collarbone.' He indicated his shoulder. 'There was something odd about each incident, it happened at the third or second to last fence and it's as though I misjudged the striding and asked the horse to take off too late or too soon. The thing is I know I didn't do anything wrong.'

'Hmm. Well, I'd need to see all the races and go through them with a fine toothcomb.' He gave Nat a considering look. 'It maybe your eyesight, you know. Perhaps you need glasses, have you ever thought of that? You could easily wear contacts for riding.'

Nat shook his head. 'I've thought of that and had my eyes tested recently but my vision is 20.20'

'OK. Is there anything else you can tell me about these races?'

Nat nodded. 'Just that it's always when there's other horses around me and my horse in each case has started and been spooked by them. It can happen when another horse comes up alongside you, your mount sort of rushes, but for it to happen four times, it's too much of a bloody co-incidence.'

'Right. I'll look at the races.' Finn couldn't really comment until he had seen them. Privately, he wondered if the whole thing wasn't psychological. Maybe the articles criticising Nat's riding had eaten into his subconscious and undermined his self confidence? Unlikely but possible. Nat was after all a consummate professional and was especially good at finding a stride and a gap, in fact he was known for it. And he had self confidence by the bucket load. Finn picked up the newspapers, noting that the articles were all printed in The Yorkshire Echo and read the articles with interest.

'Bloody McGrew,' he exclaimed having noticed who the author was. 'He used to be a half decent journalist. I wonder what happened?' Then he looked through the last article. 'McGrew again. How did he know you'd been arrested for God's sake?'

Nat shook his head. 'It's almost as though they've been watching me. And as for the girl from the awards, I can't see her talking to the press.' He sighed in disbelief. 'And I certainly did not flash at the journalist, I came down the stairs to answer the door because I thought it was Livvy. We'd both forgotten about the interview and Liv went out to get some cake and flowers, that was all. It was all a massive misunderstanding but thankfully the police believed me and let me go.' He paused and looked at Livvy. 'We wondered if we could hire you to get to the bottom of all this, perhaps with Harriet. I mean properly. I was involved in that last case and saw how well you worked together, so what do you say? I want to pay you.'

Finn shook his head. 'I'll definitely take the case but won't accept any payment. You are my oldest friend, don't forget. I'll talk to Harriet. I'm sure she'll want to help too.' He thought for a minute. 'You can stay here as long as you need to, whilst this story dies down. Does anyone know you're here?'

Livvy gasped. 'I don't think so.'

'Were you followed?'

Both of them shook their heads.

'Well, you need to be alert and wear a hat or something when you go out, something of a disguise. You're both too well known. The last thing we need is the press finding out. What I suggest is that you get an early night and we'll plan a course of action tomorrow. Of course, I have my normal job to do too, but it can be helpful as it allows me to ask legitimate questions.'

Nat grinned and began to look more like his old self. 'Thanks, I really mean it, mate. I knew you wouldn't let me down.'

It was only when he was back in his bedroom where he had left his phone to charge, that Finn noticed he had several messages. Two were from his boss, Tony Murphy and there was a text from Harriet.

'*Ring me when you get a minute*', then he had left a longer voicemail. The other messages were from Harriet. Both told him essentially the same thing, that his young conditional, Sinead O'Brien, had been drugged and raped before being run over and that Sam Foster had been taken in for questioning. *We need you to investigate,* Tony had added in his voicemail. Harriet's text read.

Looks like we have another job, Tony has just rung me. Speak soon x

157

Finn took this in and questions circled in his mind. He thought about Nat and Livvy in the next room and their dilemmas. Had Nat really lost it, or was he being set up? Nat's comments about him being followed hit home. But who would do such a thing? Then his thoughts turned to Sinead's death. Sam arrested! He knew him well. He was a fine rider and an upstanding lad, with the moral courage to stand up for what he believed. Could he be implicated in the rape and murder of Sinead O'Brien? It was shocking and he didn't want to believe a word of it. But if Sam wasn't involved then another one of his conditionals could be, but who?

Chapter Twenty-One

Harriet and Finn were sitting in The Singing Kettle café, sipping their drinks with Tony Murphy, Finn's boss at the BHA and Harriet's when she was working for them. They were seated in a quiet corner of the place to avoid being overheard. Tony produced a sheaf of papers in a buff envelope and passed it over to Finn.

'I don't need to tell you that Sinead's death is a real concern to the BHA but if one of our lads or lasses is found to be the murderer, then this will not look good for us, so I want you two to find out what you can.' He frowned. 'Of course, the girl had something of a difficult past so it could be that she was assaulted by someone she knew from then. Who did you say was at your last BHA session?'

Finn ran through the list of conditionals who had been in attendance.

'Hmm. And Sam Foster was being questioned by the police, I hear. Funny how trouble always seems to follow him around.'

Harriet and Finn exchanged a look. They both knew the lad well and were doubtful about his involvement. But they couldn't be sure.

Finn frowned. 'But many people can be interviewed during the course of an investigation, as you know, so it doesn't necessarily mean anything.'

Tony nodded. 'Hmm. Keep an eye on him though. Do any of the other conditionals seem likely? Liam Flynn, Gavin Clary, Kyle Devlin, Joel Fox, Sam Foster or Connor Moore? Or any of the girls?'

Finn shook his head. 'No, I can't see it myself. Gavin is the brother of the chap who was murdered, James Clary. He was depressed but was referred to a therapist and seems fine. Nothing of any concern is known about the others.'

Tony frowned. 'But Sinead was drugged and raped, awful. I can't think it'll be anything to do with any of them, but we need to check it out. A hit and run is one thing but a rape and a possible murder is quite another and one that we really need to look at as a matter of urgency.' He nodded at the envelope. 'In there is all the information my sources could muster. You might want to consider the new owners of The Blacksmith Arm's too. It's all in there but they seem to have come into a lot of money, have spent a lot on refurbishing the place and could be into crime, maybe even drug dealing.'

'Do the local police know we're involved?' Harriet asked. She knew that DI Taverner who was involved in their last case did not know of the BHA involvement, and they had felt that they needed to hide from him which made things rather awkward.

'We have contacted the local DCI and asked him to talk to the Detective on the case in confidence, of course, but you must pass all relevant information onto the Inspector.'

Finn nodded. 'Of course, all our conditionals might be entirely innocent. There was some sort of pub quiz on and a lot of people in the place so anyone could have been involved. Do we know if the same person drugged, raped her and then ran her over?'

'Well, this is where it gets interesting. The girl was alive when she was run over but had collapsed. The driver running into her caused her to fall into the ditch where she hit her head on a rock. The impact from the vehicle left minimal marks so it is possible that they did not know they had even run into anyone, certainly if they stopped to look, they wouldn't have seen anything as the poor girl had fallen out of sight.'

'Christ.' Finn shuddered and shook his head. 'Poor kid.'

Harriet felt slightly sick and remembered Sinead's energy and zest for life. She took a deep breath to calm herself. What an awful way to die!

There was a silence as they contemplated the terrible circumstances of Sinead's death and the implications for the conditionals. Eventually, Tony gathered up his things.

'Well, good luck. Let me know if you need anything and Finn, no heroics like last time, just liaise with the local detectives and let them deal with arrests and so on. We don't want another situation like someone being held hostage or being shot.' His eyes narrowed. 'How is Nat Wilson these days?'

Finn took some time to compose his answer. 'He recovered from being shot, started off well but now is injured, busted a collarbone, but I'm sure he'll bounce back.'

Tony threw down some notes as payment. 'Course he will, despite what some may think. Best get on. I've lots to do. Good luck.'

They made their way into the gloomy streets which were glistening with drizzly rain.

Finn watched Tony climb into his blue Range Rover. 'Time for a drink in The Blacksmith's Arms? I've another job for us. I'll just wait for Tony to go.'

Harriet frowned and was about to say that this job was more than enough for them, but curiosity nibbled away at her. Finn smiled realising that Harriet would be impatient for details.

'Come on, let's get out of this rain and I'll tell you all about it.'

'So, let me get this straight. Nat thinks he is the victim of a smear campaign and also thinks he was made to lose four races but doesn't know how?' Harriet looked genuinely puzzled.

'Yes, one journalist in particular is writing about him having lost his nerve because of those four races, but also has reported that he has been having affairs and has been arrested for indecent exposure, so there seems to be a concerted effort to denigrate him.'

Hattie's eyes widened. 'And they're staying with you?'

'Yes, they are lying low, waiting for the whole thing to die down.' He took a sip of mineral water. 'But more importantly, Nat wants us to find out who is behind the smears.'

Hattie gasped. 'Christ, we are going to be busy. Where on earth do we start?'

Finn opened the envelope Tony had given him. 'Hmm. For Sinead's case, we need to find out more about what was going on the night she died. The key is probably this place or rather someone who was here that night.'

Harriet looked around, taking in the décor. It was almost unrecognisable from the place she had visited previously, sort of more themed with more dark wood panelling, farriers' tools and old photos with oak flooring and old leather chesterfields. There was an extension too, which had been turned into a classy restaurant. It would certainly have been open on that night. Even in the early afternoon, there was still a reasonable crowd. Lads and lasses from the yards, having finished their riding and mucking out, were having a quick drink before going back for evening stables, some trainers were also in there, Vince Hunt who raised a hand at Finn and Hattie, Jeremy Trentham and a couple of other men. Behind the bar were a young couple, a handsome fair haired man with well groomed stubble and a glamorous blonde woman wearing a tight pair of trousers and lots of makeup.

Finn nodded at the folder. Harriet read;

Steve and Beth Armitage purchased The Blacksmith's Arms in March and undertook extensive renovations including adding a larger restaurant and snug. Steve previously ran a pub in Manchester where there was a lot of drug dealing. It is not known whether or not he was involved but his bar manager was suspected of some involvement. His name is Marcus Lee.

'Marcus, can you change the barrels?' shouted the man. A dark haired young man with a chiselled face and bulging muscles appeared.

'Sure thing, Steve.'

Harriet raised her eyebrows. 'Looks like Marcus came too.'

Finn nodded. 'Hmm. The police will have the CCTV from outside, but we could talk to some of the regulars, someone who may have been there that night. Why don't you get another drink in whilst I make some lists.'

Hattie made her way to the bar where Marcus beamed at her having clearly passed on the barrel job to someone else. He was a lot better looking closer up, well muscled under his t shirt and had amazing blue eyes with dark hair and lashes, a sort of dark Irish look that she had always liked.

'Now, what can I get you?'

'Just two cokes that's all.'

Marcus peered round to where Finn was sitting. 'Are you here with your boyfriend then?' He was clearly fishing and she found that she was actually a bit flattered. He was certainly easy on the eye, that was for sure. Then she pinched herself, remembering the allegations about him.

163

'No,' she found herself saying. 'He's just a friend.'

He grinned and handed her the drinks. 'Well, in that case perhaps you'd like to give me your phone number then?' He flushed. 'I mean, seriously. I think we'd get on.'

Harriet blushed. 'How do you work that out?'

Marcus grinned. 'It's just a hunch but I'm never wrong about these things.' He gave her a penetrating look that she found faintly unnerving.

'I don't know anything about you, nor you about me.'

'Well, we can remedy that easily enough…'

Harriet was quite taken aback by his forthright attitude and irritated by his confidence too.

'Well, let me think about that…'

She turned on her heel and walked back to where Finn was sitting.

Finn looked up from his writing. 'Looks like you've made a conquest there. He can't take his eyes off you.'

Harriet flushed. 'Bloody cheek, he asked for my phone number. I suppose I could meet up with him and find out more?'

Finn suddenly looked serious. 'If he's involved then you could be placing yourself at real risk. I know you're doing much better emotionally now, but we'll have to find another way.'

Hattie sighed, realising that Finn was right. 'So, what is the plan then?'

'Well, that's easy. We are off to Cheltenham and we're going to find a journalist, a certain James McGrew. He is the person who wrote all those articles about Nat.'

164

Harriet remembered the red haired, middle aged chap from Charlie and Tara's party. He was often hanging around the racecourses.

'When?'

'Friday.'

Harriet sighed. 'OK. I'm doing some training in Newbury for work and Cheltenham is on the way back, so I'll meet you there. I'm due a day off. OK?' She frowned. 'Will McGrew reveal his sources?'

Finn contemplated this. 'Possibly, or possibly not. The photographer is credited in the articles, a Michael Lofthouse. So, it may be worth speaking to him too.'

As they stood up to leave, she noticed Marcus staring at her and wondered. She was feeling so much better about things after her work with Tara, but even so she'd be mad to knowingly put herself in harm's way, wouldn't she? Would she ever feel like going out with anyone again, she wondered? Give it time, she told herself, then you can get back on the horse.

Chapter Twenty-two

DI Taverner reviewed the video of the interview with Sam Foster conducted by DC's Ballantyne and Haworth, the morose Scot and the jolly Yorkshireman. It was definitely a good cop, bad cop type of interview, with Ballantyne pressing the jockey about slipping Sinead a roofie and Haworth flattering the lad with the number of winners he'd had so far. Sam had come to their attention as he had bought a round at The Blacksmith's Arms which included Sinead's last drink. It was likely to have contained the drug that incapacitated her.

'But I didn't give the drink to her,' Sam frowned. 'There were a few of us around the bar and I think one of the other lads or lasses may have handed her the drink, but I can't remember who. I was too busy asking for the order to notice.'

Sam was a slim young man, dressed in a hoodie, joggers and a pair of trendy black trainers with an air filled sole. Taverner watched Sam's body language minutely and went back several times over the clip. Sam looked to his upper left when he recalled the incident, a sign that this was likely to be accurate, but still, Taverner had read about his history and noted that the lad had gone missing last year, something to do with avoiding getting involved in race fixing. He'd ended up being found in Shetland of all places. Sam had been seen as the victim in the case, but supposing there was more to it? He appeared to attract trouble and Taverner wondered if he was just unlucky.

'So, you didn't fancy Sinead or have a relationship with her?' Ballantyne had asked.

Sam shook his head. 'No, I barely knew her,' he frowned. 'Besides she seemed a bit weird, prickly, trouble I'd say.' He shrugged. 'I gave her a wide berth, to be honest. She had cheeked the guvnor and was on a warning already.' He gulped. 'I mean I think it's awful how she died, but I can't tell you anything else. We all stayed to have a drink, she'd apologised to Joel then said she'd get back as she didn't want to be late again and have another warning.'

Taverner went through the clip again and wondered. He had read about Sinead and knew she had come from a troubled background. She had not long started her apprenticeship but had not made a favourable impression so far. Ballantyne had gone on to ask about drugs in Walton and the racing community and what Sam knew.

'Well, I daresay you could pick up some if you wanted to, I mean drugs are everywhere, aren't they? But I don't use anything, and I don't know anyone who does.'

Nor did he appear to know anything concerning about the landlord of The Blacksmith's Arms.

'Seems alright, that Steve, done a good job of doing up the place anyway.'

Sam had no criminal record but had been a victim of crime when he'd had some items stolen from his car and home. Then there was the Shetland incident. Taverner went through the statements of the other jockeys and people who had been in the pub at the same time. All had said roughly the same thing; that Sinead had calmed down, had a drink with the other conditionals and seemed perfectly fine which told them precisely nothing about how she had acquired the drugs and who had given them to her. Yet, he sensed that Sinead was likely to have

167

been attacked by one of the other conditionals. She was troubled and in many ways, the perfect victim because who would believe her? Yet, there wasn't enough to pin anything on them. He wandered around the office to see what his team were doing.

Patel was going through the CCTV from the pub that evening, Cullen was cross checking witness statements and DS Wildblood was on the phone to Sinead's social worker.

'Where are Ballantyne and Haworth?'

Patel looked up. 'Doing some more interviews, I think.'

'Anything?' Taverner stared at the computer screen.

'Not so far. I can see Sinead setting off on her own and I'm just seeing if she's followed, but there's nothing so far.'

Taverner sighed. The clues were drying up at an alarming rate. Trawling through hours of CCTV was painstaking and tedious work, but he knew that if there was something to find, then Patel would find it. They were having a press conference later which he was heading up. Council staff were going to be in attendance rather than Sinead's mother who'd had very little contact with her daughter recently.

Wildblood finished her call, a triumphant smile on her face.

'That were Sinead's social worker, Ella Morton. Sinead were in a home before she came here, and you'll never guess what? There were a lad there that really took to her, they were in a relationship but he became quite obsessive, always following her and getting annoyed if she spoke to another male. They had to warn this lad off, but he were devastated when she left and came to Walton. Supposing he came after her?'

Taverner was suddenly alert. 'What's his name?'

'Zack Archer, he's 17 and listen to this, he were also into cannabis but Ella reckoned that he had progressed and had started to

168

dabble in uppers and downers and was a small time dealer, so he'd be able to get roofies.'

'Right. Where does he live?'

'York. He's at The Laurels, same home as Sinead was.'

Taverner looked thoughtful. Most women were raped and attacked by men they knew, so this was definitely worth following up, and the boy had form. Sinead's phone had been recovered but it would take a day or two to search all the messages. Archer could be their man.

'Let's go there on the pretext of speaking to the staff about Sinead and see what we can find out. And keep looking, Patel. What about the owners of the pub and their staff?'

'That's who Haworth and Ballantyne have gone to speak to,' added Wildblood. 'Let me just ring the home and then we can get going.'

Taverner felt his mood lift. The lead about Zack Archer would definitely need chasing up and he hoped that the press conference would provide more clues. This might just be the breakthrough they were waiting for.

Chapter Twenty-three

Nat and Livvy were in the living room watching the racing when Finn arrived home. The trainer Nat rode for, Michael Kelly, had three runners at Newbury and Jamie McGuire was riding all three. Nat's face fell as soon as McGuire came into view.

'Bastard,' muttered Nat. 'Now he may well be worth a look. He was well pissed off when I came back to Michael's and he was relegated to second jockey again. I wouldn't put it past him to do me down. He's top of my list.' He nodded at the notes he had made at Finn's request, together with a list of people who may resent him enough to instigate a smear campaign. Jamie McGuire's name was top of the list and was underlined and starred several times. Livvy rolled her eyes. Obviously, she had heard this all before, many times.

'Finn, I've cooked a spaghetti bolognaise for supper. It's a low calorie version but very tasty.'

'Thanks. What have you two done all day?'

Livvy frowned. 'We went jogging and then Nat worked on his list and watched the racing.' She sighed. 'I don't think it's helped actually.' Finn could see that Nat was in a foul mood so after supper he attempted to harness that energy whilst Livvy was out of the way chatting to her sister on her mobile.

'Come on now, we'll find out who is behind this, Nat. We just need to think, that's all. Now what is true is that James McGrew has written several negative articles about you. Why would he do that?'

Nat chewed his lip. 'Dunno. He was always a decent, fair journalist, so God knows what's happened to him.'

'Have you ever had any run ins with him, anything you can think of?'

Nat's frown deepened. 'Nope. Unless of course he lost a lot of money on a horse I rode. I know he likes a good bet and he is a tipster, but he's not done well lately. Maybe someone asked him to write all that rubbish about me.' He shrugged and nodded at his list. 'He's number three on my list after Colm McNally.'

Finn frowned. 'What I don't get is how the photographer knew you were arrested. How on earth did they get that piece of information?'

Nat shrugged. 'Maybe the police tipped McGrew off?'

Finn considered this. 'Or you could have had someone following you. Have you ever noticed anyone hanging around?'

Nat looked horrified. 'Christ! I haven't noticed anyone but that suggests something much more sinister all together.'

Finn nodded. 'Did you come in your car?'

'Yeah, Livvy's is an underpowered, eco thing.' He smacked his head. 'Hell, if you're right then whoever it is will know I'm here.'

'Well, it's certainly possible.' Finn thought for a minute. 'Hmm. I was going to Cheltenham on Friday to see some conditionals ride. I'm doing a course walk with a lad but as it's a decent card, McGrew is bound to be there. I had thought I might bump into him and talk to him. At least I can warn him off. But how about I go in your car and wear some of your clothes? Your coat and hat maybe. That way if you are being followed, I can lay a trap for them.'

Nat's fists clenched and unclenched in sheer rage. 'Christ, this needs nipping in the bud, it really does. Yep, you can certainly take my car if you think it will help. I couldn't bear to go anyway as I'd only thump McGrew. I could not keep my hands off him. I don't want to see the pity in folks' eyes, if they believe all that rubbish about me losing my nerve either.' His expression suddenly became serious. 'You don't think they will believe it, do you?'

Finn smiled. 'Nah. Course not. It's probably better if I go on my own anyway.' He had hoped that Nat would say that. He really didn't want the responsibility of dealing with his hot headed friend when he was confronted with the enemy. Finn decided a more subtle approach than a public brawl was definitely called for.

Finn glanced at the list Nat had written. There were several more jockeys on there and some names he did not know.

'So, Colm is on your list too? Why?'

'Same as McGuire. He won the Championship and probably thinks he can win it again if I'm not about.'

'And Gerry King?' He was a solid, safe pair of hands as far as Finn was concerned.

'May have had a thing with his girlfriend, now wife, a few years back and caused him to fall in a race or two.' He scowled. 'He never complained though and the fling with Karen was long before me and Livvy got together. Honestly.'

Finn sighed and pointed at some other jockeys' names on the list. 'And these…'

'Same.'

Finn scowled. 'I bloody well hope you never cheat on Livvy, Nat. I mean it. I won't stand by and let you hurt her, you know.'

Nat gasped. 'As if, mate! I'd never do anything to her. I'm strictly a one woman man now. She has ruined me for anyone else, honest.'

At that point Livvy walked in. She was dressed in coral silk pyjamas, had her hair twisted up into a bun and had removed all traces of her makeup. Her features and bone structure were so perfect, she did not need any cosmetic enhancement. She looked wholesome, fragile and absolutely beautiful. The silk pyjamas clung to her slender figure as she sank down onto the sofa next to Nat with the grace of a cat. As Finn looked at her, he wondered if the same was true for him. Had loving her ruined him for all other relationships? He mustn't think like that. He forced himself to drag his eyes away from her and steeled himself to concentrate. After a while, Livvy announced she was tired and went off to bed which certainly helped him keep his focus.

'Right. Talk me through those four races again. There must be something that links them, some common denominator.'

Nat turned the page of his notebook. 'I've already made some notes.'

Finn peered at the paper but nothing obvious sprang out. Then he and Nat went through videos of each of the four races as best they could using Sky Sport's racing channel. Sometimes it was difficult to see Nat and his mount because the camera was often directed at the leaders. Finn couldn't see anything particular that had made the horse fall. Nothing obvious at all.

Nat stared at the screen, mentally re-riding each horse. 'Look, the horse rushes, I'm not sure why. What the hell!' Nat shook his head and frowned as in each case the horse either put in an extra stride or took off from too far out, basic mistakes. There were other horses within the group next to Nat's mount on each occasion, but then again this was not unusual.

'What do you think?' asked Nat.

'To be honest, there doesn't seem to be any pattern that I can see. I really don't know.'

Nat stretched and yawned. It was now quite late; they had been at it for hours.

'Me neither, mate, me neither. But when you see that swine McGrew, make sure you give him a good kick in the balls from me. It would make me feel better, nevertheless. As if he's ever even ridden a horse! Tosser!'

Finn laughed. Maybe Nat's mysterious falls were something and nothing. Every jockey had lean spells and times when things just did not go right no matter what they did. Maybe even the great Nat Wilson? He'd see James McGrew, put him right on a few things and hopefully that would put the journalist off writing nonsense about his friend. If he went in Nat's sporty Merc and looked to see if he was followed, he could find out who was involved. Someone had to have tipped McGrew off and he was determined to find out who it was.

Chapter Twenty-four

Friday came around quickly enough. It was a chilly December day and Cheltenham was decked out with Christmas decorations even though there were still three weeks to go. Before he left in Nat's car, he had donned Nat's beanie hat and his tweed coat which luckily fitted him. He has also taken the trouble to ask the concierge at his flats to keep an eye on the CCTV outside at the front and rear of the flats, and to keep a copy of the recording. He guessed that anyone following him would not bother to go to the racecourse but might lay in wait for Nat or drive into the car park and follow him at the end of the day. He was due to meet Hattie later at the racecourse. She'd been on a two day training course at the Professional Jockeys' Association in Newbury, so had opted to meet him there. On the way down, he didn't detect anyone following him but he guessed that someone employed to spy on Nat Wilson would be skilled at hiding away, possibly a professional.

The atmosphere was excellent, he loved Cheltenham and had some great memories of his wins there. He quickly found Kyle Devlin walking from the jockeys' car park. He was a young conditional who had already ridden 30 winners and was based at Jeremy Trentham's yard. Tristan Davies was also with Kyle and by all accounts had really helped him when he had started out. Jeremy's yard had expanded and there were plenty of rides for them both.

'Now then, Finn. How's it going?' asked Tristan.

'Great. How about you?'

'Mustn't grumble. How is Nat doing? It was bad luck to get a serious injury so early on in the season.'

'Yes, it was. I have spoken to him recently, but I'm sure he'll bounce back as always though.' For some reason Finn did not want to reveal that Nat and Livvy were staying with him. Not that Tristan would say anything to any journalists, he was sure of that, but the more people who knew, the easier it was for Nat's whereabouts to get out, so he decided to play dumb. 'Anyway, I might just call him and arrange to see him later. There's been some pretty bad press about him recently and he might need cheering up.'

Tristan shook his head. 'That McGrew has really gone down in my estimation, writing all that stuff about Nat. Everyone knows he's *the* top jockey and as for all that rubbish about him cheating on Livvy, we all know he's besotted with the woman. Christ! It's almost as though someone has got it in for him. Mind you The Yorkshire Echo has changed hands and the word is that they're in financial difficulties and out to make cutbacks, so Topper's probably fighting for his job.' Tristan sighed. 'Anyway, did you hear about that poor girl in Walton? All the lads have been interviewed, even Kyle here. And Maura is devastated.'

Kyle grinned shyly. 'Yeah, the cops wanted to know about the session we had with you, Sinead being sent out and everything that happened in The Blacksmith's Arms afterwards. They went on and on about it, kept asking questions about who was there, how long Sinead stayed, who bought her a drink and that. They took poor Sam in for more questioning. Maura is really cut up because she started out at the same time as Sinead. Proper bad, innit?'

Finn nodded. He had already spoken to Maura. 'I don't suppose you knew Sinead, did you?'

Kyle looked down and suddenly looked awkward. 'Well, I was in foster care and did come across her once or twice. Me social worker, Poppy, asked me to speak to her about doing the course at The National Horseracing College. She wanted to go, and Poppy asked if I would help her. She were at one of the kids' homes in York. Said it were bad and one of the lads was making her life a misery or summat. He was obsessed with her, by all accounts.'

Finn suddenly became alert. He also knew that Poppy was a social worker and Tristan's girlfriend. She had worked with Kyle when he was a stable lass at Jeremy's and had started to go out with Tristan. Finn had met her a time or two and liked her a lot. 'How long ago was this?'

Kyle shrugged. 'Maybe a few months ago. She must have done the course, I told her the staff were good but it were going to be hard work.'

'Can you remember the lad's name?'

Kyle frowned. 'Zack summat or other. They were at The Laurels in York, that were the name of the place.'

Finn committed this to memory and tried not to look too interested. 'Might be worth talking to the police. They need all the help they can get.' He looked at Tristan.

'Yep. Poppy is coming later, so I'll mention it.'

'Great. I'll catch her later. Now, how about this course walk? You're on Horatio, I see, who's second favourite to Tristan's horse, Lillimae.'

Tristan's mount was a new addition to the yard and showed a lot of promise having won a couple of times already. Horatio would have to go some to beat him.

'Hey, don't help him too much, will yer,' joked Tristan. He fluffed up Kyle's hair. 'Can't have the lad beating me so early in his career, can we?'

Kyle grinned. 'Bound to happen sometime though, isn't it?'

Tristan shook his head. 'In yer dreams!'

In good spirits, Kyle and Finn walked the course and discussed where the good ground was, how to ride each fence and how to position his horse. This was often a problem for conditionals who sometimes couldn't find a gap or left it too late to make their move. The fences were quite tough, the fourth last coming very sharply after the turn, although there were only two hurdles in the last six furlongs. However, the last half mile was uphill, and positioning was crucial.

'On the rails is best around the bend, but don't be afraid to pull your horse wide if there's no space, better though to go for the gap as soon as you see it. Alright?'

Kyle asked a few questions and seemed to be taking it all in. They arrived back at the stands and Kyle rushed off to change for the first race.

'Good luck,' Finn called after him, pleased that Kyle had been receptive. He had already seen him ride and was pretty sure that he had a bright future. He thought back to what Kyle had said about Sinead and the lad who was obsessed with her. Zack could have felt abandoned when Sinead left and may have followed her and cut up rough, so that was worth pursuing. He also researched The Yorkshire Echo, taking into consideration what Tristan had said about it changing hands. It was certainly true from what he found on Google, so that could explain McGrew trying to firm up his position as the new editor had a reputation for more sensationalist journalism.

Finn wandered about taking in the sights of Cheltenham, the statue of Best Mate, the celebrated three times Cheltenham Gold Cup winner and recently erected statue of A.P McCoy, many times Champion jockey, as he waited for Hattie to join him. He flicked through his racecard and saw that Joel Fox was also riding for Dan Richards, so he wondered if he could catch up with him too. It was bitterly cold and he was glad of Nat's warm coat and hat.

'I'm bloody freezing not to mention starving,' Harriet announced as soon as she arrived. She was dressed in a huge fur collared coat and had a furry headband in her auburn hair. She looked him up and down approvingly.

'Hey, like the coat. New, is it?'

'No, it's Nat's. Let's pop in the bar and have a drink, whilst I explain.'

Finn ordered some drinks and told her his thoughts about Nat being followed.

'So, I've come in his car and I asked the concierge to train the camera on the road outside as well as in the car park.'

'I suppose it makes sense. Do you think they're here?' Harriet's eyes were like saucers as she looked at the racegoers in the bar. It had filled up with punters, as the first race approached.

'Probably not. Listen, I need to pop and see Kyle and Joel Fox who are both riding today. Look, there's Poppy, and Jeremy. Let me introduce you to her. If you have an opportunity, see if she knows a Zack who used to be in care with Sinead. He was a bit obsessed by her, according to Kyle. Maybe he felt abandoned when she left and attacked her in a fit of rage.'

Hattie nodded. 'OK, I will if I get the chance.'

Poppy was delighted to see Finn and pleased to meet Harriet. Poppy was a slight, dark haired woman with long hair and a heart shaped face and glossy good looks. The pair chatted as Finn spoke to Jeremy.

'Hi there. Tris has mentioned you. I hear you work as a dietician for the PJA. That must be interesting.'

They continued to talk as Finn rushed off to catch up with his conditionals.

'Yes, it is. Not as interesting as your job working as a social worker with kids in care, though. It must be very rewarding.'

Poppy's eyes sparkled. 'Well, though I love all the kids I work with, it can certainly be challenging.'

Hattie nodded. 'Did you know Sinead O'Brien, the girl who was involved in the hit and run in Walton?'

A shadow crossed over Poppy's face. 'Sadly, yes. I did come across her. It's absolutely shocking, poor kid.' Her eyes filled with tears. 'I can't understand how whoever did it could just drive off and leave her like that!'

Harriet patted her arm. 'I know, I know. Kyle said that he knew her and that she had told him that a lad at the home, Zack someone or other, was making her life a misery. Do you think he might have harmed her?'

'Zack Archer? Really? No.' Her eyes widened in surprise. 'I can't see it.' She smiled. 'Look, why don't we finish this drink and then we can brave the cold and watch the races. Tristan is riding so I'll be biting my finger nails, I'm afraid and I could really do with the company.'

Harriet instantly warmed to this woman. She seemed genuinely enthusiastic about her job and besides, Finn was going to be busy and she might pick up some more information about Zack.

'Great idea.'

Tristan was riding in four races and Poppy was a bag of nerves, although she was trying very hard to keep a lid on her emotions. She was pleased though when he won the first race and her face flushed with pleasure. They went down to cheer him on into the winner's enclosure and then made their way to inspect the horses for the next race in the parade ring. It was then that Harriet saw Dan Richards and Lloyd Fox huddled together. Dan grinned at the sight of her and Lloyd waved.

'Hi, Harriet. Can me and Lloyd buy you two ladies a drink after the fourth race?' Dan looked inquiringly at Poppy. 'We're a bit busy until then.'

'Certainly. This is Poppy, Tristan Davies's girlfriend, Lloyd Fox and Dan Richards. Lloyd is an owner and Dan trains for him.'

'Tristan, he's a great jockey,' commented Dan Richards. 'G'day it's nice to meet you, Poppy.' They chatted about Tristan's rides and then they arranged to meet in the stands to watch the fourth race when Dan's horse was being ridden by Lloyd's son, Joel.

'It was a late decision,' added Lloyd.

'Finn's here somewhere about. He saw Joel was riding and wanted to catch up with him before,' added Harriet.

'Great stuff. We'll see you then, I just need to make sure Paperweight is settled and get him ready for the next race,' added Dan. 'But we'll catch you later.' He stared hard at Hattie. 'I could still do with your advice about diets, you know. And you never did contact me.' He made a sad face. 'I'll see you later.' With that, he rushed off.

Poppy nudged Hattie. 'Hmm, someone has an admirer. That Aussie Dan, couldn't keep his eyes off you. He's rather nice. What do you think, unless of course, you and Finn are an item?'

Harriet laughed. 'Finn and I are just good friends. I hardly know Dan, but he seems nice enough. Anyway, how did you meet Tristan?'

'Well, I filled in for another social worker visiting Kyle when he was a stable lad, met Tristan and he asked me out.'

'Right. I think Finn said something about you working with Kyle. He seems like a really nice lad.'

'Oh, he is. I'm so glad he's doing well.' She frowned. 'I wish all my young people were like that.'

'You mentioned Zack. I suppose the police will find out all about him. It would be awful if he did harm Sinead.'

Poppy looked sceptical. 'I'd be surprised. He's hanging around one of my girls and has moved on emotionally. It's out of sight, out of mind with Zack, I think.'

Harriet took this in. Maybe his interest in someone else was a smoke screen? But if not Zack, then who the hell did murder Sinead? It certainly turned the spotlight onto someone in Walton, someone likely to have been in The Blacksmith's Arms including the conditionals.

It soon came round to the fourth race and Lloyd, Dan Richards and Finn joined Hattie and Poppy in the stands. Kyle was riding Horatio in the race. The other main contenders were Montecarlo ridden by Jamie McGuire, and Tristan was riding Lillimae, with Joel Fox riding Paperweight. So, all parties had a vested interest in the contest.

Lloyd turned and smiled at Poppy. 'May the best horse win!' It was clear that he was feeling the tension and was highly competitive if his stiff, whispered conversations with Dan were anything to go by. Finn had returned from seeing his conditionals and was keen to watch both in action. He had asked Lloyd if Joel wanted to walk the course with him, but his father had said that Dan had already done that, with a tight smile. Poppy just looked anxious.

'I'm not bothered about winning or losing. I just don't want anything to happen to Tris,' she confided in Hattie. 'Though if he won that would be good, of course.' Hattie sympathised with Poppy's predicament, guessing that Livvy Jordan must have gone through hell

182

supporting Finn and now Nat in his racing career. The risks that they took hurtling over fences were enough to make anyone anxious.

The race was a two mile four furlongs Novice Handicap, so the jockeys had to negotiate a number of hurdles. Cheltenham had a reputation for stiff fences and with its uphill finish, it promised to be a competitive race. In the first circuit, Kyle was positioned in the main pack and easily held the big chestnut up. Joel was just behind Kyle, but both were going well. Fine drizzle started to fall and the skies darkened. The ground was clearly getting cut up as the horses' hooves kicked up clods of earth as they galloped past. Finn kept his binoculars focused on the two conditionals and was glad that both were up there in the main group as they finished the first circuit. Kyle began to gain ground as they came up to the fourth last, Kyle rode on strongly in second as the fence quickly appeared after the turn for home with Joel in third place. The horses began to jostle for position coming up to the third last. Finn felt himself stiffen with anticipation as the crowd began to roar, as the race was about to reach its climax. Tristan's horse faltered a little but still landed narrowly in the lead, closely followed by the bay, Montecarlo, who pecked badly and lost a lot of ground with Paperweight and Horatio battling it out for second and third. He could barely hear the hooves thundering towards the finish line, against the roar of the crowd who had braved the rain to watch the finish. He saw whips being raised, one being let loose into the air as the jockeys rode on strongly and battled for the winning post. In a blur of colour and sprays of mud amidst the shouts of the crowd, Tristan and Lillimae won by three lengths closely followed by Joel Fox on Paperweight and Kyle Devlin came a creditable third on Horatio. Finn felt the familiar adrenalin buzz, highly delighted that his two conditionals had been placed.

Poppy was flushed with pleasure and went to see Tristan in the winner's enclosure whilst Lloyd and Dan looked bitterly disappointed. In fact, both men rushed off before the finish after muttering to each other.

'Let's just go and have a word with the lads and then we'll have a bite to eat, shall we?' suggested Poppy.

Hattie nodded. 'Great. Both lads did well and Tris rode the winner, of course.'

'Well done, guys,' shouted Finn as the riders rode their horses into the winner's enclosure. Just as he was about to say more, he spotted someone he knew, a florid faced, large man dressed in a tweed suit that was rather too tight, topped with a grey mackintosh. Shit, James McGrew. Finn saw him write down the names of the winners. Then he saw McGrew dash off with unusual haste. He explained to Harriet that he'd meet her later then he followed him. He found him in an empty bar with Christmas carols playing in the background and sat down on a bar stool nearby. McGrew's gaze slid over him.

'Finn McCarthy! Long time, no see. How are you? Have you got a story for me? Drink?' He motioned to the barman.

'Scotch, please.' Finn took a sip and felt the fiery fluid burn his throat. 'Not as such, but I do want to talk to you.'

The journalist's eyes narrowed and he looked a little uneasy. 'Well, I'm afraid I have copy to complete, so I really don't have much time at the moment…'

Finn looked into the dissipated eyes, which had many more fine lines around them than he remembered and took note of the scuffed shoes, threadbare mackintosh and overall bulk of the man. It was clear that James McGrew was aging badly and was in poor shape. His greying strawberry blond hair was greasy and in desperate need of a good cut. All that remained was the cutglass accent and the air of entitlement. James made to stand up.

Finn glared at him. 'This won't take long, just sit down and listen.'

James climbed back onto his bar stool and raised an expectant eyebrow.

'A little bird told me that you have been writing some inaccurate stories about my friend, Nat Wilson. I could hardly believe it, you were always such a thoroughly decent and competent journalist...' James could not resist a self satisfied smile at this point, such was his excessive vanity. 'But imagine my surprise when I read that you have written three such articles, one claiming that my friend has lost his nerve, on the basis of four races which you say he fell in because he missed his stride, another article implying that he is cheating on his fiancée, and another about him being arrested for indecent exposure.'

James started to look discomfited, but tried to brazen it out. He waved his hand in the air aiming for nonchalance, but didn't quite pull it off. 'My dear chap, I have given Nat plenty of opportunities to respond so I can give his comments, and he has blanked me. I mean, what's a journalist to do? And those races were all badly ridden by him and as for the photo of him leaving another woman's flat in the wee hours, well that speaks for itself. I certainly did not fabricate him being arrested either, of course.'

Finn pursed his lips. 'But if you'd stopped to ask more questions, you would have found that Nat was released without charge, the races are something and nothing and the girl was someone he dropped off after a do because she was so drunk. If the photographer had waited a few more minutes, they would have seen Nat leave.' Even the great Topper McGrew looked embarrassed at this. 'You have no idea what it's like to ride horses day in day out for a living. Occasionally, of course, things do go wrong, they don't go according to plan, but horses are not machines and neither are jockeys and to draw such ridiculous conclusions from a few races, is frankly libellous and absurd...'

'Well, I may not ride, Finn, but I've seen enough jockeys lose their nerve in my time to know the difference...' replied McGrew. 'Something *is* wrong with him...'

Finn shook his head. 'What gives you the right to make judgements about a jockey's riding? Have you even so much as sat on a horse? I *know* Nat is a true champion, because I *know* the sport, I was a professional, and I know how bloody hard it is. I knew I was never, ever going to be as talented as Nat is. And as for him cheating on Livvy, well that's ridiculous, he adores her.' McGrew looked mildly chastened by this. 'Do you ever stop to think of the harm you do when you write such inflammatory nonsense? Did someone pay you to do it? Well? Or is this how desperate you are to get stories these days?'

James looked a little deflated. 'Nobody paid me, of course not, I do have some integrity despite what you may think. The information behind those stories came from a reliable source.'

'Ah, Michael Lofthouse, freelance photographer, I presume.'

The journalist flushed. 'But it's up to me to provide the story behind the photograph. I am Topper McGrew the best racing journalist there is, but I do have to keep audiences interested, keep them engaged, you know how it is? What better copy than the tale of the faltering comeback of Nat Wilson, his fall from grace, so to speak…'

Finn sipped his Scotch, fighting the urge to sock the other man in the mouth. 'Now listen, McGrew. I advise you to cease and desist, do I make myself clear? Nat is taking legal advice and wants The Echo to publish an apology explaining the facts behind those stories. If you had anything about you at all, any natural curiosity then you would wonder why someone is trying to discredit Nat. That is the big scoop here and if you can't see it then you have really lost the plot. A few words here and there and your name will be mud in racing, and I'm not sure your editor would approve of you making stuff up just because your star is falling, especially when he receives a letter from Nat's solicitor.' He noticed McGrew wince and swallow nervously at this. He was glad he had completed his research about the paper after the tip off from Tristan Davies. 'New chap, isn't it? Christian Lamont? It will probably give him the excuse he was looking for to fire you and can be very easily arranged, not to mention incurring the wrath of Nat Wilson who can get very riled up at times, as I'm sure you know.'

Finn downed his drink and stood up, glaring at McGrew as he walked away. The expression on the journalist's face said it all. He knew he'd hit the mark. He went to find Harriet and settled down to a gin and tonic and a club sandwich.

'Sorry, I've been a bit busy with the conditionals.' He bit into his delicious sandwich. 'At least I managed to have a word with that bloody journalist and told him that Nat was taking legal advice. How did you get on with Poppy?'

Hattie nodded as she nibbled a chip. 'Very well, she's really lovely.' Her eyes roved around the bar. 'I wonder where Dan Richards and Lloyd Fox are? They said they'd buy us a drink, but they left before the end of the race, something to do with losing a whip or something. Poppy heard them talking about it.'

That must have been the whip that Finn saw sailing away in the air towards the finish. Still, Joel seemed to have his in the winner's enclosure, or maybe he was mistaken.

'Hmm. Whips are ten a penny, so it's no great loss. Probably they're disappointed about how their horse ran. Anyway, did you find anything out?'

Hattie grinned. 'I did. I asked Poppy about Zack, just mentioned him like you suggested. Poppy certainly knows him. She couldn't say too much except that he was now involved with another girl, someone she is working with, so she doesn't think he would have had anything to do with Sinead's murder. She thinks he's moved on and it was a case of 'out of sight, out of mind.''

'Hmm. Interesting. We'll let the police follow him up in that case, though knowing Poppy she always sticks up for her charges, so perhaps she's cutting him too much slack.'

Harriet could well believe it, she was so enthusiastic about her job.

'So, what about Nat?'

'Hopefully, I have made McGrew think twice, but it may be worth having a word with Michael Lofthouse, the photographer, who sold him all those photos. The real question is who tipped Lofthouse off about Nat? It seems to me there has been a concerted effort to bring Nat down. But who would do such a thing?'

'Presumably, the same person who has followed him, which reminds me, do you think you might have caught someone on the CCTV?'

Finn grinned, pulling down his hat. 'I don't know, but I can't wait to find out.' His mood lifted. Not only had his conditionals both been placed, it felt great to have said his piece to McGrew and even better, it was clear to him that Hattie was back, recovered from her PTSD and firing on all cylinders.

As they left the racecourse, Finn noticed Topper deep in conversation with someone, a jockey judging by his slim build. The jockey had his back to them but as Finn and Harriet walked past, he could see the man's face. It was McGuire. Jamie McGuire was talking and Topper listening carefully and nodding. What on earth was that about? Then Finn realised that it could be about anything, Topper was a racing journalist after all. But there was an intensity to their conversation that troubled him and seemed to suggest something other than a normal interview. Supposing the conversation was about Nat? Maybe it was Jamie who had been feeding the information to Topper?

Chapter Twenty-five

Taverner and Wildblood settled themselves down whilst the residential worker sought permission to share information with them. They had travelled to the children's home, situated in a leafy street in the suburbs of York having rung ahead, but the powers that be were still deciding what information about Zack Archer they could share, which was infuriating Taverner. The press conference for Sinead had gone well on the whole. Ella Morton, Sinead's social worker, had been in attendance which was a sad situation. Ella knew that Sinead would not have wanted her mother anywhere near. The team were working through the calls and leads the conference had generated, following everything up. DCI Sykes, of course, wanted Zack arrested but DI Taverner had advised a more softly, softly approach, but he could do with more co-operation from social care. It was time to be blunt.

'Can I remind you that we are investigating a serious crime certainly rape, possibly murder so I am simply being courteous. If I have reason to believe he's involved then I won't hesitate to arrest him, whether he's in care or not.'

Maggie Montgomery smiled nervously and hurried off to ring her manager. Moments later she came back looking more relieved.

'Zack's social worker is on her way, so she'll be able to fill you in. Can I get you a cup of tea or coffee? She'll only be five minutes.'

Vicky James was slim with blonde hair pulled back into a ponytail. She walked in wearing a grey suit and was carrying a laptop bag. She looked every inch the young professional.

'Excuse the clothes, I'm due in court later.' She gave an apologetic shrug and turned on the laptop. 'Right, fire away. I have authorisation to share information from Zack's mother too. He's in voluntary care and as such she still has parental responsibility for Zack, so I did need to ask her permission.'

'I appreciate that. We would invite her if we did interview him although I understand Zack is on a referral order to the Youth Offending Team too, so a worker could attend from there.'

'Yes, he was involved in TWOC'ing. He stole a car from the home and was found to be driving on 'A' roads at 80 mph. That was over a year ago and since then he has complied with the terms of his order and has done much better.'

Taverner nodded. He was aware of Zack's criminal history car theft, Taking Without The Owner's Consent, TWOC'ing, as it was known had featured at least twice. 'OK. Can you give us an overview of his case?'

Wildblood made notes whilst Taverner listened and asked the odd probing question. It was apparent that Zack's childhood had been challenging and his mother had been vulnerable and suffered from depression. He had lived with relatives for a couple of years. Zack's father hadn't been on the scene and when Zack was returned to his mother's care, he had been bullied and physically assaulted by successive partners who also hurt his mother. Zack had struggled at school and had anger outbursts which increased as he grew. He began to copy the behaviour that had been meted out to him, culminating in him taking drugs, truanting and assaulting his mother, hence him being taken into care. He was in desperate need of a male role model, but when he had attempted to meet up with his birth father, he had been cruelly rejected and became increasingly depressed as a result. This had turned to anger and he had started to become involved in criminal activity. Taverner listened intently.

'So, how has he been since he's been in care?'

'He has been in care for about three years now. At first, he was in foster care but after a few placements broke down, it was agreed that he needed more support. In all three placements he started off well, but then began to isolate and intimidate the female foster carer resulting in threatening behaviour, so had to move. He's been with us almost nine months now. He's up and down, refuses education or therapy but will tolerate a few hours home schooling, that's all. He refuses to work with the therapist though they have a good worker within the Youth Offending Team. It's a great pity because he would benefit from the work.'

'Can't you insist he has therapy?' asked Taverner, feeling frustrated at the lad's poor progress.

Vicky shrugged. 'Put simply, no, we can't. In my experience the most damaged children won't go anywhere near a therapist, but they do work with staff to help them help him. People need to be stable and in a position to access support emotionally and Zack isn't there yet.'

'OK. And how did he get on with Sinead O'Brien? Were they pretty much here at the same time?'

'Sinead arrived later but they were here together for around six months. Sinead was more mature and initially they got on very well, were an item but things got bad when Sinead dumped Zack. He was aggressive and he then became increasingly angry and upset when she started to do well at The Horseracing College and it was clear that she would be moving away.' Vicky's face clouded. 'She really was a lovely girl under all the buff and bluster. I used to see her when I visited

191

Zack.' She discreetly wiped away a tear. 'I still can't believe she's dead, I really can't.'

'I'm sorry to upset you, but that's precisely why we need to ask questions about her and Zack's relationship. In your opinion would Zack be capable of raping someone?' Taverner frowned in concentration.

Vicky looked distinctly uncomfortable. 'I've got to say it's possible. The daughter of a previous foster carer did make some allegations about Zack sexually assaulting her, but when he was moved she stated that she did not want to pursue it any further…'

Wildblood and Taverner exchanged a glance. 'We will need details of the girl involved. And can you tell me where Zack was on the evening of the 12th November?'

Vicky looked flushed. 'Well, that's just it. Zack has increasingly gone missing and he's very vague as to where he's been. He won't even talk to us when he comes back. He has a range of friends who are in gangs and it's possible he could be engaged in minor drug dealing. What's more, I have just checked and double checked and he was missing on the evening of the 12th November. He didn't come back until late in the afternoon on the 13th.'

'And you mentioned drug use, possibly drug dealing. What drugs would he have been able to get hold of?'

'Anything, I think. He started off using cannabis but has taken cocaine, opiates, probably the lot.'

'Rohypnol, roofies?''

'I don't think he's used them, but he could certainly get hold of them.'

Taverner felt himself leaning forward in anticipation. 'Right. And would he have been able to get to Walton? I mean it's 20 or so miles away with very poor public transport in the evenings.'

Vicky frowned. 'But that's the thing Inspector. Zack is the most resourceful young man I know. He could easily have found his way to Walton. He has friends and would have begged, stolen or borrowed to get somewhere he wanted to be. He's done it before, so I would say, yes, he could have easily gone to Walton if he wanted to.'

'In that case then we might need to speak to him informally, if you have a small photo of him for us, please? We need to show that to witnesses to see if anyone saw him there.'

Vicky nodded. 'I'll find one for you.'

Just then Taverner's phone rang out. He frowned as he listened then rang off. He turned to DS Wildblood and muttered out of earshot of the others.

'That was Haworth. Someone has just walked into the station admitting to running into something or someone on the evening of the 12th. We'd better get back to the station once we've finished here.'

'Who is it?' asked Wildblood in a low voice.

'A farrier, by the name of Ben Unwin.'

It was strange. Investigations were always like this, Taverner thought. One minute you were floundering, and nothing was coming together and then the next, clues came in thick and fast and now they had at least two suspects. He'd had an open mind about Zack Archer, but the fact that he had gone missing at the same time as Sinead had been killed, was surely no coincidence. Yet he would prefer to have more information, preferably a witness seeing Zack in the area before interviewing him. He didn't want the lad to go to ground as he had a history of going missing. Vicky handed him a recent photo of Zack. He was smiling at the camera and was a good looking lad dressed in a hoodie and jogging bottoms, dark in colour and fairly nondescript.

'What was Zack wearing when he went missing on that night?' Maggie looked at the photo. 'Pretty much what he was wearing in that picture. He has other tracksuits, mainly Nike ones in dark colours and some Nike Vapomax trainers. He's very proud of them.'

Wildblood took down the details and colours of his clothing. Taverner looked at her, his expression giving nothing away.

'Thank you for your time, Vicky, Maggie. We'll be in touch.'

'Inspector, will you want to interview Zack?'

Taverner thought it was best to play things down. 'Not at present. We have several lines of inquiry to pursue, and it depends how they develop. It's best if you don't mention our visit to Zack.'

The social worker looked relieved and agreed.

The pair debriefed as they drove back to the office.

'He's looking a lot more likely, I'd say, guv,' commented DS Wildblood.

'He certainly is, which is why I'm not tipping them off. If we can find a witness putting him at the scene, then we can arrest the lad properly. The information about the suspected sexual assault, him being missing at that time and having access to drugs is highly significant.'

'So, this Unwin character could have driven over Sinead and pushed her into the ditch after Zack drugged and raped her?'

DI Taverner nodded with a grim smile. 'Maybe or perhaps Unwin is good for both crimes? We'll have to see what he has to say for himself.'

Chapter Twenty-six

When Finn returned from Cheltenham, he and Nat sat up until the early hours talking about James McGrew and studying the CCTV footage which the concierge had given Finn. It was inconclusive to say the least, and merely showed a dark car turn round in the car park and seemingly follow Finn. The same car could be seen outside the flats when Nat arrived back, but it was impossible to decipher the number plate. It looked like a grey Astra in shape, but beyond that it was hard to identify. Its appearance could be coincidental anyway. The conversation turned to the journalist himself. Finn was keen to reassure Nat.

'No one believes a word of what he has written, and Tristan tipped me off about The Yorkshire Echo which has been taken over and has a new editor eager to make changes. McGrew is old school and my guess is he doesn't fit in and has had to write all the sensationalist rubbish about you to impress his editor. When I mentioned this to McGrew, he didn't deny it. I said you were taking legal action and that wouldn't go down well with his Editor either. So, he'll think twice about writing any more stuff about you. I have basically warned him off.'

Nat took a sip of Scotch and frowned. 'Well, that's good, at least. But, you see, the thing is, I'm pretty sure that there was something off about those four races, in fact, the more I think about them, the more sure I am.' Nat shook his head. 'It's the way the horses behaved, not like their usual selves…' He smiled. 'I am grateful that you spoke to him. How did he take it?'

'He looked worried, especially when I explained the facts behind them.'

Nat laughed. 'I bet. It's a shame really, he was a good journalist. Who put him up to it, do you know?'

'Well, the photos are all credited to a Michael Lofthouse, a freelancer. But he must have been tipped off by someone, but who?'

'The same person who has been tailing me, I suppose. Your conversation with McGrew will no doubt get back to them and hopefully they'll stop. I still think it's Jamie McGuire or Colm McNally just trying to discredit me so I don't get as many rides. Listen, now things have died down a bit, Livvy and me, we're going to go away for a few days, to Paris, just while my collarbone mends and then we'll go back home, and I'll be back riding winners again. We can't impose upon you for longer.' Nat suddenly looked thoughtful. 'Will you do me a favour though and have a look at those races again, the ones I fell in. I'm still not sure about them…'

Privately Finn thought it was a waste of time, but he decided to humour his friend anyway. 'Course I will. When do you leave?'

'We have an early morning flight, so we probably won't see you, but thanks again, Finn. You've been a real friend to me and Livvy.'

'No worries. Just let me know when you're back and I'll put you through your paces before you get back on the racetrack.'

Nat grinned broadly. 'Good idea, mate. You'll soon have my striding just right.'

Finn thought he heard them briefly as they left, whispering and trying to be quiet. He was pleased to have been able to help and noticed that now, at least, Nat was prepared to acknowledge that maybe, just maybe his falls were an everyday blip and not something to be concerned about. Finn firmly believed he'd be back riding winners in just a matter of weeks and was pleased that his old friend's good humour seemed restored.

Finn was keen to meet up with Harriet and she had been kept up to date with developments by text. They met up at The Singing Kettle over a coffee and toast. He updated her on the mystery car sighted in the car park and on the street but explained there was no number plate visible and its presence could have been coincidental as he never noticed the car tracking him.

'So, you think that's that?' Harriet asked.

'I certainly hope so. I warned McGrew off from writing such inflammatory nonsense and said Nat was taking legal action. I think a warning letter from his solicitor will do the job. I think the man's in a precarious situation and has resorted to writing sensationalist claptrap to keep his career going.'

Harriet pulled a face.

'Still, you'd have thought that Nat would know if something funny had happened in those four races, wouldn't you?'

Finn shrugged. 'Not necessarily. It could be psychological. Sometimes things get into the brain, self doubt starts to kick in and then it becomes a vicious circle. I did promise I'd review the races though, but I'm not expecting to find anything.'

Harriet bit into her toast. 'Hmm, still Nat Wilson and self doubt are two things I never expected to hear in the same sentence! Anyway, Daisy rang me this morning to say that Ben Unwin, the farrier, is helping the police with their inquiries and Gavin Clary told me that Ben was also chatting Sinead up when the jockeys all arrived on that night.'

'Interesting. What's the gossip on him then?' Finn knew that Daisy would very likely have an opinion on Ben and was bound to know everything there was to know about him.

'Well, Daisy reckons he's a serious hunk and rather shy. He had a girlfriend who he split up with fairly recently and he's a damned good farrier. Vince even thought of swapping when Steve Britcliffe, their regular farrier, got really busy but they decided to stick with Steve when he got more staff.'

'So, nothing to suggest he's capable of rape then?'

'No, nothing at all.' Hattie frowned. 'Although, Daisy spoke to Gavin Clary who also said that Kyle Devlin and Sam Foster were not there all evening either. Maybe they went to the loo and got chatting to someone?'

'Maybe.'

They were interrupted by Finn's phone beeping. It was a message from Rosie.

Have had a word with Clare and she wants to talk to you.

He showed Hattie his phone. 'I knew there was something. I think *the* Clare who Maura and Lottie were referring to, works at Rosie's yard. Rosie implied that she had been harmed in some way but didn't want to go to the police. I suggested that she try to persuade her to stop someone else from being harmed and it sounds like she may be ready to talk. Are you up for a visit?'

Hattie glanced at her watch. 'No time like the present.'

Finn texted Rosie back and grinned at Harriet's enthusiasm. She finished her toast with relish, so it was clear that she had got her appetite back which was a good sign in Finn's book.

As they drove, the December day was cold and rather gloomy, with grey clouds threatening to turn to rain. Finn drove past The Blacksmith's Arms, the route that Sinead had taken on her walk back to Robert Johnson's on the fateful night when she died. There was a wide, sweeping verge on the left hand side bordered by a ditch. The police tent was still in position indicating the place where Sinead's body had been found. Finn saw the tent and shuddered. He slowed down and scanned the surrounding area. To the rear of the tent, there was a fence and a field where a series of stables were being constructed. The whole yard was half built but had expensive equipment lying around with a wide range of timbers, joists and a small concrete mixer in situ. The yard was bordered by temporary metal fencing locked together with a chain and heavy padlock. It was not surprising that new stables were being erected, the whole of Walton was taken over by racing and he suspected this was going to be a new yard for yet another trainer. Suddenly, he swerved into the side and did a U turn making his way back.

'I'm just wondering if the owners of that new stable block have some CCTV in place? There's some expensive equipment about which they wouldn't want to get nicked. It's worth asking, don't you think?' Finn's eyes roved around the site.

Harriet was not so sure. 'Surely the police will have asked?'

Finn shrugged. 'Maybe but then again, maybe not.'

He parked his car as close as he could to the yard. 'I'll go, you wait here.' With that, he strode around the back of the car and made his way to the stables. There were a couple of men working on the site and they came over as soon as Finn appeared. The burlier of the two approached him.

'Hi, I'm Finn McCarthy, I work for the BHA.' He fished in his pocket for his card. 'I'm just wondering if you have CCTV in place since you're in the process of building? I can see you've got two cameras. There was a death here a few days ago and I'm trying to help the police.'

The man looked him up and down. 'I know you. Backed several winners you rode. What's your interest in the girl who died, then?'

'I coach jockeys now, and she was someone I worked with. Terrible business, poor lass.'

The man held out his hand. 'Twas. I'm Bill. I'm working on these stables and hoping to get them done before the bad weather kicks in. I have a couple of cameras installed just to protect the materials. They're those motion sensor ones, nothing fancy but they do the job. We've been here about six weeks, longer than we thought because of problems on another job. I put the cameras up about two weeks ago, been stung before when I've had loads of stuff nicked, see, and the police are bloody hopeless. The cameras are pretty good and record on SD cards. Let's see what I've got.'

Bill pulled up a ladder and fished out something from one camera and then went to the other. He returned with two small SD cards. 'I need 'em back though pronto.'

Finn felt in his wallet and pulled out a few notes. 'Have you had anything nicked so far?'

Bill shook his head.

'In that case, you don't need these. Can I take them and then you can buy some new ones?'

The man looked doubtful but grinned when he saw the notes Finn had given him. 'OK, cheers. Hope you find what you're looking for.'

Finn returned to the car triumphantly holding up the two cards.

'Bingo. We're in luck.'

'Shouldn't we give those to the police?' asked Harriet.

Finn grinned. 'Course, but not until we've copied them ourselves.'

Harriet smiled back. 'So, should we look at them?'

Finn shrugged. 'I don't see why not!'

Rosie was in the kitchen with the small, blonde woman who Finn had seen on his previous visit. Rosie filled up her capacious red teapot and poured out the tea whilst introductions were made.

'You can trust Finn and Hattie completely,' she explained to Clare.

Clare nodded and clasped her mug to her.

'Now me and Clare have had a chat, and she feels that she's ready to talk to the police about the assault.'

Finn nodded. 'That's brilliant and very brave. We know the Inspector on Sinead's case, but I'm thinking they will want to put you on to some specialist officers.'

Tears started to fall down Clare's cheeks.

'I know. I will have to tell them, and I think I'd like to tell you too.'

Rosie reached out her hands across the kitchen table. The old grandfather clock was ticking, Rosie handed round huge slices of coffee and walnut cake and replenished the teacups. Clare continued to sip her tea but did not touch her cake.

Rosie looked steadily at Clare. 'Only if you're sure.'

Harriet took in the girl's pale features and bitten nails and felt nothing but pity for her.

'Rosie's right, Clare. It's really up to you,' she added.

Clare looked at Finn and Hattie.

'Rosie says you have dealt with other things that have happened in racing and I want to tell you because you might be able to help other girls.'

They waited for Clare to compose herself.

'It happened a few months ago in August. My friend, Gill, and I had been shopping in York for the day. We came back and decided to call into The Blacksmith's Arms for a drink as it was a nice evening and the place had been done up, so we wanted to have a look. We were sitting in the bar and ran into some young lads from the yards, and they offered to buy us a drink. We were having a laugh, chatting about horses and that. The lads were quite sweet, younger than us. We were both up early for work the next day, so made our excuses. Gill had had too much to drink to drive home so she rang her boyfriend to pick her up and I said I'd catch the bus though her bloke offered to take me. Anyway, I waited and waited but the bus didn't arrive and the next thing I knew I was lying in a field completely out of it. It was much later, dark and cold and I could barely move. I felt like I'd been drugged and was spaced out, like I'd been paralysed or something. I found me phone and managed to ring Rosie, God knows how. She and Seamus came looking for me and found me along the footpath half way between their house and Walton.'

'How did you find her?' asked Finn.

Rosie sighed. 'More good luck than anything. We'd retraced her steps from the bus stop, and I kept phoning Clare and heard her phone ringing. We found her in a right state, clothing all over the place...'

'What happened then?' asked Finn.

Clare sighed. 'Rosie and Seamus let me sleep it off and looked after me. It took a couple of days to feel right again but I knew I'd been assaulted. I was sore down below, had bruises on me thighs and I just knew I'd been raped. I didn't want to tell anyone because I just felt so ashamed.' She began to weep, huge tears splashing down onto her cheeks. 'I was out of it and can't remember anything!'

'I know this is difficult, but do you remember who the lads were that bought you drinks?' asked Finn.

Clare shook her head. 'They were stable lads from the yards, from Hunt's, Johnson's and that new place, Fox's, no one from here though. I keep thinking about it, someone must have spiked me drink. That's why I don't go out much these days, I can't bear to think that someone did that and they raped me and I don't have a clue who it was. I just feel so dirty and so stupid.' She looked ashen, her face wet with tears. 'That's why I never wanted to go to the police, but then when that happened to that girl Sinead, I wondered if I had then she might have survived...' Rosie rushed to comfort her as she wept.

Finn and Hattie glanced at each other, grasping the enormity of what had happened to Clare.

Eventually Finn spoke. 'Is there anything that you can remember about the attacker, it may be just impressions, fleeting images, sensations, smells anything...'

Clare wiped her eyes and took a deep breath as she tried to compose herself. 'Hmm. I don't really know. But he had a four by four, newish. It had that new, plastic smell. I looked up when he drove away and thought I saw a bright strip of light in the rear window, a few inches long, maybe a sticker. I was out of it after that.' Clare frowned as she thought. 'It sounds weird but there was also a squelching, squeaky sort of noise.'

'Coming from where?' asked Finn.

'The guy's shoes, I think.' A wave of emotion washed over her. 'It must have been, as it was there when he walked. I'll never set foot inside a pub ever again.'

'So was the light like a shiny sticker in the rear windscreen, maybe a garage name?' Finn asked.

Clare nodded. 'I think so.'

'So, the new owners in The Blacksmith's, they were definitely there?' asked Hattie.

'Yes, they'd just refurbished the place and it was their opening week so that's why we wanted to go there.'

Finn and Harriet looked at one another. 'Thanks for talking to us, Clare. Do you want me to ring the Inspector and ask him to talk to you?'

Clare nodded, her face grim with determination.

Hattie chatted to the pair as Finn rang the police from the hallway out of earshot. He came back grim faced.

'I've spoken to DS Wildblood and she will phone you back to arrange to visit within the hour.'

Clare gave a faint smile and appeared relieved.

They drove back to York deep in thought.

'Christ, that poor girl.' Harriet shuddered. 'Not knowing who did that to you and being suspicious of everyone is just awful. What did you think about the strip in the rear windscreen and the squeaking?'

'Well, it's something, I suppose. I feel a bit guilty though.'

'About what?'

'The SD cards. Let's make a copy, then I can pop them into the station.'

'Shouldn't we have a look before we drop the cards off?'

Finn smiled. 'I'd rather not because at least if Taverner asks me if I've looked at them, I can honestly deny it.'

Hattie laughed. 'I can understand that. Taverner does have a way of making you feel like he can read your mind. I wonder what's on the memory cards, anyway?'

Finn sighed, the anticipation building. 'I wonder?'

Chapter Twenty-seven

DI Wildblood and DS Taverner were interviewing Ben Unwin, the farrier. The man seemed genuinely mortified about his predicament.

'So, to recap, on the evening of the 12th November, you thought you'd run over something and stopped your vehicle to take a look?'

'Yeah, that's right. It felt like a brick or a branch or something but when I got out and looked there was nothing there, nothing on my truck, so I thought I'd imagined it.'

Taverner showed Unwin a photo of Sinead wearing her riding clothes and smiling into the camera.

'Do you know this girl?'

'Yeah, it's the girl who died, that Sinead. She was in The Blacksmith's that night and in something of a state. I asked her if she was OK. Me and the barman, Marcus, calmed her down. I heard she was hit by a car and then when I saw the press conference...', his voice cracked, 'and you said the person who ran over her might not have known, I got real worried.' His face was etched with pain. 'It can't have been me what did it, can it?'

Taverner did not answer but went on to question him about Sinead, had he ever taken drugs, had he given them to her and then had he followed her?

Ben was a well muscled, handsome man with tousled dark hair and the air of a gentle giant about him. He looked genuinely horrified.

'What drugs? You have to be joking, don't you? I've never so much as had a smoke of a spliff, I'm into fitness and boxing in my spare time. I've never done any of that shit! What are you trying to pin on me? I came here of my own accord, you know. Why would I do that if I had something to hide?'

Taverner continued pressing the man for a while about the time he left the pub, when Sinead left, whether he had drugged her and what route he had taken home. Eventually, he nodded at Wildblood, indicating that they needed a break.

'We'll need to inspect your vehicle and make some more inquiries, Mr Unwin.'

Ben gulped. 'How long will yer need me truck for? I need it for work, you know. I have all my tools and me forge in there. I've got loads of horses to shoe.'

'We'll be as quick as we can,' Wildblood assured him. 'But you'll need to stay here whilst we continue our inquiries.'

Whilst Unwin was left with an officer in the interview room, the team went through his version of events and cross referenced the information he had given them with the other witness statements. Forensics inspected Unwin's vehicle. Eventually, they reached a clear decision.

'He came in of his own accord, his version of events checks out exactly with what the bar staff and other people in the pub have said,' Taverner commented. 'He has no previous record, no history of drug use, no prior knowledge of the victim or history of sexual violence. He never left the place all evening except to relieve himself, finally going home just before closing time. He left the pub and arrived home 10 minutes later, which his two house mates confirm. CCTV from the pub car park shows him leaving in his vehicle when he said he did. He and his housemates watched a film and had a few beers. He is described as a hard-working gentle giant. I don't think he committed the rape, but he is admitting to running into Sinead.'

'That's right. And judging by the size of his vehicle, which he needs to house the forge he uses for his job, it's likely that he were the one who ran into Sinead,' added DS Wildblood. 'Forensics have confirmed the tyre prints on Sinead's body are a partial match for his tyres. They're pretty common, mind. There's no match on the footprints at the scene though, but they are a bit unusual. Patel is looking at 'em as we speak, to see if they match a particular type of trainer or shoe. Might take a while though. I think Unwin is telling the truth, guv. Given the size of his truck, he'd have barely noticed running into Sinead, poor lass.'

The team sighed, as one. It was a shocking situation for the young man who had inadvertently and accidently caused the death of a young girl. They would have to charge him, yet the real culprit was the man who'd drugged and raped her and left her for dead. What an awful thing for Unwin to have on his conscience.

'Christ, who's going to tell him, poor guy?' asked DC Haworth.

Taverner frowned. He'd had worse jobs, he supposed. 'I will.'

'I'll come with you,' Wildblood added, her expression grave.

Unwin was extremely upset to say the least. He sat there with his head in his hands, tears in his eyes, after he'd had his rights read to him.

'Christ! What the hell was she doing lying on the verge out of it? Had she taken something, is that it?' He looked from Taverner to Wildblood.

'Or she was given something,' answered Taverner. 'Which is why it's really important if you can think back to what else you saw on that evening.'

'I've already given you a statement. Sinead was upset, came in early doors. Me and Marcus tried to calm her down. Then the other lads and lasses came in, they got talking, seemed fine, then she set off on her own, right?'

'Did you see anyone following her or acting suspiciously around Sinead or just hanging around?' He passed a photo of Zack Archer over to Unwin.

Unwin studied it. 'Hmm. Maybe, he looks like some of the stable staff, I can't be sure though, I'm afraid.'

An officer knocked on the door and came in with a note for Taverner. He read it and stood up.

'Thanks, Ben.'

'Please tell me I didn't kill Sinead, Inspector, I couldn't bear that.'

Taverner considered this. He tried to be sympathetic but honest. 'I don't know is the honest answer. We will have to charge and bail you, but I will do my best to have the charge reduced to failing to report a road traffic accident.' Ben groaned. 'But think yourself lucky because you could be looking at a manslaughter charge otherwise.'

Ben gasped, utterly horrified.

'I'll get one of my officers to sort out the paperwork with you,' added Taverner, as he left the young man blinking back tears.

There was new information to impart to the team, so Taverner gathered them all together.

'So, we have another young woman stating that she was drugged and raped at around the time The Blacksmith's Arms in Walton re-opened in August. Some four months ago now. Clare Hudson who works as a stable lass at Seamus Ryan's place. Wildblood and Cullen, can you go out and do a preliminary interview then pass the case on to the vulnerable victims' unit? We do need to liaise with them closely though, as it may relate to Sinead's case.'

DC Natalie Cullen nodded. A bobbed haired, smart young woman, she was shaping up well having recently joined the team and her questions reflected her growing confidence.

'Does that point to our rapist being amongst the racing community, sir? In that case it could rule out Zack Archer.'

'It could do, Natalie, but we do need to keep an open mind on this. Finn McCarthy, the jockey coach rang in the information.' They had dealt with him in some previous inquiries. 'And, of course, Sinead was a conditional jockey so the rapist might well be amongst the racing staff. It might be worth talking to McCarthy about what he knows, as he has his ear to the ground.'

'Well, that's easy enough, guv. He's downstairs. Summat about videos he's got on SD cards,' said DC Haworth cheerily. 'Talk of the devil.'

Taverner nodded. He couldn't have timed it better himself. 'Right. I'll go and have a word.'

Taverner shook Finn's hand. Although not friends exactly, there was respect between the pair. They had ended up working on some interesting cases which involved the racing yards and Finn had a good knowledge of what was going on there. He had learned never to dismiss anything the jockey coach told him.

'So, thanks for contacting us about the stable lass, Clare Hudson. We're going out to see her today. Are there any other females or males, for that matter, who appear to have been attacked?'

'Not as far as I know. Nothing has come to my attention, but I'll ask about.'

'And your conditionals, have any of them said anything that might be relevant?'

'Not as such.' McCarthy put his hand in his pocket. 'But I was passing a stable block that was being built close to the site where Sinead was found, and on impulse I asked them if they had any security cameras, given that there was a lot of expensive equipment lying about protected by metal screens.'

'And?'

'Luckily the builder had those motion sensor cameras and I paid him for the SD cards.' He gave an envelope to the policeman. 'Here they are. Might be useful, that's what I thought.'

Taverner was pleased but embarrassed that his own team hadn't noticed the stables being built and had the initiative to see if there were cameras in place.

'Thanks. That's really helpful. You know you'd make a good policeman if you even fancied a change of career.'

Finn grinned back. 'No, you're alright. I love my job.' He realised as soon as he had spoken the words outright that it was true.

'I suppose you haven't looked at these?'

Taverner's gaze was penetrating.

'No, of course not.'

'But you are making your own inquiries via the BHA about Sinead O'Brien's death?'

Finn gave him a man to man stare but didn't exactly answer the question. 'I've just been asked to keep my ear to the ground, that's all, but I'll report anything I do find out to you. I've learned my lesson after the Shetland case.'

'Hmm. I'm glad to hear that, Finn. Keep in touch and thanks again.'

Taverner watched as the ex-jockey made his way out of the station. He didn't believe him entirely. Still, he was glad that the ex-jockey was involved in a way. He and his friend, Harriet Lucas, had a habit of finding information out and the imagination to see how it could be useful, and that could be very helpful. As he made his way upstairs to his office, he tried to remember who had been tasked with scoping out the crime scene as they were definitely in for a bollocking. McCarthy had made him and his team look like a bunch of amateurs and it wasn't the first time he'd done it.

Chapter Twenty-eight

Topper drove away from his pleasant Arts and Crafts era ex-marital home with a sigh. He waved to his two sons Tim and Giles, as they stood on the steps. They were frozen in his headlights as he reversed on the gravel drive and pressed his horn in a chummy way, giving them a chirpy wave as he left. It hid his utter desolation. Their mother, Jacqui, ushered the two boys indoors before he'd turned out into the lane heading back to his dingy, lonely flat.

It had been a pleasant outing, he and the boys had visited the Jorvik centre, the day marred only by the frostiness of Jacqui as he handed them back again. Damn and blast the bloody woman. He had managed to focus on the boys. Tim was proving to be a bright spark, keen to excel in his school history project, hence the visit to the Viking centre so he could research his essay. Giles was an excellent sportsman and keen rugger player and their next trip was to watch a game if he could cadge some free tickets. As he drove through the darkening city, he remembered Tim's astute questions,

'Could you read my essay before I send it in? I want to enter it in the house competition, you see Dad, and you know about writing, don't you?'

Yes, I bloody well do, my son, he had wanted to shout. And then to add, it's my writing skills that have kept you boys and your mother in the lap of luxury all these years. My pen is my sword and all that. The respect with which Tim regarded him, clear in his approving gaze, cheered Topper enormously. Maybe one day he'd pack in working for The Yorkshire Echo, and finish the racing thriller he'd started writing a couple of years ago. He might even become the next Dick Francis and make a fortune. Why not? He had the connections, and he knew all the tricks which trainers, bookies and jockeys employed. As he approached the flat, his mind turned over what Finn McCarthy had said to him at Cheltenham. The memory was like dark storm clouds on his horizon. Christ, he needed a drink.

Back in the dismal, chilly kitchen diner cum sitting room, Topper made for the corner cupboard where he kept the whiskey. He lifted down the bottle of Bells. Bugger, it was virtually empty, just a half inch left. Mmm. Tim's face floated before his eyes, his keenness, his apparent faith in his father's writing skills. Bugger it, a coffee would do whilst he checked out the stories he'd written about Nat Wilson.

McCarthy's comments about the unfairness of the allegations against Wilson rankled. As did Finn's assertion that Topper was trying to sensationalise his copy to ingratiate himself with his trendy new editor, Christian Lamont. Of course, like many shrewd guesses, McCarthy had hit the nail on the proverbial head and touched the heart of the matter. He had probably rushed out the stories, been too eager to believe his sources and failed to cross check his facts. Even Finn's prediction about his editor's reaction to the legal letter from Nat's solicitor, which was yet to arrive, was likely to be accurate. He waited for it with dread and knew the temporary reprieve he had been granted from Christian would disappear in a puff of smoke when it arrived. What if Wilson had simply suffered a run of bad luck? It happened all the time in racing and Topper had not tried to talk to Nat, well not tried hard enough anyway, had not checked out his side of the story. Maybe, Nat wouldn't have visited a solicitor, he hoped he had thought better of it. But then again, supposing he had? Bugger. That crafty sod, McCarthy, had been on the money. Topper was definitely trying to impress Lamont and keep his job so that he could maintain Jacqui, the boys ticking over. Not to mention saving for future school fees. But what about me, he thought sipping the scalding black coffee? What about my reputation and integrity? Mmm. He knew he had to look further into what were, on the face of it, easy scoops, stories practically spoon fed to him by a certain Micky Lofthouse. Supposing he'd fallen for fake stories like a complete novice cub reporter? He needed to take a closer look and there was no time like the present and with a clear head too.

Topper found the relevant footage and studied several of the races, where for one reason or another, Nat had come to grief unexpectedly on a well fancied horse. The most recent one, when Wilson rode Portland Bay at Worcester, made him wince. It was a hell of a fall and had led to a broken collarbone to boot. There were a few other races to study. Topper frowned and watched them several times. Each time the horse Nat was riding either veered to the side or most often took off too soon or too late. Bugger, he thought, Finn was exactly right, Topper had only ever ridden a little as a child and young man when he'd hunted with the local pack on an old schoolmaster horse of his father's. He realised that he did not know enough about riding and nothing about race riding at all, to be able to judge whether Nat Wilson had made a mistake. And it all seemed to happen so quickly and even slowing down the footage didn't help. Annoyed, he made another coffee and tried to think of other ways of analysing the races. He got out his notebook and sipping the scalding hot drink, went through the list of jockeys riding in all the races he was interested in. Certainly, he also needed to ask Lofty more about where the information about Wilson had come from, but that could wait until he was next on a racecourse later in the week. Lofty was notoriously hard to get hold of and tended to drift in and out of bars at the races like a spectre. He was as elusive as trust amongst thieves and twice as slippery. So, if he knew that about him, why had he trusted him? Why, indeed?

By midnight he'd drawn up a comprehensive list. It seemed that Colm McNally or Jamie McGuire were riding in all of the races, along with a spotty faced conditional called Joel Fox. Topper immediately dismissed the young jockey, he seemed no particular threat, but McNally and McGuire certainly were. Colm McNally had won the Jockeys' Championship for the first time last season and was clearly a close rival of Nat Wilson's. Colm must have been seriously annoyed when Wilson made his comeback this season. And as for Jamie McGuire, he was the second jockey at Michael Kelly's, behind Wilson and had had a great season last year, riding many of the stable's best horses including St Jude, as Nat was injured. Could these pair be working together, trying to ruin Wilson's comeback somehow? It wasn't unheard of for jockeys to hold grudges and shove another off around the quieter parts of the racecourse. They had even been known to land punches and fight whilst riding, but all these incidents of Wilson's took place near the final few fences, well in view of the crowd, the stewards and of course were filmed. It seemed unlikely, but maybe it was worth investigating further. He tried to think back to his recent conversations with the pair. He had recently spoken to McGuire about rides and prospects and he hadn't exactly criticised Nat, but he sensed that the first jockey's return had put him on the back foot. Supposing he had fed the stories to Lofty? And Colm was a taciturn chap and would be wanting to hang on to his champion's title, so could he have had Nat followed and tried to find some dirt on him? Topper yawned and switched off the laptop. Time for bed. As he undressed, he considered the two jockeys. McNally was a quiet chap, almost sullen and interviewing him was like getting blood out of a stone. He had a thick Cork accent which was hard to understand as he tended to mumble, and all you could reliably hear was 'hoss' every so often. McGuire was more talkative, he was also from Cork but could adapt his speech when interviewed to sound quite intelligible. Both had not a scrap of charisma like the likeable and jokey Nat Wilson, but both had very good reasons to stop him winning.

Topper brushed his teeth, deep in thought. He knew that the jockeys' changing room was sacrosanct and he wouldn't be able to visit there. He needed some excuse to interview the two of them, to ask a few searching questions and see if he could tell if they were hiding something. After all, he had a nose for that sort of thing.

Then he had a brainwave as he padded over to the cold, single bed with its lumpy mattress. What about doing a piece on jockeys' pedigrees, in the same way as you might about a horse? Both jockeys were from Cork and McNally's father was definitely an ex-jockey. And wasn't McGuire related to him, some sort of cousin or something? He could use some of the other racing families too, like interviewing Simon Barclay and his sister Eva, the broadcaster and wasn't the late trainer, Josh Powell's daughter a top three day eventer, what the heck was her name? He could call it 'Bloodlines'. All sorts of thoughts chased around his head. He only needed to start with these two and then see where it went. No need to carry on if the idea didn't have legs, but Topper was sure he would be able to sniff out good stories if they were there to be found. Sod Christian Lamont, maybe it was time for him to think big? As he fell into an uneasy sleep, he dreamed of journalistic fame, maybe even writing a regular witty column about racing folk and their relatives. He felt strangely heartened and optimistic about his career. There's life in the old dog yet, he thought, as sleep overcame him.

Chapter Twenty-nine

Finn and Hattie shared a pizza at Finn's flat whilst they reviewed the footage from the SD cards. The place was spacious and tidy, rather stylish and had been converted from an old Rowntree's chocolate factory. It was open plan in design, all beams, large factory windows and wooden floors. Hattie always thought she could still smell the chocolate that had been made there, but maybe that was just her overactive imagination.

'Did Taverner suspect anything?' asked Hattie.

Finn grinned. 'He did ask if I had looked at the footage and said he supposed we were making inquiries for the BHA regarding Sinead's death. I said we were just keeping our ear to the ground. I was going to tell him about what Clare had said but he would think we'd overstepped the mark. She's bound to repeat it to them, I mean about the squeaking noise she heard and the sticker on the back of the 4x4.'

'Hmm. I wondered about that. I suppose the sign could be fluorescent if she saw it at night, so that at least is something to go on.'

Finn nodded. 'Yes, of course. I'll check the cars the conditionals drive for starters.'

'Do you really think one of them is involved?'

Finn shook his head. 'No, I don't think so. They're all good kids. It's probably someone else who was in the pub that night. I hope so anyway.'

'Ben Unwin was released according to Daisy.' Hattie took a mouth full of pizza and frowned at the computer. 'Come on, Finn. The suspense is nearly killing me!'

Finn grinned and pressed some buttons on the keyboard whilst the footage began to load. They scrolled back to the day of Sinead's death and watched closely. The camera showed pictures of cars driving past the stables in the day, cats and squirrels wandering about the scene until gradually the pictures darkened as the daylight fell. Again, there were images of cars driving along the road, their bright lights illuminating the darkness.

'Christ, this is slow!' complained Hattie.

'Do you want a drink?' asked Finn.

'A glass of red would be nice if we're here for the long haul.'

Finn laughed. 'Fine, just keep watching that screen.'

He came back a few minutes later with two glasses and a bottle of Rioja. Hattie was hunched over the computer and was rewinding the footage.

'There, look. That car stops outside the stables and stays there for ages and look it has something in the back window, a rectangular strip, quite small.' They both studied the screen and watched, horror mounting as they imagined the depravity of what was happening to Sinead at that time.

'Sinead must be out of shot, thank God!' Hattie sat with her hands across her mouth, her imagination running wild. Eventually, after about 30 minutes, a figure approached the vehicle. Dressed in dark colours, it was impossible to make out any distinguishing features, but the figure seemed slim and was wearing a dark jacket, cap, loose

219

trousers and trainers. The vehicle moved off, the strip in the rear window still visible. They watched the footage again, searching for more clues but found none. Their mood dipped as they re-imagined the horror of Sinead's attack. They saw the car drive away. Then they fast forwarded to three hours later and saw another vehicle stop by the stables, a driver exit the vehicle and look on the side of the road with the light from his phone, and presumably finding nothing, drive away. He was noticeably broader in stature than the first person and was wearing different clothes. They stared dazed at what they had just seen.

After a while Finn spoke. 'So, it looks like the person that raped her left her by the road and someone else ran over Sinead. The first person, that's the real culprit.' Finn said after a while. 'Sinead wasn't murdered by her rapist. Presumably the second guy is Ben Unwin. And the rapist in the first vehicle, definitely did have a sign in his rear windscreen. So, it looks like Clare and Sinead's attackers are the same person.'

Hattie nodded and took a sip of wine, her expression serious. She found she had lost her appetite for the pizza and pushed her plate away.

'It could be anyone, someone we know even.' The thought terrified her. She looked at Finn and could see he was alarmed too.

Finn sighed heavily. The reality of what had happened to Sinead was beginning to sink in.

'Christ! We have to find them before they attack again.'

The next day, Finn set out for Lloyd Fox's place to see his son, Joel, ride. He had been studying his rides and was struck by the really good quality horses his father had and how often he trusted his son to ride them. Dan Richards obviously bowed down to Lloyd in allowing the conditional to ride ahead of several more experienced jockeys in the area such as Tristan Davies, who had occasionally ridden for them when his own guvnor didn't have a runner. Tristan, it had to be said, did a better job. Although promising, Joel found it hard to judge a race and often left it too late to ride his finish and also struggled with positioning his horse. Finn had to admit though, that the lad was doing well and had clocked up a respectable five or so winners. He suspected though that Lloyd was pushing him too hard too soon and wondered how to broach this. He googled Lloyd Fox and saw that he'd had a very successful online clothing business which was tipped to go global when his wife had died of a rare form of cancer at the age of 43. Lloyd had then sold his business for millions, deciding to devote his time to bringing up his young son, who was then aged 14. So that explained Lloyd's attitude towards Joel, thought Finn. A successful and astute businessman, he had channelled his grief into caring for his son.

The reporter doing the feature had asked why Joel hadn't gone into the family business. Lloyd had replied that Joel was not remotely interested but had a passion for horses and racing, '*I will help him in every way I can,*' Lloyd commented. '*His mother was really concerned about the safety of riding, so I owe it to her memory to make sure that we make it as safe as we can, but Joel has talent and I want to do everything in my power to help him succeed.*' There was mention of Joel training with the eventer Lloyd had spoken about previously. Finn felt uneasy. There was a fine line between being supportive and bullying. Finn suspected that Lloyd had pushed his son too much and was one of those men who didn't really understand racing but thought he could buy his son success by money alone. He resolved to talk to Lloyd about this if the situation allowed.

The stables looked very smart and well kept and there were even some hanging baskets with a few straggly flowers and greenery in them, even in mid winter. At the rear of the stables was a large farmhouse, that had also been beautifully renovated. The family cars were parked on the gravel driveway, and Finn studied them carefully. There were several vehicles, a silver Aston Martin, no less, a sporty Mercedes and a new grey Land Rover. The staff's cars were there too. He studied them closely. Some had garage stickers in their rear window, but none were in the right place to fit the images from the SD cards, and the Land Rover had one at the top of the rear windscreen in the centre. None appeared to be fluorescent either. Well, that was something at least, thought Finn, mentally crossing them off his list of suspects, as Dan Richards and Lloyd came into view.

'Great to see you.' Lloyd shook Finn's hand and Dan clapped him on the shoulder, grinning broadly. The men's clothing was in marked contrast to each other, Lloyd was dressed formally in a checked shirt and tie topped off with a tweed jacket and shiny boots, whilst Dan was wearing more casual clothes, a polo shirt and waxed jacket.

'Joel is just in the yard,' explained Lloyd.

'Are we off to the gallops in town?'

'No. We have an all weather track here and some fences in the paddock.'

Finn smiled. That did not surprise him. 'As you're so close to the town's gallops, I thought you might use them.'

Lloyd smiled tightly. 'We do from time to time, but not when we want to avoid prying eyes.'

Finn frowned at this which seemed overly paranoid, but he supposed Lloyd had the money to put down his own track, so fair enough.

'Right. Listen, before I see Joel, I just wanted to ask if you intend using an experienced stable jockey alongside him?'

Dan opened his mouth to speak but Lloyd quickly interjected.

'We do use the services of experienced jockeys and as we expand, we intend to employ one.'

Finn nodded. 'Good. It will really help Joel learn and develop to have an older more experienced jockey to work with. It's very hard starting out as a conditional and he needs someone to help him learn.'

Lloyd gave Finn a frosty smile. 'I rather thought that was your role, Finn.'

'In some ways, yes, but I can only do so much. Besides your horses would achieve better results with an experienced jockey on board which really is the point of racing, isn't it?'

Lloyd's expression hardened. 'Are you suggesting that my son is not competent, Finn?'

Finn was taken aback by the hostility from Lloyd and was careful how he answered.

'Not at all. It's just that too much responsibility and expectation on his young shoulders could prove too much and he might struggle. I've seen it happen before.'

Lloyd looked momentarily less annoyed. 'Hmm. Well, I'll start looking for someone. Who do you recommend?'

Finn named a few jockeys who lived locally. 'Of course, the best jockeys in the area are Tristan Davies and Charlie Durrant but they both have commitments to yards. How about Jed Cavendish? He's also really good and is not attached to a stable.'

Dan nodded enthusiastically. 'Sound idea, mate.'

Finn added, 'I suppose it all depends on what your plans are. How many horses are you thinking of having in training?'

Lloyd gave him a considering look and seemed slightly less hostile.

'We have 10 at present, six I own solely and the other four I have an interest in, but we do hope to expand to about 40.'

'You'll certainly need a professional jockey then. And that will help Joel develop at his own pace.'

Finn smiled, feeling that the conversation had gone better than expected.

Lloyd nodded thoughtfully. 'Yes, I can appreciate that. I am a newcomer to racing and am just learning, you understand, which is why it's so helpful to talk to you. I will speak to Jed Cavendish.'

Finn was relieved. 'Good. At least we understand each other. Now perhaps I can see Joel?'

'Of course.'

Joel was busily tacking up a smart, bay horse. He smiled at Finn. He was dressed from head to toe in expensive riding clothing and Lloyd's vow to his mother about safety was much in evidence by the fluorescent hat band on his red hat silk and the fluorescent strips on the arms of his jacket. The lad's complexion had not cleared up, Finn noticed, and his stammer was still very much in evidence.

'Hi ttthere, Mr MmmMcCarthy. What did you wwwant to sssee me dddo?'

'You can call me Finn. Can you just take him up into your gallops, do some warm ups, have a run round and then we'll see how you tackle some of the fences. What's the name of this chap?' Finn patted the horse.

Joel contorted his mouth as he tried to say the horse's name. Tension and embarrassment seeped out of him. Finn waited for the block to pass, but his father was far less patient.

Lloyd tutted loudly. 'For God's sake, Joel. We haven't got all day, it's Palisade.' Joel flushed with humiliation.

Dan looked uneasy. 'He's five and has won a few hurdles. We're thinking of sending him steeplechasing as the fella has a great jump in him.'

'OK, Joel, let's see what he's made of, shall we?'

The gallops which Lloyd had had constructed were all weather and sited on an incline. No expense had been spared, Finn noticed, though he couldn't understand why the town's gallops wouldn't have been just as effective. Finn watched as Joel walked, trotted and cantered in a circle before giving the big bay a blow out on the gallops. He came to a halt.

Finn patted the big bay.

'Well, so far so good. You have a good seat on the flat and this boy has a bit of speed, but let's see what he can do over the jumps, shall we?'

Joel grinned at the praise and steered his mount into the jumping paddock. Lloyd had a set of hurdles and there was even space for a couple of larger chase fences. After some flexibility exercises and a warm up over poles, Finn had Joel jumping round the four hurdle fences. Palisade clearly loved jumping and pricked his ears as he jumped effortlessly and with great skill and enthusiasm. Joel got left behind a little and struggled on take off.

'Go again and let him have his head coming up to the fences,' yelled Finn. 'He knows what he's doing so don't interfere too much. If you were on the track, you would have plenty of time to slow him down in between the fences, so you can afford to give him his head on the approach to the jump.'

Joel steered the horse and this time both horse and rider completed the line of fences much more smoothly.

'Grand, that was much better. He's a real natural over fences. See how he jumped much more smoothly when you weren't holding him up? Fancy a go at the chase fences?'

Joel beamed. 'Yyes.''

'OK. Take him round two of the hurdles then come back here over the chase fences.' Finn pointed out the route he wanted the horse and rider to take.

Joel cantered round for a couple of circuits then took on two of the hurdle fences then pointed Palisade at the chase fence. They jumped the hurdle fences well, but Joel reverted to holding the horse up over the larger fences.

'You're doing it again. Just let him go over the chase fences like you did with the hurdles. He's a good jumper, you just need to trust him. Go again.'

This time Joel did as Finn had asked and cleared the fences effortlessly. After a few more attempts with differing approaches, Finn was satisfied.

'Much better, Joel. That's enough for today. Just cool him off now, will you?' Finn walked alongside as Joel walked the horse around the jumping paddock on a long rein. Finn remembered that Joel had ridden at Cheltenham recently.

'How did you find Cheltenham?'

'Oh, it was great. I loved it,' replied Joel, with no trace of a stammer. He smiled at the memory of the ride.

Finn remembered something he wanted to discuss. 'Did you lose your whip in the race?'

Joel flushed and nodded.

'Right, you'll probably need to practice using it with your left hand as you're right handed, aren't you? And you know about the BHA whip rules?'

'I think so.'

'Well, I'll remind you. You can only use the approved type of whip, you know the sort with the padded end. The clerk usually checks the whips beforehand to make sure they're the right sort and of course, you can only whip a horse eight times in a race. You have to allow the horse time to respond before striking him again and must only hit the horse on the hindquarters not the flank.'

Joel nodded, taking it all in.

'Why are you asking about whips?' asked Lloyd who had suddenly appeared at their side.

'I'm just making sure that Joel knows about the whip rules, that's all after I noticed he lost his whip in his ride at Cheltenham.'

Lloyd frowned. 'He's just clumsy, that's all.'

The lad flushed at his father's comments. Finn noticed the tension between them, it was hard to ignore it. He arranged to meet up with Joel again and go through his positioning. Finn was going to go through past videos of his races to see where he needed to improve. He felt he needed to end the session on a high.

'Well done, though. You have lots of potential.' Joel flushed at the praise.

Finn drove home in a troubled mood. The visit had had mixed success. He hoped he had won the argument about the yard needing a professional jockey to work alongside Joel. The young conditional clearly had ability, but he was increasingly worried about Joel's relationship with his father. The lad was lacking in confidence, and this clearly wasn't helped by his father's overbearing, pushy attitude. No wonder the lad stammered. He felt that Joel would flourish in a more supportive, less pressured stable yard away from his father's influence, but he knew that his father would never allow that to happen. He felt desperately sorry for the young jockey but was at a loss as to how he could help him. Joel would need to gain the confidence to stand up to his father, which could take time. At least, having checked the vehicles at the yard, Finn realised he was able to rule the family and their yard staff out in the search for Sinead's attacker, which was something he supposed.

Chapter Thirty

DC Patel was bristling with excitement.

'I've got something, guv.'

The team all pricked their ears as DI Taverner stared at Patel's computer screen.

'That partial footprint which was found at the site near Sinead's body, well the imprint was quite unusual, so I researched trainers that had a similar pattern and I've found a match.'

'Right, go on.' Taverner frowned, deep in concentration.

'It's from a particular type of trainer, a Nike Vapomax. They have an air-filled tread that matches perfectly. I have also estimated that the size is an eight.'

Taverner grinned. 'Well done, that's amazing. Good work.'

Patel flushed. 'And there's more. I went through the description of what Zack Archer was wearing when he disappeared and he was in a pair of black Nike Vapomax, size eight, just the same.'

There was an audible gasp from the assembled officers.

'I'll go and speak to DCI Sykes about picking the lad up, but I'm still worried that there is no actual sighting of Archer in the area in the correct timeframe.'

DS Anna Wildblood frowned. 'Gi' over, will yer. Sykes will say that Archer had a motive, he was missing on the night Sinead died, he had access to drugs and wore Vapomax, so you know what Sykes' decision will be...'

DI Taverner grinned. DCI Sykes was nothing if predictable. He would still like to wait until Haworth and Ballantyne had come back. They had been talking to potential witnesses to see if they could place Archer at the scene,

'I'll go and do the necessary, by then the others will be back and we'll head out and pick Archer up.'

Clues had been thin on the ground but now they had the SD card footage from McCarthy, which Cullen was currently poring over, and now they had another great lead. He felt a surge of optimism. Things were coming together at long last.

Nat Wilson was at a loose end. Livvy was off working, and he was injured and unable to ride. His collarbone was feeling better but there were still a couple of weeks before he could go back to riding, let alone race competitively. He decided to pop into Michael's yard. They'd spoken over the phone about the bad press he'd received but he wanted to talk more face to face. As he drove into the yard several horses' heads appeared over their stable doors to see who had come to call. The place was quiet now, it was midday and all the horses had been fed, exercised and mucked out. He patted the nearest horse and pulled the ears of a grey called Snowy Mountain. He noticed, with a pang, that Saint Jude's stable had been filled by a large chestnut he couldn't place. He felt momentarily depressed at the loss of such a good horse, but it was racing and horses moved yards all the time. Michael came out and invited him in for a drink. He sat down in the homely kitchen and after initial pleasantries, talked to him one to one about those articles.

'I just wanted to let you know that the girl I was pictured with was from an awards ceremony. I dropped her off home because she was pissed. Then I was questioned about this damned girl who came to interview me and Livvy. I opened the door to her with a towel wrapped round me as I thought it was Livvy. I'd just come out of the shower. My towel slipped and I went running back upstairs to put some clothes on, and the next thing I know, she reported me to the police. They accepted my explanation, so that's that. And as for all that stuff about the fallers and me losing my nerve, it's bollocks, you know that!'

Michael patted Nat's hand. 'Course, I know. No one believes that eejit, McGrew. Whatever you do in your personal life is up to you as long as it doesn't affect your riding, and as for the falls, well yer know that's what racing's like, it's part of the job. Horses are not machines, and that bloody McGrew should know that. Take no notice of the man!'

He was relieved to hear that Michael didn't have doubts about him.

'Good. Because I'm going to come back stronger than ever, I've been to the gym, I'm in shape and when I pass the doctor, I'll be raring to go. I don't want you thinking I'm not up to the job.'

Michael nodded. 'You might want to have a word with that McGrew, though. He can't be writing that sort of nonsense and expect to get away with it.'

'It's all been taken care of. One of me mates spoke to him, I have consulted a solicitor and asked him to write an apology, so that should sort him out.'

Michael gave a rueful smile. 'Grand.'

'How's Jamie doing?'

Michael frowned and shook his head. 'He's not as good as he thinks he is, that's for sure. He lost a couple of races you would have won, and he still can't get on with Portland Bay.'

Nat grinned. 'Porto is a quirky one, that is for sure. I see Saint Jude's gone.'

Michael looked pensive. 'It's a shame about Saint Jude though, isn't it? We were going to win everything with him until that damned fool actress made the owners an offer they couldn't refuse. She's got more money than sense, that Regan woman. The horse went ages ago. I suppose Charlie Durrant will ride him now he's at Jamieson's place.'

'Yes. Charlie will do well with him.'

Nat had to agree that the yard losing Saint Jude was a major blow. He was a horse who could have won the Gold Cup, the King George, the Grand National, the Betfair Chase even, after his Charlie Hall win. Still racing was like that, there were always ups and downs, everyone knew it and it didn't do to dwell on the lows.

Michael's eyes sparkled. 'But did I tell you, I've got some new owners? The Herringtons have moved their horses from Granger's yard. So, we've got Huntsman and Detonator. I've put Huntsman in Saint Jude's stable and Detonator is in the other block. Now I like the look of that Huntsman. He's a great jumper and has a lot of stamina, so we'll let him acclimatise then he should be running in a nice handicap at Haydock.' Michael grinned. 'You'll be back by then, of course, so we've got that to look forward to and the other horse is handy too.'

'Great, that's good to hear, Michael. I won't let you down.'

The older man gave a brief nod. 'Are you at Worcester tomorrow? We've a few runners, Jamie's riding them but you need to show your face on the racecourse again, you know.'

Truth to tell, Nat had been worrying about this. The great racing public could be fickle, and he knew very well that any sniff of gossip, especially anything to do with sexual misconduct, was highly emotive and his popularity could take a serious nosedive. OK, so Finn had insisted that McGrew write a further article explaining the truth about the photos, but mud had a habit of sticking. He had been uneasy about facing the public. It seemed that Michael's abilities were not just confined to horses, he could read Nat like a book. He made a quick decision.

'Good idea, I'll definitely be there.'

Michael gave him an approving look. 'That's right, fella. Hold your head up high and face them down.' He frowned. 'You know what? Have you ever wondered how that photographer just happened to know you'd been arrested? I mean how would he have found out?'

Nat had wondered. He knew that sometimes even the police tipped off the press for a backhander and he assumed that that was what had happened here.

'The police maybe tipped them off, I'm not sure.' He thought back to the officer who had interviewed him, DC Horton. She had made no secret of the fact that she disliked him, but would she risk informing the press? He wasn't sure, as she seemed to be someone who'd do things by the book.

Michael looked pensive. 'Strikes me that McGrew just got lucky, or somebody tipped him off. Do you have any enemies?'

Nat grinned. 'Maybe the odd husband or boyfriend, but not since I met Livvy. I'd never cheat on her. Or maybe it's another one of the lads, keen to get ahead perhaps...?'

Michael raised an eyebrow. 'Well, you can discount Jamie, if that's what you were thinking. The lad wouldn't have it in him, he's competitive but he's not that bright, to be honest with you.'

Nat had been suspicious of Jamie, but he was glad to hear Michael's assessment of him. He was probably right, he realised.

'I know that.'

The older man gave him a penetrating look. 'And Livvy is still supportive of you, is she, after all these revelations?'

'Of course. She knows I'd never look at another woman.'

Michael nodded in approval. He'd made no secret of the fact that he liked and respected Livvy.

'I'm glad to hear it. She's good for you. But think on, Nat, in this game it always pays to stay one step ahead of the enemy.' Michael gave him a shrewd look and tapped the side of his nose.

Nat nodded. It was good advice and he intended to heed it, but if it wasn't Jamie who'd tried to engineer his downfall, then who?

As good as his word, Nat dressed smartly in a grey suit and warm overcoat and set off for Worcester the following day. He'd dressed in his best clothes and looked around him as he drove from his Cheltenham home. He remembered what Finn had said about him being followed, but he didn't see anyone unusual lurking in the street, any vehicle pulling off as he drove or anyone following him. It was a bright winter's day and he felt his mood lifting. He was going to do as Michael had suggested and hold his head up high. He'd done nothing wrong, in fact had been the victim of some stupid idiot trying to wreck his career. He'd been very reassured by his talk with Michael. If his guvnor was not concerned, then neither was he. He was naturally a confident, optimistic person and if someone was trying to do him down then the best thing for him to do was try even harder and be even more successful. He was glad to hear Michael's views about Jamie's riding and although he picked up a lot of jealousy and envy from the lad, he thought Michael was probably right, he didn't have the brain power to plan a whispering campaign against him.

The other person who might possibly be involved was Colm McNally. He was the current Champion jockey who had picked up the title when he was off with his thigh injury. Perhaps, Colm had got a taste of success and didn't want to let it slip away from him? Colm was a quiet man, taciturn even, but maybe still waters ran deep? It still felt like a stretch, but Colm was something of a closed book. Still, the sun was shining, bathing the road with its rays and he found he was looking forward to the day. He was glad now that his solicitor had demanded that McGrew print an apology about his allegations in relation to the charges, his riding and the alleged affair. McGrew had agreed to do so, but there was still the issue about the four races when he had fallen in mysterious circumstances. He'd thought and thought about each race and still hadn't reached any real conclusion and he was beginning to think that it was in his head. Finn had implied that it was and perhaps he was right. He decided to just enjoy a day at the races without the stress of competition. He put the Mercedes through its paces, enjoying the thrill of the acceleration, arrived in plenty of time and bought a racecard. Settled in the bar, he ate a sandwich, and leafed through his copy of The Racing Post, studying form.

Michael had three runners all of which were being ridden by Jamie McGuire, all pretty good prospects. He saw that there were several horses from Walton, Tristan Davies was riding three, as was Charlie Durrant, Gerry King and Colm McNally was also there riding the much fancied Desperado in the fifth race in which Michael had Moonbaby, ridden by Jamie, of course. The Owners and Trainers bar was filling up and he found that he was attracting a lot of attention. There were a few nudges and winks from some people, most were friendly from his many acquaintances, but he noticed a group of women staring at him. He suspected they had read McGrew's article and were wondering if he really was guilty and how much they should hate him. He decided to square his shoulders and then gave the group a wide grin. Then he felt a tap on his shoulder and turned round. It was Michael along with some owners who were introduced as Maggie and Peter Wilmott, owners of Hedonism who was running in the next race.

'Glad you came, lad.' Michael was pleased to see him. 'We're feeling quite optimistic about Hedonism. We're just having a quick drink then I'd better go and saddle him up.'

The Wilmotts seemed a nice couple. Peter ran a software company and his wife was heavily involved in The Cotswold Hunt. She was the sort of woman that he remembered from his Pony Club days. She wore a furry headband, a Barbour and had the ruddy complexion of a woman who was always outdoors and had heavily lined skin that indicated she was a stranger to moisturiser. Probably had other priorities, he mused, thinking of all the lotions and potions Livvy used. The pair greeted Nat enthusiastically.

'We'd really like your opinion of our gelding when you're back riding, of course. We've always been great admirers of yours.' Maggie told him. 'I daresay you won't be off too much longer, maybe a week or so, then we'd definitely like you to ride for us.' She lowered her voice. 'Between you and me we are not that thrilled with McGuire. He sits like a sack of potatoes, whereas you on the other hand, sit a horse beautifully.' Nat knew he had to be diplomatic, but found he was absurdly pleased at her praise.

'Jamie's shaping up well though, just give the lad a chance. He's not had the benefit of The Pony Club, whereas I was lucky enough to ride for all the teams.'

Maggie beamed. 'Really? I should have known. It makes all the difference. You can always tell.' She went on to tell him about the exploits of the Hunt. 'Course we're only allowed to do drag hunting these days,' she winked. 'And we stick to the letter of the law, absolutely.'

Michael had clearly heard these tales many times and glanced at his watch.

'We'd better make our way to the saddling enclosure.'

Maggie suddenly looked nervous. 'Oh God. Wish us luck.'

235

Nat duly obliged. 'Good luck!'

He was enjoying himself hugely and was just about to go to the stands, when one of the women who had been staring at him previously came over. She was smiling broadly.

'Hi, Nat. You probably don't remember me, do you? It's Millie, from the awards. Millie The Milliner?'

Nat instantly relaxed. So that was why they had been staring at him.

'Of course. How are you?'

Millie smiled. 'Mortified and embarrassed actually after my ridiculous display at the do. I'm just so glad you managed to drive me home safely. I feel so awful, especially since that journalist tried to make a thing about it. I hope you didn't get any grief from your fiancée. I tried to explain to the man that came knocking on my door asking questions, afterwards. Some journalist, I think he was. I told him that you'd been completely chivalrous and an absolute hero. And where he could stick his money. I hope they printed that, I mean everyone is so keen to believe the worst about people, aren't they?'

Nat narrowed his eyes, his senses sharpening. What man? What money?

'Would you like a drink? Then you can tell me all about it.'

Having listened to Millie and gained a detailed description of the man involved, he sent her off with a bottle of champagne for her and her friends, much to their delight. It was the least he could do for someone who was prepared to tell the truth, despite being offered considerable financial inducements. He went to watch the main race in something of a daze. The horses looked well in the parade ring. He saw some trainers and owners he knew, all of whom appeared glad to see him and asked when he would be back riding. He nodded at some of the jockeys as they came out to mount. Jamie McGuire acknowledged him, as did Charlie Durrant and Tristan Davies, the latter making a 'ring me' sign with his finger and thumb. It occurred to him that whoever had tried to bring him down had failed, he'd only been off for a month with a broken collarbone. But would they stop there? Millie's account of her visitor left him in no doubt that this was a serious matter. It was something he hadn't really considered before. He watched as the runners came into the last two furlongs. Colm McNally's mount, Desperado, had been the front runner but was closely followed by Jamie McGuire on the stable's chestnut, Moonbaby. A third horse, Kir Royale, was also making excellent headway on the inside.

'Come on, Moonbaby,' he shouted. His eyes were fixed on Desperado who was just ahead of the other two as they approached the third last, when the horse jolted, suddenly springing forwards. The horse and rider badly misjudged the stride resulting in them falling in horrifying slow motion, as the crowd gasped. Michael, with whom he was watching the race from the stand, took a sharp intake of breath. Jamie managed to navigate the fallen horse and rider and went into the lead closely followed by Kir Royale. Moonbaby went on to win by a couple of lengths.

'To be sure, we had a bit of luck there, didn't we?' exclaimed Michael, his smile wide. He could afford to celebrate, particularly as Desperado had galloped off, no worse for his experience, and Colm McNally was on his feet, which was a relief.

'It was lucky,' Nat replied. But he knew it wasn't true. His heart was still pounding from the awful realisation that had come to him as he watched Desperado fall. The horse's reaction was identical to those of the horses he had ridden, the four unexpected fallers. He was aware of other racegoers around him muttering that McNally had had a few fallers lately and made a mental note to check them out. He watched Colm McNally make the ignominious walk back to the weighing room, his expression dazed. Nat knew exactly how he felt. He knew without a shadow of a doubt that his enemy had now begun to target McNally. He made his excuses to Michael and decided to leave before the last race. He needed to contact Finn and McNally urgently and work out what to do next. He also knew that the information from Millie was highly significant. Deep in thought, he realised he was glad he'd let Michael persuade him to go racing. It had been truly illuminating but not in the way he expected.

Chapter Thirty-one

Meanwhile, Topper McGrew had opted to go to Wetherby. It was near to home and he guessed that Lofty was more likely to be there. The course was filling up nicely by the time he arrived and true to form Topper made for the main bar but ordered a coffee instead of the usual Scotch. He wanted to keep a clear head, prompted by the epiphany he had experienced after being tackled by Finn regarding the shabby stories he had written about Nat Wilson. And he felt that Finn was probably onto something. There might be another bigger and better scoop, if only he could just sniff it out and run it to ground.

As Topper was assessing the form, flicking through the racecard, wondering how many of Topper's tips would win today, and looking to see if the wet weather had led to any non runners, Lofty sidled up to the bar.

'Hello old friend,' said Topper expansively, 'what'll you have to drink? The usual?' He wanted to get Lofty nice and relaxed and ready to reveal more.

Topper ordered whiskey and another coffee for himself. They talked inconsequentially and then Topper pressed another whiskey on the photographer before he could leave. He knew Lofty would soon melt away to take photos of the first race.

'I was meaning to ask you how you got the photo of Wilson and the girl that time, and then one when he'd been arrested. You never said...'

Lofty tapped his nose and then leaned closer so that Topper noticed his shabby appearance and grubby shirt collar. 'Got emailed them, I did...'

'Who from? And did it ever occur to you it might be a fake, could have been photoshopped, couldn't it?' Topper felt a frisson of alarm at this.

Lofty grinned showing long, yellow teeth like an aging horse. 'I asked for the real copy to be sent by post, then I could tell, if it'd been tampered with. Anyway, what are you saying, it was OK, wasn't it? It was Wilson and you got a good story out of it!'

Topper made calming gestures with his hands. 'Of course, my friend, just wondered who the source was, that's all.' He wondered how much to reveal. 'I mean, it's almost as if someone wanted to drop Wilson in it.'

Lofty shrugged. 'Dunno. Even if they did, it's the truth, isn't it? Anyway, I never found out. I just paid cash, that's all. Didn't recognise the email address either. But look, here's the envelope that the original photo came in.' Lofty rummaged about and extracted a folded brown envelope from the inside pocket of his grubby mac and passed it over. 'Anyway, gotta go, horses to snap. See you...' And he shuffled off.

Topper held the paper between his fingers and glanced at the postmark. From North Yorkshire, there was a faint, smudged name on the front of the envelope. He peered at it and made out the name. TJ Rudge. Got you, he thought and googled the name on his 'phone. 'TJ Rudge, Private Investigator, York' popped up, 'Discreet and professional service,' it read. Mmm, not so discreet thought Topper. But who would set a PI on Nat Wilson and why? I'm definitely onto something here, he thought. Time for a little more digging.

Later that afternoon after a successful day's tipping, three wins and two places, Topper revisited the bar and watching the TV, caught up with the racing from Worcester. He had considered going there but his car needed a service, and he didn't want to push it, deciding to travel more locally instead. There were some good races there and he had an interest in the fifth race where some decent horses were running, Moonbaby from Johnson's yard and Desperado ridden by Colm McNally, the champion jockey. He'd had a small bet on Desperado and clutched the betting slip tightly. He watched closely as in a tightly fought contest, Colm McNally and his horse seemed to misjudge one of the final fences, which sent him and his mount crashing to the ground. Damn. He sighed then tore up the slip in annoyance, but then realized there was something strange about the fall. He watched a replay as he sipped his coffee. Twitching with excitement and recognition, he vowed to have another look at that race when he got home. Something told him McNally's fall was a carbon copy of those that Wilson had recently had. He should know as he had studied them carefully after Finn McCarthy had spoken to him. If someone wanted a horse to fall, how would they arrange it without it being obvious? There didn't seem to be any noticeable obstruction. His mind pondered over what had happened to Nat Wilson. Who would hire a PI to dig up some dirt on him? McGuire and McNally seemed the obvious suspects but after what he had just witnessed, it looked increasingly like McGuire was acting alone. As Finn had suggested, that was the real story and he felt annoyed that he had not realised this at the time. He decided to push off home and then he was going to ask about and find out more about TJ Rudge. Like a truffle pig, he had picked up the scent of a story. Topper left the races fired up with resolve. He was definitely onto something, he just couldn't work out what it was, not yet.

Hattie was in the middle of talking Lottie Henderson through the Eatwell plate, which was designed to help people eat a better balance of carbohydrates, proteins and fats. The plate was marked out in portions for each food type which made it easier to eat the correct proportion of foodstuffs. Lottie had arrived for her appointment on time at the little office at the PJA headquarters in Walton. Hattie watched the young conditional, who seemed so tiny and slim, as she went through the details. Lottie had agreed to be weighed and seemed not to have lost any weight this week, which was good, given her history of eating disorders. Although Hattie was thrilled to at last be working like a proper dietician in her dream job, using her office for a private consultation, she also felt anxious. Was it her imagination or was Lottie just nodding and agreeing to keep her happy? Somehow the youngster did not seem really interested in what was said and it made Hattie feel out of her depth. Hattie knew from her reading and course that anorexics were difficult to treat. At least she wasn't dealing with the psychology of the situation, that was Tara's role, and Hattie found she did not envy her. She also realised that Tara had great skill, if anyone could help Lottie, she surely could. Hattie got together some leaflets and passing them over, tried a different, more friendly approach.

'So, Lottie how's it going at your yard? It must be awful. After what happened with Clare and then Sinead...'

Lottie nodded. 'Yes, terrible. I didn't really know Sinead, but I do know Clare and apparently she's spoken to the police about what happened to her. It's sort of opened the floodgates and she's talked about the incident more to me too. God, it's just awful...'

Hattie smiled and nodded. 'Go on...'

'Well, she's just frightened and a bit depressed and all us girls feel the same. I mean there is a rapist and murderer still on the loose. Seamus and Rosie are great, and Seamus is really helpful, takes us places and that, insisting we're never on our own. But we're just really wary of the lads. The conditionals, they're OK some of them but others they think they're God's gift to riding and think that we should be falling all over them too...'

Hattie's ears pricked, could this be significant? With studied casualness she said, 'Any lads in particular?'

242

Lottie leaned forwards. 'Well, that bloody Joel's a right creep, gives me the willies, he does. He's always trying to get us on our own, buy us drinks, pushes too hard. I've got so I don't go to the pub anymore. Surprising for a lad who seems to lack confidence. And he's always flashing the cash. Sam's alright though, I can talk to him, but I miss home, I dunno if I can stick it, looking over my shoulder all the time. It's no way to live. Might chuck it in or might move somewhere else.'

Hattie frowned. 'Well, you should talk to Finn before you do anything. Don't make any hasty decisions. The police might catch the perpetrator soon and then you'll be sorry you left.'

Lottie managed a smile. 'Maybe. Seamus and Rosie are great. I'd certainly miss them, and I have lots of friends here.'

'Do you want me to speak to Finn if I see him?'

Lottie nodded and then got up to leave. 'Thanks, if you want to, it's no secret. And he might be able to help.'

Deep in thought and feeling starving as usual, Hattie dashed out towards The Singing Kettle to order a sandwich and cappuccino. On the way, she collided with a young blond haired man. Sam Foster no less. The young man grinned in recognition.

'Hi Hattie, just on my way to the saddlers. Had to have my boots repaired, just gonna pick them up.'

'Fab, how're things? Finn said you've been doing well, you've had a few more wins?' Hattie noticed he looked rather more grown up than before. He was slightly broader and taller. Then she looked at his feet, noticing he wore a pair of trendy looking, black Nike trainers with quite a thick sole. That would account for him appearing taller, she supposed.

'Want a coffee?' Hattie gestured towards the café.

Sam grinned. 'Nah, got to dash. Off to Market Rasen later. Got a ride in the four o'clock, so I need to pick up me boots and get going. See you.'

As he walked off Hattie noticed a faint squeaking noise. She watched him leave, a loping, familiar figure who she knew from previous investigations. He looked vaguely comical, wearing his usual tight breeches with long socks and thick soled black trainers. He really was a nice lad. She had a soft spot for him ever since she and Finn had found him beaten up at the races. She smiled and dived into the café.

Sipping a cappuccino, she reviewed her morning. It was harder than she'd expected to engage Lottie, like the girl was just paying lip service to her. But maybe she couldn't concentrate if she was scared to death. The police really needed to find out who had assaulted Sinead then normal service would be resumed and Walton would return back to being a vibrant but safe town. Several thoughts chased around her head and feelings of disquiet engulfed her. It was very interesting what Lottie had said about Joel Fox. I'll have to tell Finn, she thought, especially as Finn had a lot of sympathy for the lad, so did she actually, with his overbearing father undermining him at every touch and turn. Suddenly as the waitress brought over her food, something leapt into her consciousness. The squeaking sound she had heard when she'd talked to Sam. Christ, was it Sam's trainers? She remembered what Clare had said about being out of it when she was attacked and hearing squeaking shoes. Oh my God, did it mean he was the one who'd attacked Clare and possibly Sinead too? Surely not Sam? Appetite gone, she jerkily grabbed her phone and texted Finn.

We need to talk. It's urgent

On the way out of the café, she nearly jumped out of her skin when a 4x4 rounded the corner and beeped at her. She could vaguely see someone waving. As she looked at the rear windscreen, trying to make out who it was, she saw no garage sticker, just a riding hat covered in a red silk with a fluorescent hat band around the base. Presumably, it was Sam, dashing off to the races having picked up his

244

racing boots. That was a relief, at least his car didn't have a garage label in the back like the one they'd seen in the video of Sinead's attack. The trainers worried her though. She prayed that Finn would contact her soon.

Chapter Thirty-two

Sykes tapped his computer keyboard for a few more seconds and Taverner stood waiting, having been called to speak to him urgently. The DI was sure it was Sykes' way of putting him in his place, of pulling rank. He fully expected not to be invited to sit down as well. Eventually, the chief turned his office chair around and finally addressed him.

'So, you say you've got a prime suspect?'

'Yes, a lad called Zack Archer. He's in care, lives at the same home Sinead lived at. They used to go out and then when it ended, he became obsessed with her and followed her everywhere. So, he's got a motive as he was spurned, and he was also reported missing on the night our victim died.'

Sykes' face spread with a beatific smile. 'Messed up care kid with a motive. Bring him in, try to get a confession out of him. Any other evidence, something concrete?'

'He wears the same type of trainers with a distinctive tread, that we found at the scene, but there is no sighting of him in the area on the night. So, do you think we have enough to arrest him?'

Sykes punched the air. 'Course! Hah, he's the one. The little bastard! You throw the bleeding book at him.' He shook his head, 'it all makes sense. Someone from her past, with anger issues and an obsession. I was beginning to worry, lad, it's been nearly four weeks, there's a lot of pressure to solve this case. But it'll be him, well done Taverner, bloody well done.'

Taverner nodded and left feeling slightly uncomfortable. For a start, they weren't there yet. They had nothing so far to place Archer in the area, he hadn't been seen in the pub, for instance. Typical too, of Sykes to see looked after youngsters as obvious perpetrators of crimes, instead as the victims they undoubtedly were. Not that the two categories were mutually exclusive of course. But being adopted himself, Taverner knew that care kids usually had a lot of emotional baggage to work through and adolescence was a difficult time, a time when things could come to a head, like it had in his own life.

Taverner found Wildblood at her desk. 'Sykes thinks there is enough to arrest Archer, now we've got the trainer print we've got enough to hold him.'

Wildblood grabbed her jacket. 'What did I tell yer! But listen, there's still no sign of Archer around the area at the time. Patel and Cullen are wading through CCTV footage from around the pub and talking to witnesses again, but nothing so far and Haworth and Ballantyne have been showing witnesses the photo of Archer. There're on their way back as we speak.'

Taverner sighed, feeling uneasy. Someone must have seen him, surely, if he had been there?

'Tell them to come straight back. I think I'll just wait for them. How far are they away?'

'Maybe 15 minutes?'

Taverner nodded and glanced at his watch. 15 minutes would make no difference either way and he just wanted to be sure. Someone was bound to have recognised him, surely?

Nat wiggled his shoulder. Hmm, no particular twinges or niggles, the swelling had gone too. He tried a few exploratory stretches, imagined holding back a headstrong horse and riding a finish. All good. It'd been four weeks and he reckoned he'd healed enough to get back in the saddle, not yet riding professionally, but that wouldn't be too long. Of course, he had the best physio, Doug, and first class advice about exercise, anti-inflammatories and the rest. He reckoned he'd pass the doc soon, he'd always healed well, he was lucky like that. I'll phone Michael Kelly, ask to ride out, give those new horses of his a try out, that Huntsman, the chestnut horse in St Jude's stable, now he looked a likely sort. The guvnor had been enthusiastic about him which was unusual. He usually played his cards close to his chest, so that was promising. He'd look back at the horse's previous races, see if he could get any tips about how to ride the horse. He felt his mood lift.

The next morning, Nat took Huntsman up the steepest gallop, riding alongside Detonator, the other horse owned by the Herringtons. Michael Kelly was watching from a distance. It felt great to be back in the saddle, feeling the muscular power of the animal beneath him and the wind in his hair. There really was no feeling quite like it! He could see Jamie McGuire hunched over the bay Detonator, just ahead of him on the track. Huntsman had a smooth, rangy gallop and felt full of running. At the furlong marker, Nat kicked on and to his immense satisfaction felt the horse respond and increase his stride, like unleashing an Aston Martin on the motorway. Nat felt a huge rush of adrenaline, a thrilling release of high voltage energy sent tingles all around his body, as his horse sailed past McGuire's mount. Elation coursed through him, because he recognised that Huntsman was a bloody good horse. As they pulled up, Nat hid his smiles and caught a glower from McGuire as Detonator cantered up and was pulled up too. Nat gave Jamie a quick nod but no other acknowledgement. Jamie could still be part of the conspiracy against him. Nat had ruled out Colm McNally because it seemed the same, mysterious type of fall had happened to him. Bloody bastard, he thought, I'll keep my eyes and ears open this time. No one's going to get me again like that in a hurry. But what exactly was he looking for? He had absolutely no idea.

Michael Kelly strode up and patted Huntsman on the neck. 'Class ride Nat, now isn't he the business, this fella? You ready to ride him in the race next week?'

'Sure guv, I'd love to. I'm seeing the doc in a couple of days, and I'll be signed back.' He grinned at the thought, catching sight of McGuire's tight, sulky face as he wheeled his mount around and headed back to the stable. Even thoughts of Jamie and of whoever was trying to ruin him were chased away by the sheer, soaring joy of the moment. McGrew had been put in his place, he still hadn't sorted out the falls and was still awaiting a call back from Colm, but not even that could dampen his enthusiasm. He had rung Colm hoping to have a calm discussion about his fall to see if he was at all suspicious. But the best thing was that he would soon be back in the saddle! His mood soared like a leaf in a flurry of wind. The Magician was back and he was determined to let nothing stand in his way.

Chapter Thirty-three

James McGrew sat in the café opposite TJ Rudge's ground floor office. It was situated in an anonymous building marked out only by a small sign, TJ Rudge and Associates, by the front door. The office was located in a side street off Stonegate in York. So, this was the place where the PI worked, but who had paid him to follow Wilson? That was the question. Topper had no idea what he was intending on doing by coming here. He hadn't really thought it through but stung by Finn McCarthy's comments and the fact that he had to publish an apology, this had set him thinking and he was not pleased with his appraisal of his actions. He had allowed the pressure from Christian Lamont, the editor of the Yorkshire Echo, to cloud his judgement and he had rushed to publish his articles without considering their source. In doing so, he had risked his integrity and reputation, which he badly needed to rebuild. It hadn't even helped his situation at the paper, with Christian's initial positive attitude towards him melting away as soon as he had read the letter. He had in fact been cutting in his criticism about being forced to publish an apology, and he had waved the solicitor's letter from Nat Wilson around in the main office for all to see and demanded an explanation. His colleagues looked enthralled, amused and then embarrassed, even dim Lindy kindly offered him a drink after the furore had calmed down.

'Have some green tea,' she had whispered 'That's what I do when I feel a bit stressed, it'll do you no end of good and it's full of antioxidants.'

He had wanted to ask her what bloody antioxidants were but instead politely declined. His mood had sunk even lower. He was now an object of pity to his younger, trendier colleagues. How had it come to this, he asked himself? He was a world away from the promise of his youth. Yet he still felt he could salvage the situation. Annoyingly, he had to admit that Finn was right. There was a bigger, altogether more sensational story here, he just needed to find it. He sipped his latte as he gazed out of the window, his eyes trained on the nondescript, grey front door that led to the office. All he needed was some sort of lucky break that might lead him to find out who was paying the PI and therefore, who was behind the campaign against Wilson.

After a while, his attention started to drift. He scanned the pages of The Racing Post and found an article about Nat Wilson, who was returning to racing later this week, after breaking his collarbone in one of those strange falls. He sipped his drink, waited for his toastie to cool down and studied a replay of Colm McNally's recent fall at Worcester which bore a striking similarity to Nat's. The horse, Desperado, appeared to be going well and jumping cleanly when he seemed to rush his fence, put in a small stride as he came to the hurdle and came crashing down. He googled Desperado's previous racing record on his phone and then the four horses which Nat had ridden who had fallen in similar circumstances. All were good jumpers, yet all had fallen. He knew that horses did fall, especially when tired, but the falls were just so similar. They occurred two or three fences from the winning post when there were other horses approaching the same fence and it was the horses' behaviour that was odd. They almost seemed scared. He scrolled back through the footage and saw that there were a couple of stray whips in two of the incidents but it was hard to see which riders had lost them. Careless. Was that significant, he didn't know? If he dug a bit more maybe he'd find some common denominator. He completed google searches on a few people. Some of

251

the trainers seemed new, so he tried to find out more about them. He felt his skin begin to prickle. One of them stood out, he did some more checking and thought he might just have hit the jackpot. He felt he was making definite progress.

He looked up and saw a man walk past the café with The Racing Post tucked under his arm. He recognised the paper as it was identical to the copy he was reading. For some reason, he followed the man's progress as he crossed the road and felt a frisson of excitement when he saw the man go into TJ Rudge's office. What were the odds on that, a client with an interest in horseracing? Then it came to him. Of course, it was highly unlikely to be a coincidence, so he could well be looking at the person behind the whispering campaign. He silently thanked the Gods, that his prayers had been answered. Topper old man, you've had two lucky breaks, just stick with it. Now all he had to do was wait and follow the chap. He wished he'd had a good look at the man's face. He had an impression of someone well dressed in a fitted coat and shiny shoes, but that was it. He ordered another latte, moved towards the window, this time abandoning his internet searches and waiting impatiently for the man to reappear.

After about an hour, when he was considering ordering something else or packing the whole thing in, he noticed the front door opposite open and the same smartly dressed man, pulled up his coat collar and stepped out into the street. Topper roused himself, pulled out a tenner, drank the dregs of his coffee and acknowledging the waitress, burst out of the door. He wished now that he was wearing some sort of disguise. He knew he stood out with his red hair and bulk, so he tried to keep his distance and fade into the background.

The temperature was much cooler as it was now early December and as he pulled up his collar, he saw a silver car navigate the traffic and turn into the side street. He saw the driver gesturing to the man on the pavement who appeared to be waiting to be picked up. But instead, he saw the car sail past as the traffic flow didn't allow him to stop. He squinted at the number plate and was unable to read it completely but thought he could pick out the letters L something 1 and some more numbers. He had no idea what make the car was and tried to make out the manufacturer's mark, but he couldn't really see. The man in the overcoat hurried round the corner following the car, he presumed. Topper followed him on to Stonegate, which was thronging with shoppers even at mid morning, but he struggled to keep up as the man strode out ahead of him. Then the figure was obscured by a gaggle of school children clutching clipboards and then a bedraggled group from a hen party dressed in tutus, the hen clutching a giant blue, inflatable penis and wearing huge 'L' plates. Bloody hell, muttered Topper under his breath as he tried to negotiate them, ignoring their shrieks of laughter. He felt hot and sweaty with the effort of trying to tail the man. The obstruction of the hen party infuriated him and when he had pushed his way through the group, he looked around and found there was no sign of his target. He walked past more shops and dodged the crowds, desperately trying to see where the man might have gone. He kept his eyes peeled for the figure, scanning the crowds as he went, but there was no sign of him. Disheartened he pulled out his phone and texted Finn McCarthy. He knew that the man would definitely try to target Nat Wilson again in his comeback race, but he still wasn't completely sure how the falls were caused or who was involved. A germ of an idea was growing, but it couldn't be that, surely? He hadn't really seen the man's face, but he had a partial number plate, so that would certainly help. For some reason he wanted to redeem himself and at least he could pass on the information he had gleaned so far. Maybe McCarthy could fill in the blanks? It was then that he realised he had a text from Lofty, his photographer friend.

Have a new photo. Want a story about the Champion Jockey? Ring me.

It took him a while to realise that this could be about Colm McNally, not Nat Wilson, as Colm was now the current champion. Maybe, he was the focus in Wilson's absence. What could they have on Colm? Deep in thought, he turned the corner and was about to cross the road into High Petergate, when he felt a sharp push in the back and to his horror felt his feet folding from underneath him and he stumbled. He heard the screech of brakes and then everything went black.

Finn caught up with Hattie in The Blacksmith's after work. It was early but the place was filling up slowly but there were still a few lads and lasses from the yards present. Marcus grinned at Hattie as she ordered the drinks, white wine for her and a coke for Finn. Even his harmless flirting didn't register, so deep in thought was she.

'So, what was so urgent that you needed to speak to me tonight?' asked Finn. 'Are you OK?'

Hattie nodded. 'I was just keen to talk to you about how everyone is feeling. I was speaking to Lottie today and the girls are all really scared about a murderer and rapist still being on the loose.' She went on to tell him what Lottie had said about Joel being creepy.

'Really? Maybe, he's just lacking in social skills. Mind you when I went to Fox's place, I studied the vehicles and there were no signs in the back windscreens, so I don't think it's him.'

'Hmm. Maybe he has another 4x4 stacked away somewhere. Anyway, you might well be right because when I saw Sam in town picking up his riding boots from the cobblers, he had trainers on and it took me a while to register that there was this squeaking noise coming from them. You remember what Clare said about the noise she heard?'

Finn gasped. 'Christ, Sam? I can't believe it. Seriously?'

Harriet nodded. She knew how he felt because she felt exactly the same. Sam Foster was a promising conditional who had shown great integrity in the past and had been beaten up for standing up to a crooked trainer. The possibility that Sam could be the rapist was horrific.

Finn took a sip of coke, his face ashen.

'I wonder where the police are up to? They seem to be concentrating on Sinead's previous life. That Zack Archer who Kyle mentioned might be a more likely prospect.'

'Hmm. Tara didn't think so, remember?'

Finn nodded rather glumly. He really didn't want to believe it of Sam and was keen to absolve him.

'I suppose lots of people could have squeaky trainers, though. The police have already interviewed Sam because he bought Sinead a drink the night she died and they released him, so he can't be the person who attacked her.' He sighed heavily.

Harriet nodded. 'But they will know about the shoes after speaking to Clare. And I know we don't want to acknowledge it, but trouble seems to follow Sam around.'

Finn nodded. 'OK. I'll ask him about the trainers and see what he says. What car does he drive, can you recall?'

Hattie sighed. 'I saw him afterwards, at least I think it was him, he blew his horn at me. He was driving a 4x4 but he only had his riding hat in the back you know, the one with the red silk and the green stripe around the bottom.'

Finn looked relieved. 'And there was no garage sign? There you are then.' He made a mental note to check Sam's car again when he next saw him.

'So, do we have any other clues to follow up on? Anything about Nat?'

'No. Nat'll be back riding soon, he says, which is good. I hope his situation is sorted now I've spoken to McGrew.'

Harriet was not so easily deflected. 'What about those races when he fell? What were your thoughts about those? I mean surely he will know if they're normal falls or not.'

Finn shrugged. 'I promised Nat I'd look at the replays again but at first sight I couldn't see anything significant. It might be in his head, these things can happen to jockeys.'

Harriet frowned. 'But to Nat Wilson? Are you sure? Listen, it might be important.'

Finn laughed. 'It might be. I think the most important thing is who gave McGrew the stories. It suggests that someone was following Nat to land all of them. I did suggest to McGrew that he look into who his source was. That has to be the main story here. But I'll send you the footage and see if you can see any links. I have looked at Nat's riding but maybe I'm missing something.'

'OK. I'll see what I can make of it.'

Finn pulled out his phone and sent the footage to Harriet. He thought about the conversation with Sam which needed to happen sooner rather than later. That was something he was not looking forward to. They both decided to go to Haydock to support Nat in his first race back since he was injured. He was riding the favourite in the Christie Cup.

'I'll text you to let you know what time I'm picking you up,' he added.

Hattie smiled. 'OK. Well, good luck with your conversation with Sam.'

Chapter Thirty-four

Nat was thrilled at the prospect of riding tomorrow after his time off due to his injury. Livvy had cooked a steak with a light salad and he really didn't mind missing out on the pudding, a lemon mousse. He'd make the weight with a sauna no problem if he didn't over indulge now.

Livvy smiled. 'Even I'm glad you're riding, you've been like a bear with a sore head since you were injured.'

Nat grinned. 'I know and I'm sorry. It is what it is, I know accidents happen but this year I really wanted a good season.'

Livvy gave him an appraising look. 'You're not still thinking there was anything wrong with those falls, are you? Surely everything will be fine now Finn has spoken to the journalist, won't it?'

'Course it will. The Magician is back!'

Privately he wasn't quite so sure. He'd looked back at the footage of the falls again and again to see if there were any patterns. They'd all happened towards the end of the race, when other horses were coming up to the same fence. But, so what? Horses were often tired by then and more likely to make mistakes and it was no surprise that there were other horses around, that's what happened when jockeys were trying to get into a good position for the home stretch. He felt reassured when Colm McNally had returned his call. He had been unconcerned about his own fall.

'Oh, me hoss just took off all wrong, that's all,' he'd said in his strong Irish accent. 'Some wee man did some research and we're all likely to fall every 14 races or so, I think they said, so put it this way, it's good to get one out of the way and move on. We're all eejits, anyway.'

Nat laughed at Colm's philosophy. If he was right, then Nat reckoned his riding would be plain sailing for a few weeks. He'd kept up with the gym, had ridden out for Michael a few times and jumped Huntsman. He was feeling well. He was thrilled by the buzz the horse gave him, not just his speed but his jumping ability and he found he was really looking forward to riding him tomorrow. Don't overthink things, he told himself. He'd lived his life being carefree and shrugged off mishaps, always believing that something good was just around the corner and he saw no reason to change his ways now. After all, it had worked so far. He studied The Racing Post cover to cover, checking the form and packed up his kitbag, anticipation mounting.

Finn was dreading talking to Sam but decided to try and get it out of the way. He thought rather than give Sam any warning he'd turn up on spec. He'd make some excuse or other but in reality, he wanted to have the discussion and move on. He arrived at Robert Johnson's place and realised he hadn't checked The Racing Post so didn't know if Robert had any runners at Haydock that afternoon. Finn was going to the races anyway, as he was keen to support his friend Nat Wilson. He'd not managed to check the footage of the falls that Nat had wanted him to look at and felt rather guilty at passing this job on to Harriet. He was pretty sure the falls were something and nothing and he didn't want to imagine problems when there weren't any.

As soon as he arrived at Johnsons, he realised that the place seemed pretty deserted and crucially the large horse box was not parked where it usually was. Maybe Sam didn't have any rides today though. He parked up and wandered around. Several horses' heads appeared over the stable doors as they surveyed the stranger, some even whickered at him. He went to stroke a large, friendly grey horse.

'Hey, is there anyone there?' he called.

A small blonde girl, hair pulled back into a ponytail appeared brandishing a sweeping brush. She grinned at Finn, clearly recognising him.

'Hi. Guvnor's at Haydock today. He won't be back till this evening. Can I help?'

'I was after Sam Foster, actually. Does he have any rides today?'

The girl frowned. 'Yes, he's gone with them. The guvnor has put him up on a couple of horses.'

'Fine. I'm going there later, I just thought I'd call in on the off chance.'

Disconsolately, he set off. Damn. He had hoped to see Sam on his own, it would be much trickier to catch up with him at the races and have an in depth conversation but he must try. He glanced at his watch. He texted Hattie to say he'd be picking her up earlier than he'd said.

DI Taverner shook his head in exasperation. They had just been about to go and arrest Archer, but this had stopped him in his tracks. He had been waiting for Ballantyne and Haworth to come back to the station to see if any of the witnesses from The Blacksmith's Arms recognised Archer.

'What? Are you absolutely sure?'

DC Patel nodded gloomily and showed DI Taverner the report he'd printed off.

'It's just come through. He's wanted by South Yorkshire Police in connection with an altercation with some lads in Mexborough, Doncaster. It's possibly drug related. He's been positively ID'ed by several witnesses as part of the gang though he wasn't involved in the assault allegedly. He's being interviewed as a witness.'

Taverner ran his fingers through his hair and frowned. He stared at the report from the neighbouring police force which clearly stated the date and time when Zack's associates had been arrested and had photos of a gruesome looking knife which had been involved in the attack. Zack was clearly listed as a witness. The dates matched. Hell their prime suspect had been in Doncaster on the evening of Sinead's death!

'OK, so that rules him out of the Walton case, since he clearly couldn't be in two places at the same time.' The team had been preparing to bring in Zack in connection with the rape of Sinead O'Brien, but despite DCI Sykes' enthusiasm, Taverner had waited for his officers to come back. Something had made Taverner try to dig a little more before setting up the arrest. He had been unhappy that no one had been able to positively identify Zack Archer as having been in the area of Walton at the time. At that moment, Haworth and Ballantyne walked in.

'Any joy,' asked Cullen.

Taverner knew what the response would be.

The two men shook their heads.

'No bugger recognises the lad,' said Ballantyne. 'No one at all.'

They now knew that was because he hadn't in fact been there on the night in question. He'd even had the right trainers which matched the footprints from the scene, had had a prior relationship with the victim and had reportedly been very upset and angry when Sinead left him to pursue her dream career of being a jockey. But they now knew that he wasn't involved. Taverner tried not to look as dejected as he felt.

'Right then, we'll get everyone together and see what else we can come up with.'

The team were suitably frustrated, except for DS Wildblood.

'Look on the bright side, guv. At least we didn't go out and arrest the poor lad, so we should be thankful for small mercies. Where does this leave us though? We've a footprint from a certain set of trainers, Vapomax, and nowt else.'

'What was on those SD cards that McCarthy brought in?' asked Taverner.

Patel looked through his notes. 'There is possible footage around the time of the attack of the potential perpetrator stopping and coming back 40 minutes later to his car but obviously I'm guessing, we just have one camera angle, and the attack is out of view. It's hard to see much from the video because of the light and the camera quality. The perpetrator's vehicle has something in the back which I have sent to get enhanced. It might be a narrow sticker. Other than that, I'm not sure.'

'Right, let's see if the tech guys have managed to enlarge the sign. The rest of you go back through the statements of the witnesses. It really looks like someone more local is involved, maybe one of the jockeys even.'

The team set to, scouring the statements they had obtained for any anomalies.

Haworth was speaking urgently on the phone and replaced the receiver with a clatter, his expression suddenly animated. 'Guv, uniform have just been on. A journalist was involved in a hit and run yesterday, says he was pushed into the road from behind. Uniform have visited him. He's James McGrew, a racing journalist, and he said he has some information about racing fraud. He also alleges that he was pushed into the path of an oncoming car by someone.' He scratched his head. 'Might be related to Sinead's case, sir.'

261

Taverner thought for a minute. He had learned that vital intelligence sometimes arrived in unexpected ways. This could be one such occasion, in fact, he was sure of it. There was no time to lose. He grabbed his coat.

'Racing fraud, hey? It certainly sounds more than a coincidence. Come on, Anna, let's see what this McGrew character has to say for himself.'

Hattie could feel tension seeping out of Finn as he drove. They'd decided to go to Haydock anyway to support Nat, but since she had told him about Sam Foster's squeaky shoes, he had made the obvious link between Clare and Sinead's rapes, and was wondering if Sam was the attacker after all. He'd not been able to see Sam before he went to Haydock and was now desperate to see him to rule him out. So much for setting off early, there'd been an accident on the motorway and the traffic had been at a standstill for an age. Eventually, they were able to move. Harriet tried to make conversation.

'Never mind, we should get there just in time for the big race at three.' She scanned her phone where she had the runners and riders listed. 'Sam's riding in it, that must be a last minute decision, 'cos you didn't know, did you? And Joel Fox, as well as Nat, of course. Hope his shoulder's mended properly, he's riding Huntsman of course, the favourite. Is a month and a bit too soon to be back?'

'No, we jocks are tough. You know I do think Lloyd Fox should get another jockey in to help out, it's a bit too much pressure for Joel to be riding in the Christie Cup. I mean, Sam I can see, he's had over 30 winners now, but Joel has only had a handful. He's just starting and he's a lot to learn. Which horse is Sam riding again?'

'Lucky for Some. You know, I've been thinking about those trendy trainers. When I was competing, I was into trainers and there were those air soled ones, Vapo something or other that were all the

262

rage. They used to squeak when the air started to seep out of them. They were really trendy so probably Sam has just got a pair of those. They're common, so there's bound to be lots of them kicking about.'

'Yep, you may well be right. It might not mean anything', added Finn, his eyes on the road as he overtook a slower car. He knew in his heart it was significant though, and he just needed to talk to Sam one to one, he'd know for definite if he had anything to hide.

Hattie took in Finn's fixed expression. 'I had a look at the tape of those falls you sent me.'

'And?'

'On a couple of occasions there's a stray whip in the video, someone seems to lose it. Is that common?'

Finn nodded as he steered the car off the motorway. 'Well, it does happen sometimes when a jockey is transferring the whip from one hand to another. Usually, one hand is better at holding it than another. Did you notice anything else?'

'Not really. I was just going to make a list of which jockeys and trainers had been there to see if there any themes.' Harriet pulled some pieces of paper out of her bag and began to leaf through them. 'I'll have a look now. We might be wrong about Sam, you know. We can all make mistakes about people.'

Finn sighed. 'I know. But I'd never forgive myself if another girl was harmed, which is why we need to get there quickly so I can talk to him.' Finn pulled off the A road and followed the signs to Newton-le-Willows where the racecourse was situated. They were nearly there. As they pulled into the racecourse, Finn drove slowly past the jockeys' car park.

'What sort of car does Sam drive again? We can look at the rear window.'

'I'm not sure it was Sam's. Someone blew his horn at me, and I saw a riding hat in the back, Sam's, I presume, with the red silk with the lighter stripe round the base.'

Finn thought for a moment, his expression suddenly serious. 'Hang on, Sam always rides out in a blue hat silk, so it can't have been his.'

Harriet shrugged. 'Who has a red hat silk with a lighter, greenish stripe around it?'

Finn gasped as several facts filtered through to his brain. Surely not? How could they have missed it?

'The lighter stripe, could it be a hat band, a fluorescent one, the type that is visible at night...'

Hattie looked at him as understanding dawned. 'You mean like the sign in the back of the 4x4 we saw on the SD cards?' She gasped. 'Suppose the sign was from the riding hat shoved on the parcel shelf, you mean and not sticker at all...'

Finn drew his car into the car park as they both sat dazed at what they had just potentially uncovered. The air was thick with tension. Finn was frowning as he tried to process the information and gauge its significance. It meant that one of his conditionals was likely to be the rapist and there was only one of them who routinely used a hatband on his skull cap.

'You know who it is, don't you?'

Finn nodded grimly, the enormity of what they had just found out was just beginning to dawn on him. 'There's only one of the lads that wears that type of hat band and uses a red hat silk. It's Joel Fox.'

'Joel Fox? Really? Oh my God.'

'Come on, we can't do anything yet. Now we're here, let's go and see Nat's race and then we can contact the police.'

Then his phone beeped and he looked at the message and saw that it was from Topper. He realised it had been sent the day before but because of the poor signal locally, it had only just arrived.

Warn Nat to be very careful at Haydock. Check the whips.

He showed his phone to Hattie.

'What on earth does he mean about the whips? Don't jockeys all have the same type?'

Finn nodded. 'Rules are very strict and the clerk checks them all beforehand, so I have no idea what he means.'

They both made their way into the racecourse, deep in thought.

Chapter Thirty-five

As they reached the parade ring, the jockeys were making their way into the ring for the big race. Bringing up the rear was Sam wearing black and red striped colours and waving his whip, as if he had not a care in the world. He raised his hand at them in greeting. Finn nodded but was concentrating on scanning the jockeys and studying their whips as they came out.

'Good luck, Sam.' Hattie turned to Finn. 'Did you notice anything unusual?'

'No, they're just standard issue whips as far as I can tell.' He nodded at Nat as he came past them with his customary swagger.

'Should we warn him?' hissed Hattie.

Finn considered this then yelled. 'Keep your wits about you, Nat. Take care!'

Nat winked, smiling. He made a 'phone you later' gesture with his fingers then went on to speak to Michael. He looked supremely relaxed and unconcerned, despite the warning.

Finn looked on helplessly, aware that his message had missed its mark.

'Christ, Hattie. I don't know what to warn him about. All the whips are standard issue ones…'

Hattie touched his arm. 'Maybe McGrew is wrong. Come on let's watch the race.'

The two scrambled towards the stand to get a good vantage point.

'Twelve runners, two and a half miles and lots of chase fences to jump. It'll be a stiff test and there's some good horses,' said the commentator.

Even though they'd missed the build up and the earlier races, the tension in the ground was palpable and despite the time of year, the racecourse looked in fine form and was well cared for. It was set in beautiful parkland and the trees on the far side of the course were still hanging onto some of their autumn leaves. There were Christmas themed stands selling mulled wine and mince pies and a sense of well informed anticipation from the spectators, as the runners and riders made their way down to the start. The crowd gave a huge roar as the tape went up and the field set off just to the right of the stands. Hattie clenched her fists and looked around at the well dressed crowd, racecards open, betting slips in hand. A woman wearing a trilby and tweed coat proclaimed loudly,

'My money's on Tabasco Bay,' she said, waving her racecard.

Hattie sensed something sensational might be about to unfold and she stood alert, ready to act and tried to calm herself by taking deep breaths. But the first circuit was fairly uneventful.

Finn grimaced. 'So far, so good. Keep your eyes peeled though.'

As the runners came past the stands for the first time, Nat was in about fourth place on Huntsman, with Sam at the rear on Lucky for Some and Joel up in fifth on Tabasco Bay, an outsider which no one knew too much about. Finn's eyes were trained intently on the field. All was going well for Nat, so far. Huntsman appeared to be jumping magnificently. Then the field gradually began to stretch out with the riders running along the far side of the track. Suddenly there was a groan and the commentator said,

'And Lucky for Some pecks badly on landing.' There was a pause and then he added, 'but a good bit of riding there has kept Sam Foster in the saddle, although Lucky for Some has lost a few lengths. And we're coming to the final half mile as they turn the far corner. And now Huntsman begins to move up passing Blue Butterfly and seems ready to make his run.'

Hattie could see one horse was far behind. 'Fairy Ring is tailed off last and has pulled up,' confirmed the announcer, 'whilst Huntsman now passes Lucky for Some and is a length behind Tabasco Bay with another length to Native Brave, the leader, as we come to the third last.'

Senses on full alert, Hattie took another quick look at the packed stand and at the area in front. Suddenly she froze as if ice cubes had been dropped down her neck,

'Christ, look Finn, I think that's Taverner over there and that nice DS, Anna someone or other. In fact, there's loads of officers. What's going on?'

Finn followed her gaze and looked at her cryptically. 'Well, they certainly look like they're looking for someone, we'd better have a word...'

The two pounded down the steps and dodged through the crowd to intercept the detectives.

Taverner reacted first. 'Ah, McCarthy and Harriet too. Thought you might be here. We're looking for a suspect. We need to talk to him urgently about an attempt on a man's life and racing fraud.'

'You need to arrest Joel Fox too. We've worked out he's the one who attacked Sinead and you need to look at the jockeys' whips,' said Finn.

268

Taverner took this in, seemingly unsurprised and motioned to several uniformed officers. He was clearly here to make arrests and had brought uniformed back up.

There was a massive groan from the crowd and the commentator's excited voice rose an octave. 'And there's a faller there. It's Huntsman who's hit the deck, getting in very close to Tabasco Bay who's cleared it and is running on well making his challenge and gaining on Native Brave with Lucky for Some third.'

'Shit,' said Finn, 'I don't believe it, it's happened again, poor Nat. I better just catch the end of it, my lads look to be fighting out the finish.'

They all watched as Joel Fox got to work on the outsider, Tabasco Bay, and using his whole body, rode out a tight finish just catching Native Brave to win. Lucky for Some was third. Hattie spotted the woman in the trilby whooping and jumping up and down like a demented jack in a box.

Taverner coughed loudly get their attention back. 'Look, I need to get going…' But his voice was drowned out by the cheers of the crowd. Taverner motioned for uniformed officers to get into position.

They jostled their way through a big crowd just as a steaming Tabasco Bay was led in, followed by Native Brave and Lucky for Some. Neither Finn nor Hattie knew exactly what was happening. As they reached the rails, Finn spotted a furious looking Nat running towards them still carrying his whip. In fact, he held two. He reached them panting and burst out.

'Finn, I know how they did it. That trainer Dan Richards was trying to find this whip, but I grabbed it before he had a chance to. Found it on the track as I walked back. Feel this.' He thrust the end of the black whip into Finn's hand.

Finn jumped back in alarm. 'Christ, what the hell is it?''

269

'Look, really look.' Nat thrust the whip into Finn's hands as he dismantled it. Understanding flashed through Finn's brain. It seemed that the newer, slightly thicker whip was in fact collapsible, which presumably could be easily hidden possibly in a riding boot. It had a button on the handle that Nat depressed again, causing Finn to jump back again, as the shock coursed through him.

'It's a bloody jigger, an ingenious one at that. Of course, you mean one of the jockeys has used this to make your mount fall? I bet I know which one.' Finn's face showed dawning recognition. 'And he must have swapped the usual whip for this one mid race, put it down his boot or something. No wonder he sometimes dropped it...'

Taverner, Wildblood and Haworth elbowed their way into the winner's enclosure followed by uniformed officers. They grabbed hold of a shocked Lloyd and then Joel Fox, who was mid interview with Tim Giles, the course announcer. Tim looked on in astonishment at the scene that unfolded before him. Lloyd struggled and began to protest,

'There's been a mistake, some mix up. I shall call my legal team and sue the arse off you!'

'You do that, sunshine,' said Taverner, staring dispassionately ahead.

In contrast, Joel seemed to fold into himself, looking ashen and resigned. He did not protest as he was handcuffed, and it was as if he knew without doubt that the game was up.

The winner's enclosure was in chaos as the sponsors, standing on a podium ready to welcome the winning owners, trainer and jockey realised what was happening. The Foxes were read their rights in front of a ready TV camera and marched off by uniformed officers while Taverner and Wildblood watched.

'Ah, I think there's been a slight change of plan,' said Tim Giles into the microphone, in the understatement of the year. In the manner of a seasoned professional, he pressed on regardless. 'No doubt we will find out what just happened in due course. But now ladies and gentlemen let's focus on the next exciting race.'

'It's worse than just horse fixing,' Finn told Nat, 'it seems that Joel is going to be interviewed about Sinead O'Brien's death too.'

Nat gasped. 'But he seemed such a little squirt, I felt rather sorry for him....'

'Me too. Listen, where's Dan Richards?'

Hattie gave a shout as she realised that he had come back to the paddock after his failed attempt to retrieve the whip, and seeing the scene, had made a run for it.

'He won't get far,' said Taverner, 'we've sealed off all exits...'

Hattie, however, was in hot pursuit, sprinting down the track and ducking under the rail to reach the middle where Richards was running ahead, clearly making for the trees over on the other side of the course. Following Hattie was DS Anna Wildblood. Dan soon began to tire, and Hattie's superior fitness and youth showed as she gained on her prey. What many people didn't know about her was that before focussing on the modern pentathlon in her youth, she had in fact been a promising junior runner. Concentrating now, she got to within two feet of Dan and focussing on his legs, dived, gave a great roar and rugby tackled him to the ground.

'Christ!' exclaimed a crumpled Dan Richards, 'felled by a bloody girl!'

DS Wildblood arrived panting and pulled out her handcuffs. 'Gi' over,' she shouted as Dan struggled.

'Good work, lass,' she added to Hattie, as Dan was hauled to his feet and led away by two uniformed officers. Taverner strode up to Hattie and Finn.

'Right,' said Taverner glaring at Finn, 'you and Hattie better accompany us down to the station. You and she clearly know much more, and I need everything before I interview them. And I mean everything.'

After their interview with the police, Hattie and Finn called in to the hospital to see Topper McGrew. He had a bandage on his head and was sitting up in bed with an iPad in front of him.

'Good of you to come, both of you. I wanted to thank you actually McCarthy, you did me a favour. Because you pointed out that Wilson was not past it, and making me see the error of my ways, I've got an exclusive.'

'So, you realised a private investigator was following Nat, taking photos and you followed him?' asked Finn.

'Yes, it was someone called Rudge. I realised that the perpetrator, Lloyd Fox, had just visited and followed him. I think I was a bit careless and Fox must have spotted me following and saw I was on to him. Silly sod tried to push me in front of a car. The best of it is that the police have it on CCTV. So now I've got the exclusive as well as being interviewed by the nationals. It'll be in tomorrow, Top Tipster Tackles Trainer or some such headline, I believe.'

'But you don't seem too worried,' added Hattie, who'd expected to see an angry or a mortally wounded man, noting he was relishing making up headlines, ever the journalist.

'No, my dear, I've been offered a new job at the Press Association, Senior Racing Correspondent, as it happens. I pitched them an idea about writing a column about Bloodlines in racing families and they loved it. And I only had a broken ankle and mild concussion from the accident, so I was lucky. But I wanted to thank you for pointing me in the right direction. No more dodgy stories for stupid editors. Bloody amazing, actually. I feel like a new man. Anyway, excuse me, I better crack on, I've copy to write and a deadline to meet.'

The next day most papers carried the story.

272

Sly Foxes in Race Fix Scandal

In a stunningly farcical end to the Christie Cup Chase at Haydock Park yesterday, the father and son team, Lloyd and Joel Fox, were arrested in the winning enclosure where Tabasco Bay had triumphed. But footage showed that the favourite Huntsman, who fell at the third last, had been hit by a jigger, a specially adapted whip which administers a shock to the horse. Under caution both men admitted regularly deploying jiggers in races, where Joel Fox used them on the horses of top jockeys such as Nat Wilson and Colm McNally, causing their mounts to miss their stride and fall. Nat Wilson said, 'I knew I wasn't losing it and something had happened to make my horses fall. Now I realise what it was.'

The trainer in the yard at Walton was Dan Richards who has also been arrested. Suspicions were aroused when yours truly researched Richards and found that he had been suspected of similar offences in Australia under a different name. In a further grim twist Joel, 19, is also being held and interviewed as a suspect in the rape, earlier this year, of jockey Sinead O'Brien. Enquiries are ongoing.

Epilogue

The private function room at the rear of The Yew Tree was packed as a crowd gathered. It was several months since the Christie Cup and the end of April. The occasion was the celebration of the conditional jockeys' Championship, won by Sam Foster. There would be a formal celebration but this was a local one arranged by trainer Robert Johnson and Finn, to congratulate the popular conditional. The young man, flanked by his parents, sister and girlfriend Maura, silenced the crowd.

'I just want to thank everyone for coming. I'm thrilled to have won this year with 60 wins.' There was a huge cheer, 'obviously I've had a little drink as the season's ended.' There was a light murmur of laughter. 'I'd particularly like to thank my family of course, my coach Finn McCarthy, my trainer, Robert Johnson, for all his help and Hattie Lucas, for all the advice about my diet. And I'm pleased to see Nat Wilson, the runner up to the jockeys' proper championship and of course Colm McNally, the winner here. Make the most of it you two, 'cos I'm coming after you,' Sam added with a cheeky grin.

Everyone dived into the buffet and Hattie, Finn, Nat and Livvy stood together.

'What a bloody season,' said Nat, 'I'll win it next year, you know.' He gave Livvy a squeeze and grinned. She rolled her eyes.

Finn smiled. 'Ah, you're lucky to be only one behind Colm, after that terrible start you had.'

'I'm still puzzled as to why Lloyd and Joel did it,' said Harriet, 'I mean it wasn't even as if Joel as a conditional was going to be a threat to anyone, let alone the top jocks, he had lots to learn...'

Finn grimaced. 'I think he was so scared of his dad, he'd just about do anything. And Lloyd, well he knew nothing about racing, thought he could buy success and didn't really get the whole nature of it, how hard it is, how people spend a lifetime learning about riding and training racehorses, so decided to cheat.'

'I suppose it was easy for Richards to exploit that, he had form for it,' reflected Nat. 'We'll never know who egged who on and who started it. But they're all behind bars now.'

'It was a new twist on an old con. The jigger is usually used at home to get the horse to associate the whip with a shock to make them race faster, but they used it in a different way on the course to spook other horses and cause them to fall by pulling up alongside and using it on a rival's horse,' Finn explained.

'The damned thing was actually quite ingeniously made, collapsible so it could be hidden in a riding boot. Joel used a normal whip and switched it for the jigger but sometimes lost it as he tried to put it back in his boot, like at Haydock. Bloody swines.' Nat chewed his lip. 'Still, it's a relief to know I wasn't completely losing it.' He brightened. 'I nearly beat McNally and I'll definitely do it next year.'

Livvy touched his shoulder. 'Terrible what Joel did though, to Sinead, I mean, he's not a victim in that respect, is he?'

Hattie sighed. 'I know Tara thinks that somehow all the bullying and abuse Joel suffered at the hands of his father, made him want to bully and dominate other people he saw as weaker than himself, young lasses in his case. Sexual abuse is often about power and control.'

Hattie had discussed it all with her new friend, psychologist Tara Regan. Joel had also been charged with the rapes of Sinead and Clare. They all contemplated Sinead's fate and were silent for a minute.

'Come on, let's lighten the mood and circulate. Old Topper's over there, gosh he looks different, he's lost loads of weight and has grown a beard, he looks, well, pretty good,' said Hattie. She had given him a lot of dietary advice and now with his new job, things were looking up for Topper. There was even talk of him signing a book deal for his racing thrillers, with rumours of very large advances. 'Oh, and Taverner's dropped in, look…'

DI Gabriel Taverner made his way over to Finn and Hattie. 'Well done, you two, another case solved and as usual you both played your part.'

'Pity we can't take any real credit,' said Finn, with a grin, 'BHA rules and all that. We don't want to blow our cover.' Their identities would be protected so that they could undertake other inquiries for the BHA if required.

'I think it was good how we worked out that those Nike Vapomax trainers squeak as they begin to wear and when Clare spoke to us, she mentioned the squeaking from her ordeal. So that was a huge clue. We realised that Sam had some but then he told us he'd bought them off Joel, second hand,' said Hattie.

Finn nodded. 'Then all the stuff about the fluorescent strip on the hat and about Joel being a bit mollycoddled by his late mother. He always wore a hatband when riding out, in her memory, you see.'

Taverner raised his hand to stop them and took a sip of his pint. 'Yes, we couldn't have done it without you.' He gave a mock grimace. 'Mmm, I'd like to say I won't see you for a bit, but then you never know. Racing certainly brings out the worst in people, it seems, and most things here revolve around racehorses, don't they?'

Finn and Hattie laughed and she added. 'Course they bloody do! You don't have to be a detective to work that out! I suppose racing just attracts good and bad people, just like anything where huge sums of money are involved.'

Taverner nodded thoughtfully. 'That's true. In that case, I may see you two again, sooner rather than later.'

Hattie grinned. 'Maybe. Anyway, at least Topper McGrew came up trumps, so it's not all bad.' She looked over to where Topper was chatting to a couple of stable lasses, who were enthralled by his story of escaping death at the hands of the now infamous Lloyd Fox. She suspected that he would be dining out on the story for years to come.

Finn suddenly looked solemn and raised his glass. 'To Sinead, may she rest in peace. Justice has been served.'

'To Sinead,' they chorused.

'And here's to working together on the next case,' added Harriet wryly, as she glanced at Finn and Taverner. The detective half smiled and shook his head, but on the whole, he didn't seem too unhappy at the prospect.

About Charlie De Luca

Charlie De Luca was brought up on a stud farm, where his father held a permit to train National Hunt horses, hence his lifelong passion for racing was borne. He reckons he visited most of the racecourses in England by the time he was ten. He has always loved horses but grew too tall to be a jockey. Charlie lives in rural Lincolnshire with his family and a variety of animals, including some ex-racehorses.

Charlie has written several racing thrillers which include: **Rank Outsiders**, **The Gift Horse, Twelve in the Sixth, Making Allowances and Hoodwinked.** He has also written a detective novel**, Dark Minster,** set in the city of York and featuring DI Gabriel Taverner and DS Anna Wildblood.

You can connect with Charlie via twitter; @charliedeluca8 or visit his website.

Charlie is more than happy to connect with readers, so please feel free to contact him directly using the button on the website.

www.charliedeluca.co.uk

If you enjoyed this book, then please leave a review. It only needs to be a line or two, but it makes such a difference to authors.

Praise for Charlie De Luca.

'He is fast becoming my favourite author.'

'Enjoyable books which are really well plotted and keep you guessing.'

'Satisfying reads, great plots.'

Printed in Great Britain
by Amazon

79023676R00161